THE FOREIGN BOY

Mariano M.

This is a work of fiction.

Names, characters, places, events and incidents are either the products of the author's imagination or used in a fictitious manner. Any resemblance to actual persons, living or dead, or actual events is purely coincidental.

All the characters written on this book are fictional and their actions/thoughts/opinions do not represent the author's beliefs.

This is not in any way an autobiography of the author or any other person.

12/RTPI–009738/2007

12/077238.7/07

Safe Creative 1304084911924

ISBN: 9798712302499

A LETTER FROM ABROAD

1st Dec 1998

Dear Farah,

I was so happy to hear that you were fine and that our big problem was nothing but a false alarm. I was almost sure that it couldn't be that…, but you never know with these things. I know you must have had an awful time these last days, so did I, but let's try to forget it now.

To cheer you up a bit, here I am sending you a compilation of my misfortunes in Madrid and the strange chain of events that took me from creating trouble in the *Barrio* to bumping into you that Friday afternoon in Danetree Town Centre.

I've called my little book Yobbo 98. Yobbo as I was a bit of a trouble-maker those days, a yobbo as you say in England, and 98 because… well is not difficult to guess why. The story is in the blue disk that came with this letter. I'm sorry, but I wasn't going to spend a fortune printing and sending the whole thing. You told me you didn't have a computer at home, I know, but you will have to be creative. I'm sure that at your old school, or at the local library they won't have a problem letting a pretty girl like you use a computer for a bit.

I also want to remind you, as I have learned how small-minded you Brits are when it comes to foreign babble (tongue in cheek), that English isn't my native language and that some three years ago I couldn't speak it to save my life. Although I have somehow improved, I'm sure that this little horror of mine will have lots of grammatical and spelling blunders. Please, don't make a big deal about them and focus on the story itself.

Well, that is pretty much everything. I hope that you enjoy reading my story as much as I have enjoyed writing it. I bet you will, you have a very important role in it.

Lots of Love

Chencho

INTRODUCTION

Hey amigos, allow me to introduce myself. My name's Chencho, I'm 18 years old, and we're in Madrid, Spain, at the start of 1998. It's eight months after the tragic death of Lady Di and the year that the French dishonestly won the World Cup by maliciously playing better football than the rest of us[1]. There's nothing special about my life; I don't read books, don't go to the movies, I don't do sport, am not a musician, I have no specific talent. When I fancy a good time, I buy litres and litres of drink and go to some square with my mates to get rat-arsed on *kalimocho*[2], beer and cheap whisky. So that's my weekend; drunk in the street, smoking reefers and getting into trouble. I spend the annoying gap between weekends falling asleep in class, bored, waiting impatiently for Friday to come so the whole thing can start all over again.

Makes me proud to think someday we'll be known as the *Botellón*[3] piss-up generation, a generation of slackers who were given everything; an everything that our lives turned into idleness, boozing, and the consumption of other recreational drugs in the barrio. Our progressive, tolerant parents are both our accomplices and benefactors in this, letting us get away with any old nonsense, with the excuse that we can enjoy a freedom they never had, provided we do just enough at school to give us some kind of future.

Studying from Monday to Thursday, shooting up from Friday to Sunday is my life and the life of most of my friends. For how long? I don't know, the only thing I know for sure is that today's Friday and as soon as I'm done writing this crap I'm getting ready to go out, to party and get a hit. After all, I'm young, aren't I?

If you wanna come with me, I'll see you in Madrid tripper heaven.

---

[1] Tribute to Lord Edmund Blackadder pantomime "We must invade France".

[2] A mixture of Coca-Cola and low quality red wine.

[3] Alcohol drinking session, usually in a public place.

FROM MADRID TO TRIPPER HEAVEN

At eight that Friday I met my friends at the Café Comercial to go to Malasaña neighbourhood[4]. The second phase of exams had just finished and everyone from our secondary school class wanted to celebrate an end to the torture, with a huge piss-up in the Plaza del Dos de Mayo. For a couple of years we'd been meeting up there to drink, not only the people from my class, but most of the higher certificate crowd from our private school.

In 1998 you could still drink alcohol on the streets of Madrid without risking a hefty fine from the public order squad, so our main weekend pastime was for fifteen or twenty of us to go to Malasaña, buy a load of cheap wine and coca cola, mix it in the wine boxes and sit in the square, drinking. We called this kind of al fresco piss-up *botellón*, and it was fucking great; with just three notes you got off your tits on *kalimocho*, a local style mixture of coke and red wine, free from the rules and noise of a bar. The only downside was the barrio ended up looking like shit. Piss in every corner, the streets full of rubbish, and the poor locals kept awake into the early hours. Moreso because we weren't the only ones; in recent times the area had become rather fashionable, and half of Madrid was getting pissed there.

On that particular day we didn't sit in the square. The place was heaving so we went to the end of Velarde, a street leading off the square. Quickly we formed a kind of circle, with half of us leaning against the wall and the other half facing them, sat on the pavement. The whole barrio was full of groups of youths sitting on the sidewalks, so if you wanted to go up a street you had to walk in the road. Fortunately, fearing it would get blocked in or damaged, few people would risk leaving their car parked in the narrow streets of Malasaña over the weekend, so we could mill about with ease. Within central Madrid, Malasaña was the territory of the punks, the skinheads, and generally of all those of an alternative stripe, while the neo-nazi scumbags hung around in the *Bilbao* zone. Each urban tribe had its own patch, the ravers met up in the squares of *Argüelles*, the rich kids in *Alonso Martínez* and *Castellana*, the gays in *Chueca*, our very welcomed tourists in *Huertas* and the foreign thugs in *Lavapies*. We, who were neither poshos nor ravers, and obviously not Nazis, identified more with

---

[4] Bohemian quarter in Central Madrid. A working class area in the past, now heavily gentrified.

the lefties of Malasaña, so we had our piss-ups there. Although we went partially disguised as some kind of urban gang, in reality we were just nice kids from a private school, playing at being weekend rebels.

Having sat on the pavement, some of my mates set about rolling some spliffs while the others discussed who would go and buy the kalimocho from the Chinese shop up the road, at the corner with Corredera Alta St.

"Let me roll one," I asked my friend Davo, who was sitting next to me. Davo was a true marijuana enthusiast, and keen on all drugs, as well as being a drunk. But he blew me out.

"No, Chencho," he replied, "you never cough up the money, but you're always smoking other people's weed."

"Okay, I'll roll it, but you smoke it," I insisted, knowing the unwritten rule that whoever rolls a spliff has a right to at least the first drag.

The ploy failed and he answered, "No, Gutierrez can roll it. He does it better," and he handed Guti a piece of hashish. Guti the lad got swiftly to work and constructed a reefer within a couple of seconds. He and Davo smoked it, offering me nothing. You'll soon shoot up and be giving me a smoke without knowing it, bastards, I thought resentfully. Fortunately, the two who'd gone to get the booze were coming back down the street, loaded up with boxes of wine and everything needed to start the session. Seeing as I didn't have a joint to smoke, I consoled myself with a plastic cup filled with three ice cubes and equal parts of plonk and coke.

We started drinking and talking about our studies, our lives and many other subjects. When boozing and chatting we had a series of rituals that would be repeated almost every weekend. The first was to ask a cigarette of anyone passing by, though I never quite understood why. If every one of us had given some *pesetas*, our old shitty currency, doubtless we'd have had enough to buy two packs of *Fortuna*[5] cigs, but no, we had to ask for the smokes themselves because that was better entertainment. At this too, Guti was a master. I don't know how he did it, but his tobacco harvest was always the most impressive, by quite a margin.

---

[5] Popular cigarette brand in Spain

Once we had cigarettes the next thing was to roll spliffs and negotiate how these should be smoked. In our group there were some, like Davo or Diego, who always coughed up the money, and others, like Guti or myself, who never spent any dosh in drugs. The game was based on there being those who had weed, and those who had none but wanted a smoke it. The latter group had to achieve their goal without a minimum of scrounging. The problem was it was seen as bad form for someone to smoke a spliff all on their own, it was customary to pass it around. Because of this, it was common to see spongers like Guti and I sitting next to the ones with the weed, to see what we could get. Davo was the best to sit next to because, as well as smoking, he'd get mortal drunk and would finally have to ask for help rolling his spliffs. So I always made sure I was near him, but that *cabrón* Guti was ahead of me and was usually the chosen one.

Personally, there were two reasons I didn't buy hash. One was that I didn't enjoy smoking it much, I much preferred alcohol. The other, more important, reason was that we scroungers had just as much fun as the buyers. Us trying to smoke without paying, and them letting people sponge off them, and feeling important for it. If I'd wanted I'd have bought my hashish every weekend, but doing it this way was more amusing. In fact, as time went on, we invented a multitude of rules and laws on the whole matter, such as "roller gets first drag", "a spliff ain't asked for, it's passed" and many more, which we'd repeat like parrots until someone passed us a smoke.

Something else we did there was watch the street for anyone we knew, to say *hola* and invite them to sit and drink for a while. As we'd spent several years hanging around that area we knew a load of people, and there were also the kids from other classes in our school, and old pupils who were now undergraduates. This was great, since we'd never get bored, but it also had a downside. If you got too stoned and ended up causing a scene, everyone in school would soon know about it. This could seriously affect your rep, especially with the squarer chicks.

Sitting there in Velarde Street or Dos de Mayo Square, every Friday night would follow a similar sort of script. We'd start drinking kalimocho, cheap wine mixed with coke, one bottle after another, while Davo would discreetly invite seemingly anyone for a smoke, and Diego and Pedro would monopolize all the reefers. Each guy would spend the night in his own characteristic way. Davo usually got sick and fell asleep. Guti got up to his pranks, making himself the centre of attention, and Diego would manage the party, deciding when to go up the road for more drink. Others, like Gabo and Florian, occasionally chatted some girl up, and Pedro, being a very sociable type, would embark on interminable discussions with anyone he knew who came by.

There were so many guys there that night that it's impossible to tell you what each was up to. I would generally do a bit of everything, and didn't stand out for anything in particular, although I'd get off my head, smoke if I could, and try to be friendly if I saw someone I knew. When I needed a leak I'd go to the end of Dos de Mayo square to piss in some corner, and if I wanted a bite to eat I'd buy a snack in one of the old traditional bars that competed for drinkers with the sleazy dives round there.

By midnight I was already pretty drunk, having a good time there, in Malasaña, surrounded by all my mates. Some of us were planning to go to a bar or some other place as soon as we'd finished the umpteenth box of wine we'd just started. So much alcohol was making me a bit crazy. I wanted action; to get out of our shitty street corner, to some decent place where we could meet some birds.

Couldn't do that yet though, we still had a load of booze to get through, and we had to watch the street. It wouldn't have been right to let someone we knew go by without inviting them for a drink, for a few swallows of wine-cola. In one of these encounters, we saw Troya, a guy from our class, coming down the street with a group of people. Troya was one of the most notorious guys in school, he painted graffiti and was deeply involved in drugs. Even so, Troya was charming and funny. Everyone really liked him because although a bad boy, he never bullied anybody and was always fooling about. I was good friends with Troya because he really helped me to fit in at school. When I entered the first year my previous school sent me having to repeat the year. I also had a black eye and a miserable face on me. I had just been expelled from a state school for bad behaviour, and few of the kids at the new private school wanted anything to do with me. For the first two years there Troya was my only friend, and he gradually introduced me to everyone. Without his protection I'd have had an even worse time than I did, and for this I was truly grateful to him.

As soon as I saw him I greeted him and invited him to sit and drink a bit of kalimocho with us. Troya accepted, but did it more for me than anything else, seeing as he didn't get on too well with my other mates. With him was a guy called Abel, who was older than us, and three older girls. They sat with us for a while, though keeping a bit distant from the others, and rolled some spliffs. Troya and his group didn't drink much but they were never short of weed, and in truth were always involved in drugs beyond marijuana. On that particular day it was LSD, the week before it had been speed, and the next it would be uppers, cocaine, ecstasy, mushrooms or God knows what.

While Troya made one spliff after another, sharing them with me without the stinginess of my other friends, he told me what they planned to do that night. The house of one of the girls was free, her parents being away. To make the most of this they'd decided to sleep there, though of course that wouldn't be until morning, after having spent the night at a nearby club.

It wasn't a bad plan at all. Tripping out, then back to the girl's house where he'd surely end up fucking one of them. Troya's group were well into free love, and were forever doing it with each other, though they tended to stay with one individual for a while at least. As well as offering me some smokes, Troya tried to convince me to come with them. I wasn't sure what I wanted to do, because though I had great trust in Troya and enjoyed his company, it wasn't quite that way with his other friends. They were quite a sealed clique, and though they were nice to me out of respect for Troya, they were always a bit distant.

While hesitating over what to do I was smoking incessantly. As soon as I passed a spliff on another would magically appear. Not being used to such generosity, I didn't want to waste the opportunity. I refused nothing, neither the weed, nor the half dose of acid Troya put in my mouth on something of a whim.

"Try this, mate, see where it takes you!" he said, and I started sucking the small piece of card, first very cautiously, ready to spit it out at the slightest appearance of winged dragons or flying pink elephants. That was my first experience with LSD; I'd heard lots of stories about hallucinations and severe psychotropic effects.

As nothing was happening I kept sucking for quite a while, not noticing any effect. Load of crap, this acid lark, I thought, just before starting to feel very strange. It all began with a light dizziness and a strange sensation of irrational anxiety, although this could be blamed more on the spliffs than the other. Alarmed, I felt the dizziness increasing in intensity, and soon felt like I was riding a rollercoaster; a rollercoaster inside my head. To this was added a great feeling of weakness, as though a weight had been laid on my chest and I couldn't move.

It'll soon go, I thought. The most important thing was to carry on with the party, and avoid creating some pathetic scene in front of all my friends. For a while I sat there in the circle, saying nothing. Around me people were talking fast, and I couldn't follow their conversations; I tried to appear normal. I felt gradually worse, until I reached a point where I decided I wasn't enjoying this and wanted to go home. Yet I didn't dare move, so as not to attract attention. I was sure that if I'd gotten up or gestured that I was going, the others would have started asking questions, and even prevented me leaving. The situation was worse because due to being surrounded by people I didn't totally trust, and from whom I wouldn't have been bold enough to ask for help. On one hand, Troya's friends would have laughed and made fun of me if I'd gotten sick, and on the other I could feel my other friends more hostile to me since I'd gone with Troya and his crowd. Even Troya, my first friend at school, was taking on a cynical and vaguely threatening air.

Things got worse when one of the girls, Cristina, started talking to me and I didn't know how to reply.

"Chencho, are you all right?" she said, "You look very pale." I didn't answer her; I couldn't and I was scared. But that just made it worse because she told the other girls and soon all three started bombarding me with questions and comments.

"Are you OK?"

"You look so pale."

"You're white as a sheet, see-through."

"Look like a vampire."

Soon, thanks to those three witches and their lack of discretion, I became the centre of attention and others joined the interrogation. I quickly got the impression, or rather became certain, that everyone in the group was talking about me, and not in very kindly terms. That Chencho's a prick, always making a fuss and causing trouble, I imagined them saying. One of these days we'll have to teach him a lesson.

While I was fielding the barrage of questions as best I could, responding monosyllabically and trying to stay calm, an idea entered firmly into my head. They're all against you, Chencho, better get out of here while you can. This interior voice was answered by another, recommending prudence and that I wait until I was no longer the centre of attention, before escaping unseen. The two ideas fought inside me, but a worsening of my state convinced me to immediately seek the safety of home, before I really got sick. Now I was sweating, and to the earlier dizziness was added a tickling feeling all over my body and a strange sensation of my head being enveloped in fire, but this fire was cold, electric and light blue.

I could stand it no longer, and I got up. When I did so I felt like the whole street and the nearby Dos de Mayo square were in stone silence, and that everyone was watching me. Why can't they fucking leave me in peace, I thought desperately, while walking as best I could up Velarde Street. Behind me my so-called friends were shouting and calling, but all this did was make me afraid. "Come here Chencho! Come back. Are you all right? We're your *amigos*, we're going to kill you," and a lot of other stuff of confused meaning.

Going up Velarde Street was a terrifying experience. To start with, I felt my friends were chasing me to prevent me leaving, or maybe for more sinister reasons. I was also scared by the people getting drunk up both sides of the street. And if that wasn't enough, I now had electromagnetic rays all round my head, so people looked at me with hate as I passed by. I felt dizzy and very weak, and with each step I took reality seemed more jumbled. The safety of my house seemed thousands of kilometres away, and I was convinced I would die before reaching home. I was vulnerable in the street; there were lots of people wanting to harm me. Little by little my field of vision was blanking out, and there came a point when I was walking blind. Then, on the corner of Fuencarral Street, I fell into a doorway.

I didn't know if I was still alive or had died and followed a light up to tripper's heaven, the only thing I knew for sure was there was someone or something near me. After a long time with my head on some cold surface I started to recuperate a little and regain my vision. When I opened my eyes I saw with relief that it was Troya sitting at my side. I soon closed them again because I still felt like crap. I think Troya was trying to talk to me intermittently, but I didn't pay him much attention. I felt so bad that I didn't even have the strength to listen. Fortunately Troya wasn't the typical sober friend who helps you and lightly chides you when you get drunk or sick, putting you in even greater misery. Troya was tripping too, and this helped him see my need for understanding and support. The first thing he did was give me a bottle of coca cola that had some kalimocho in it. Although it was a heady broth, the Kali, or rather the sugar in the Kali, helped me recover from the drop in blood pressure that had knocked me out. As I recuperated we started talking, but it wasn't a normal conversation; it was more like a conversation high on acid.

"You."

"Like it?"

"Umm, I like it!"

"Kalimocho?"

"I like it!"

"Smoke?"

"No, it makes us paranoid!"

"Shall we go?

"What?

"Whaaaaaaaaaaaaaat!"

And so we continued for quite some time, and maybe our conversation made no sense, but between us we reached an almost perfect level of communion and understanding. I was so much in agreement with everything Troya said that I had no fear that others might harm me. Troya was with me, and together we were indestructible inside our blue force field. Suddenly we began to laugh, a laugh that would have seemed idiotic to others, but that for us had both a profound meaning and a life of its own. From that point we didn't stop laughing the whole night, regardless of how much my cheeks hurt or how high my eyebrows had to stretch. I just couldn't help pissing myself laughing at everything Troya said to me.

At some point we met Abel and his chick friends and we set off to a nightclub they knew. This gang no longer scared me, I felt confident and self-assured after having recovered from the earlier incident. It must have been the spliffs that had made me so unwell, so paranoid, having added to the symptoms of the LSD. Luckily, from what I could understand, Abel, as well as some of the girls, were also tripping.

The journey to the nightclub was exciting, mainly because it was well hidden among the alleyways of Malasaña. As we made our way through them we looked with fascination at the slightest little details, from a group of passers-by to a sign stuck on a wall. Occasionally something frightened us, such as an old woman who suddenly emerged from a doorway, a weird man we came across, or a big puddle in the road. Most things were of intense interest to us. In a way I felt like a little kid who was just discovering the world and was excited by any little thing, and it must have been the same for the others because we stopped every few steps and for the slightest of reasons.

After going round in circles in Malasaña we finally found the nightclub in one of the streets close to Tribunal and we went in, after paying a small fee for entrance and the cover charge. Inside it wasn't bad. Though small, it wasn't crowded, and we could walk about and dance without trouble. The electronic music seemed incredibly beautiful to me, and put me in a state of simultaneous relaxation and high activity. If that hadn't been enough, the walls were covered with mirrors, so while dancing I found myself staring at my reflection and the lights with great concentration, so as not to miss any detail of this new universe that had been set before my eyes.

Time passed, sometimes quickly, sometimes slowly, and the experience was generally pleasant, though with the small quantity I'd taken I didn't get spaced out, nor did I hallucinate or discover the hidden meaning of human existence. The only time I felt anxiety was when I went to the bathroom and got inexplicably lost, returning via a series of dark corridors and passageways containing a load of doors, hidden traps, and rather annoying tornados.

When Troya told me he was going I was surprised; we were having such a great time. I said we should stay a bit longer but he replied that the place was closing. In the blink of an eye I found myself alone in the street and it was daytime. I decided it would be a good idea to go straight back to my place because, even though I wasn't tired, I had the absurd feeling that a dog was chasing me, wanting to bite me. After a half-hour stroll during which nothing of note happened, I opened the door of my house to be met by my parents' shocked expressions. They had just gotten up and were mad as hell.

At that point the wisest thing would have been to say sorry, give them a convincing explanation as to why I was arriving home at eight in the morning without prior warning, and take my punishment with humility. Instead I said "Fuck it, you're both paranoid!", and my father got so furious that he had to go out and walk the dog – *Piletus* – so he could calm down and resist the urge to kill me.

Getting the impression that, in trying to explain myself, I had somewhat pissed on my chips, I decided to run up to bed so as not to create further annoyance. But that was where the second half of the party got started. With eyes like plates, and unable to sleep, I unceasingly rolled about on top of and under the sheets while the whole room fell onto me. I wouldn't manage a wink of sleep until well into Saturday night.

LOW LIFE IN LOS BAJOS

"How embarrassing, spaced out on nothing, making a scene, looking ridiculous in front of your *amigos* and worrying your poor old parents." Once most of the effects had worn off, I spent Saturday night and Sunday morning repeating this over to myself. Fortunately, the weekend wasn't totally lost, as Monday was a holiday, meaning Sunday night would be a kind of poor man's Saturday, and we could go out.

I was determined to go out on Sunday night, but I wasn't sure what to do because I would spend most Saturday nights in Malasaña, and no doubt it would be empty on a Sunday. Luckily I heard that a big group from school, containing quite a few girls, were off to get pissed in Parque del Oeste, a pretty big park in western Madrid. Not in principle any great plan, but in those days, when you're barely eighteen and drinking for drinking's sake is still exciting, and knowing there'd be chicks there, well, it gives the prospect added interest. Of my real friends, those I trusted, only Gabo and a rocker from *Los Bajos* called Barry were going. The others were really acquaintances, but having nothing better to do I decided to turn up at the park at the agreed time.

When I got there I went straight over to Gabo and started drinking, with a disinterested air. Gabo was my best friend at school; I got on with him better than anyone, we just hit it off. For three years we'd been doing the same course, and never exchanged a word. Then, one day, by happenstance, we started talking, and within half an hour we were inseparable friends, partners in adolescent japes and knocking about. I liked hanging around with Gabo because together we were a right pair; always looking for trouble. Even so, lately, since he'd started seeing Lola, an upper class girl, Gabo had been a bit sniffy, and didn't join in the fun with the same spirit as before. The other guys and girls there weren't from my usual circle and at first I couldn't help feeling a bit out of place. But, gradually, the alcohol reduced my inhibitions and I could relate normally to most of them, like I was part of their gang.

It would have been about six in the evening when we started drinking the kalimocho, all sat about on the grass, and there we stayed till around ten. When the drink ran out we decided we'd go to a bar in a dodgy spot called Los Bajos de Argüelles to lark about to the in the party atmosphere. We chose Los Bajos because it was the only clubbing area that wasn't dead on a Sunday and also for the interesting combination of cheap alcohol and tacky music offered by the many little bars round there.

I remember feeling particularly down that evening, maybe because Sunday is a depressing day during which the hopes you put into your weekend turn into resignation at the imminent arrival of the five mind-numbingly boring days of the week, with the added frustration of not having got your end away. For the whole evening I was constantly taking the piss out of people, with cheeky comments, jokes and various nonsense, while I entertained myself with wilful little acts of vandalism against the bars we were in and the street furniture we came across while moving from one place to the next.

Finally we ended up at "Tubos bar", a club where the concept of seediness is like an article of faith. There we kept necking it down and got to dancing like idiots to the summer hits of 73. Suddenly, amid all the messing about, and the drunken yelling of my mates, who were trying to shout out the song lyrics, something caught my attention. Leant up against one of the bars was a box of Pepsi, seemingly left to make its own way in the world, and simultaneously destined to excite my most kleptomaniacal instincts. I swallowed and dwelt on how much I'd like to go over, nick one or two bottles, and quietly drink them outside.

Being drunk, I decided to do the dirty deed, and my first considered act was to check whether the bar staff had noticed me greedily eyeing the colas and had perceived my criminal intentions. Let's remember that I wouldn't have been the first person to betray themself with a too-worried look, like when spying a classmates exam paper, or sneaking a look at some girl's knockers - showing the enemy your intent far too early. There was hardly a barmaid serving the other bars and it seemed there were no other waiters, doormen, or other hostelry fauna to be seen, so I felt that the coast was clear.

Now that I'd tested the viability of theft, and given my willingness to do the deed, all that remained was to find some excuse to justify my antisocial behaviour to myself:

1. The owners of this place sell drinks at abusive prices.

2. The owners of this place sell alcohol to young adolescents, inciting them to ruin their health.

3. The owners of this place, in flagrant violation of environmental legislation, produce a large amount of noise pollution.

4. This bar is a fucking hole.

5. The music is terrible.

6. I'm pissed out of my head, and I don't care.

Conclusion: the theft is merely a redistribution of wealth by unorthodox means, and can be justified, especially if the thief is yourself and the victims of the theft are someone else.

After so much lofty debate came the time to act, and to act with the wiles of a cat. First I approached the box containing the dark nectar, and leant casually against the bar, looking at the arses of the girls dancing on the dance floor, in order to appear normal. I felt a slight acceleration of my pulse and a shivering sensation as I bent down pretending to tie the laces of my hacky old Adidas trainers. Then, after checking for the last time that my movements hadn't been noticed, I quickly grabbed one of the Pepsi bottles and put it the left pocket of my tight trousers as I got up and made quickly towards the door. That guy's got some erection, people must have thought as they watched me scarpering out with an elongated bulge next to my groin. The next time I nick something I'll wear a tracksuit.

Once outside, and sure that no one had seen me, I felt safer and retrieved the bottle from my pocket. The drunken sensation of victory soon vanished when I saw the bottle was open, and worse, empty. With resignation I twigged there'd been as many empties in the box as full, and that inwardly exulting in my good luck had only resulted in me picking one of the empties. But I didn't lose hope, and quickly went back to steal another.

The filching process began over again, first I casually approached the bar and bent over, pretending to look for a dropped five cent coin. I took another bottle but this time made sure it was unopened and full. I now honestly think the bar staff must have been busy with other stuff, because I did all this totally drunk and hardly discreetly, though at the time I felt like I was doing a pretty professional job.

I went outside for the second time, but now with a good bottle and quite a shot of adrenaline coursing through me. By the same club door I took out the bottle, opened it with my teeth, and took a long swig. This time it was Fanta lemon, a drink I don't normally like. But on this occasion, being associated with a cloak and dagger crime, it took on a much more interesting flavour. Really, that was the only reason it did so. With the money I still had, I could have bought at least five or six of those soft drinks, but buying just wouldn't have been the same. The attraction didn't lie in the tempting citric flavour, nor in the refreshing bubbles, but in the excitement of having been stolen, taken from under the noses of the guys who had bought them honourably, and getting to laugh in their fucking faces...

Given my burgeoning alcoholism, it was only a matter of time before I put my foot in it and got caught. My weekend vandalism was getting progressively bolder and I was finding it harder to discern the thin red line that separates innocent messing about from drunken fights. I returned to the bar and had another glass of whisky, this time paying, and went to dance for a while. When I got bored of larking about with my friends, my eyes fell upon a much riskier, more ambitious target. The bottles of liquor behind the bar.

Unfortunately, this time I wasn't at all discreet. I clumsily and noisily leapt over the bar, landing on glass bottles and banging myself in the process. Once there, instead of abandoning the idea, I grabbed the first bottle I saw and shot out towards the exit. Both the bar staff and my friends were gobsmacked, not believing what I was up to and, though at the time I was blind to anything that didn't involve me delighting in my own misdeeds, the whole bar was watching in disbelief as some show-off jumped the bar and ran out with a bottle of Malibu pina colada.

Soon after leaving the bar I was stopped by one of the barmen, a guy of about my own height and build, though older. From that point on, my whole recollection is confused due to being in such an alcoholic stupor that it was hard to distinguish imagination from reality. I remember the guy tore the bottle from my hands with an indignant gesture, and it's entirely possible I struggled a bit. I even think I insulted him, though the thing I remember most was just standing there with a huge feeling of disorientation. "OK, they caught me. And now what do I do?" was how I was thinking. "Do I scarper or react casually, run or invent some implausible bizarre excuse?" What I didn't know was that, for the barman, it was a little more serious than that. He had already gone back inside, but not to return the bottle to the bar, rather to call up the reinforcements, the cowardly professional lynch mob for defenceless youths, the infamous bouncers.

The ones to react quickly and effectively were my friends, who saw how dangerous the situation had become for me, and probably for themselves too, due to me being with them. Gabo came out first, almost immediately after the barman entered, and he pushed me forward just to get me to react. He did it with such force that I almost fell. Then I realised the situation was out of control, and we sprinted off while the rest of my schoolmates, especially the girls, remained in the bar, trying to mollify the doormen.

After running through several streets of the celebrated, grid-like, barrio of Argüelles, including a few close shaves with cars, a sharp pain in my side forced me to slow to a stop. I sat on a car, trying to catch my breath.

"We should go a bit further, the bouncers will probably look for you all over the *barrio*," said Gabo, "they get pretty bored on Sundays."

"I don't think so!" I struggled to say, "They'll already have forgotten us."

Gabo looked at me, surprised, and nodded. He knew how futile it was to reason with an argumentative drunk. "Stay here and don't make any more trouble. I'm going to see what's happening." He returned five minutes later, visibly worried.

"The bouncers have called all the neighbouring bars people and they're looking for you."

"For me!" I said, angrily "they'd kill their own mother over one fucking bottle... doesn't seem... hic...fair."

"Come on, let's get out of here, you can tell me your opinions later," and that said, we set off for his house, which wasn't far. In those moments of silent return I decided to intone the classic 'mea culpa'.

"Okay mate," I told him, "I know I fucked up and spoilt everyone's fun. I was trying to nick a bottle so we could all have a piss up, I just wanted to be the man. Other times it's worked."

"No problem, brother." Gabo answered tactfully, trying not to plunge me any deeper into the misery.

"Fuck yeah there's a problem. I almost put you all in real trouble, for sure. What did the bouncers say to you?"

"Nothing intelligent, at first they were going apeshit, but Barry knows one of them, what with him practically living in the bars round here. Then the girls started on them and gradually convinced them you didn't come with us, that you were just a solitary pisshead who was bothering us."

"So they're all OK with it."

"Yeah, they're all OK, but you could have thought a bit more before trying something like that on."

"I'm sorry, very sorry," I said, dying of shame.

Then Gabo stopped and, very serious, told me "Really, I don't know what's wrong with you. You've been a nightmare lately. You're always up to some nonsense, apparently for no reason, but you won't always be so fucking lucky and get away with it like today. You are eighteen now, for fucks sake"

"Yes, you're right. I'm gonna try and calm down a bit."

"Let's wait and see if that's fucking true," and saying that he shook my hand and made for his front door, taking out his keys.

"I'll see you in class on Tuesday."

"Go straight home, and don't get in any more trouble."

"Bye."

And that was the end of my little Sunday altercation. After saying goodbye to Gabo I kept to myself and didn't dare go by Moncloa metro station, thinking the bouncers could be waiting there for me. Every few seconds I looked round, expecting to see someone following me; the dark street corners filled me with trepidation. When turning to look back I would feel a premonition of seeing a gang of muscle-bound guys who'd make me crap myself, or maybe worse if you pay attention to gossip. Even so, nothing happened, and I arrived home safe and well.

Always after such trouble I liked to reflect on events and draw conclusions. The first was that now I knew myself a bit better, and even though I was a generally thoughtful kind of individual, alcohol and party music nevertheless turned me into an impulsive guy. Well, myself and many others. The second thing was that if I hadn't managed to escape during the first confused moments in the bar, I would be facing up to some pretty substantial consequences. You've got to behave yourself in these clubs, because one of the greatest dangers hanging over a youth, apart from apparently harmless drugs like marijuana or acid that later leave you crumpled in a heap, or the exciting but dangerous mixture of cars and alcohol, are the disco bar bouncers. These characters are judge, jury and executioner in all nocturnal altercations, and they're apparently inclined to pick on anyone they like. Cockier than the police, bigger arseholes than the riot squad, more provocative than the pimps, and bigger drug pushers than the drug pushers themselves. Like Judge Dredd but seedy with it. Security, my arse! These guys just spent their time making people's lives a misery.

MALASAÑA NEIGHBOURHOOD

After my unpleasant Sunday incident and the Friday trip, I spent the following week trying to make amends while hiding from the reproachful looks of my friends, who were also my 1998 pre-university course classmates. I remember having shyly asked one of the girls how things had turned out with the bouncers and having used my tone of voice and some pansyish pouting to implicitly ask for forgiveness. But generally I preferred not to mention it again to anyone, hoping everything would be forgotten.

From nine on Monday morning to three on Friday afternoon, my priority was to be invisible and concentrate on the boring lessons. In the afternoons I'd soon be home to study, something I'd been neglecting. There were only a couple of months left until the final exams and the three day University access test that would decide my life's direction, and I hadn't been doing too well with the syllabus.

My main problem with studying was concentration, particularly in the subjects requiring some mathematics. I found Reading things such as texts difficult and boring, but equations, mathematical demonstrations and formulas in general were completely insufferable.

Even so, showing off an innate audacity, I had enrolled in the sciences course option, intending to go on to University to study engineering. Neither family nor friends had managed to dissuade me from such a preposterous plan, so I had a lot of physics, chemistry, maths and technical drawing to learn - and little time or desire to do it - before the feared University test.

Before exams I'd usually spend quite a bit of time studying, but my difficulty in concentrating meant that four hours of torture amongst the books boiled down to about one. My study sessions were all the same. I started enthusiastically, but after half an hour my strength began to flag and I'd distract myself with any little thing. After an hour my gaze would drift from my notes with shocking ease, fixing on some point off in infinity. Two hours into studying, I'd realise I'd only studied a little percentage of what I'd intended to. After this would come an anxiety attack, followed by a compulsive intake of complex vitamins to improve performance. To top it all, my first break very often turned out to be my last. I'd leave the books for fifteen minutes to drink a glass of water and take a leak, and when I wanted to get back to work I would realise, with surprise, that it was already time to go to bed.

For five days, and despite the problems I've just mentioned, I forced myself to study the syllabus, make good notes and behave myself. I think I managed it, so I was feeling quite pleased on Friday afternoon. "Watch out!" I thought, "Now that I feel confident I'm gonna fuck it up. Well, no, this Friday I'll behave myself and won't fall into past errors. To begin with, I'm not going out; I'll stay at home, playing on the computer." I decided this at five in the afternoon, but after studying for a while I became nervous and started debating with myself:

"OK, so it's Friday. Should I go out or not?" On the one hand, if I stayed in I'd be safe and there'd be no unpleasant incidents. I could watch TV and then go to bed early. In fact, I probably wouldn't be missing anything interesting; doubtless the night would consist of drinking kalimocho in Velarde street with my schoolmates, before going home, having done nothing of note. Also, Malasaña, our clubbing zone par excellence, didn't interest me as much as it had the year before. The same thing would always happen. A place would be great for a night out - for a few months - until its reputation spread around Madrid, at which point the riffraff would descend to fuck it up. Malasaña was a great place to go out during 1996 and 1997, good people, a bit too keen on alternative lifestyles, but basically normal folk. There was a party atmosphere in the street, relative safety and good vibes, but in 1998 the scum started seeping in, attracted by people enjoying themselves. Suddenly you started seeing gangs of shaved-head thugs, but with the obligatory left wing badges to distinguish themselves from neo-nazi skinheads. There were also pimps, junkies and other lowlifes. Rumours started circulating, from God knows where, that a friend of a friend had been beaten up or that the police had infiltrated their agents into the crowd, to arrest anyone smoking a spliff. At the end of 1998 the place had become so depressing that we ended up going to the Alonso Martínez and Tribunal area instead, which, before long, would also be ruined by the same process.

On the other hand, if I didn't go out maybe I'd miss something of interest. Seems like whenever you spend a weekend in, as soon as you enter the class on Monday your friends are telling you everything that happened and what you missed. If I stayed at home it was guaranteed that nothing bad would happen to me; but nothing good either. Actually, I prefer not to use euphemisms, and to speak with total clarity. When I say something good or something interesting I am referring uniquely and exclusively to meeting some nice girl and chatting her up, or at least affording myself the illusion of having been close to a conquest. In reality that wasn't very probable, statistically speaking. It had hardly happened to me at all in years. Most of the time my nights out were limited to hanging around in the street with other putzes, boozing like it was going out of fashion, and pissing in some doorway, but we did recognise this wasn't the best way to impress the feminine sex. If we'd at least gone to more decent areas there'd have been an outside chance, but I preferred not to foster such ambitions; it was impossible to get my friends to do anything other than sit in the street drinking kalimocho.

Also, don't forget that when you're 18 years old, going out on the weekend is your first priority in life. At that age the most important things are your friends and partying, as well as having your hormones going crazy, all which fuels natural curiosity. For an older guy the matter of going out isn't so important anymore; you've already drunk, danced, partied enough; you're not gonna discover anything new. And if you already have a partner, sex is what keeps you in on a Friday night; for the adolescent it's the other way round. When you're 18 years old the night is a world of fascination. Everything's new, everything's cool and freaky, there's a load of ways to enjoy yourself… or get into trouble.

After much hesitation I decided to go out, but just for a while, and intent not to go mad. Going out on Friday and resting on Saturday was a reasonable option, and quite moderate during a time of life when standard behaviour was going out two or three times a week. So, this decided, I set myself to studying for a while with my usual wandering concentration. Half an hour after starting I was forced to surrender to the overwhelming case that Fridays weren't a good time for swotting. So I closed my notes and bid them farewell until Sunday. Now that the first obstacle dividing youth from happiness had been eliminated (study) there was one more reef to navigate before I could go out with my mates; this being sport.

From the age of fourteen, every Monday, Wednesday and Friday I went to a gym on San Bernardo Street to practice WTF[6] taekwondo. I'd loved this sport since still very young, and while most of my friends stuck to football or basketball, I hit my opponents in the gym or, more frequently, they hit me. Taekwondo is a martial art similar to karate, though much more spectacular, in which high kicks, spins and jumps predominate. Not that it's the best style of martial art for self-defence, since it more or less ignores dislocations, holds and strangulation. However, at first sight, it certainly tends to impress. After training for a bit more than a year, I could do all the specialised kicks and aerial

---

[6] World Taekwondo Federation.

manoeuvres, and when you're fifteen that gives you a lot of credibility in the schoolyard, or, in my case, in the stuck-up private college yard.

The problem was that after five years training I'd tired of the same old routine. And the new trainer focused the sessions more on the sporting competition side and was very demanding. He got rid of the mystic martial art part, and though the others at the gym seemed to love it, it just put me off.

Lack of desire combined with lack of time. As I said, I would train Mondays, Wednesdays and Fridays at the gym, and sometimes on my own at home, but at fourteen I hardly needed to study at all. But with the pre-uni course you can't waste Monday and Wednesday evenings on leisure activities. Also, when you're an adolescent you don't have many leisure time options. There's sport or the flicks and then on to the burger joint, and between these two choices taekwondo always won for me; but when you're eighteen there are many more possibilities. There's alcohol, friends, girls, drugs, piss-ups in the street, Malasaña, sexual exploration, radical and alternative lifestyles, and a thousand other things. Suddenly sport starts moving to the margin and is then abandoned, only to be resumed in your thirties when you realise not much of your youth is left.

So the gym knew where it could stick its taekwondo. This was going to be my night of fun. I would study tomorrow, and on Monday I'd use some excuse to do with the family, because saying I just happened to be ill on Friday wouldn't wash.

The next step was to call my friends to arrange going out. It wasn't really necessary because we'd almost always meet up on weekends at ten o'clock in the same place; the Plaza del Dos de Mayo in Malasaña. Even so, I made a call to confirm the time and place, and started getting ready.

The pre-going-out ritual in those days wasn't very elaborate. We were so young that the nights usually weren't long, and when all you're doing is sitting in a square getting pissed, there's no great requirement to look sharp. For me the ritual started with a big meal based on pizza or some other high carb food. After that, and in the correct order, I'd have a crap, shower and get dressed. Clothes were usually casual, maybe a bit alternative, giving a nod to some urban tribe or other, for coolness purposes, though not overdoing it, so as to avoid problems with the lowlifes. Tight jeans, checked shirt, 70s wool sweater and retro Adidas trainers. A quite discreet mod-punk-skin look occasionally complemented with some left-wing badge or emblem, like a red star or squatters rights symbol. The reason for the latter was to avoid being seen as a neo-nazi due to my short hair and amateur skinhead getup. I had to be careful, making sure my real allegiance was only identifiable once I'd reached a safe area within Malasaña. On one occasion I'd left home with an antifascist badge on my lapel rather than hidden in my pocket, and at the Sol metro station some Nazis smacked me about a bit. No serious injuries, but it was pretty humiliating being beaten up in front of dozens of people stood there waiting for their trains.

The only cosmetic I used in those youthful days was deodorant. Later, when I discovered that rather than simply drinking kalimocho all night, I could pull, I branched out into aftershave, hair gel and other stuff. In 1998 the word 'metrosexual' wasn't yet popular, so apart from having a shave and spraying my pits, there was no funny business.

When it came to money, I always asked my folks for a thousand *pesetas*, and they'd give me it no problem. This, along with the three or four hundred I had saved, was more than enough to go out on. In those times, prices and our spending habits still allowed you to go out without squandering your parents' money. Prices in those days are certainly worth recalling as a matter of historical curiosity:

A one litre box of red wine cost about a hundred and twenty five *pesetas*, fifty pence in UK currency, the same as a two litre bottle of Coca Cola and about the same as a litre of *cerveza*. A bag of ice was two hundred pesetas and a small plastic glass between twenty and fifty pesetas, all these being Malasaña prices, be they from Chinese cornershops or different nationalities. For a thousand you could buy eight litres of kalimocho on special offer from the *Chinos*, and six hundred got you a bottle of DYC whisky. What's more, al fresco piss-ups were perfectly legal and the small bars were also reasonably priced. At one of our regular bars, the *Más Allí*, a glass of hooch and mixer was three hundred and a beer two hundred, though it could range up to a fiver if you went somewhere better, like *La Vía Láctea*. At these prices you could go out with a thousand, drink like a Cossack, and still have money for food.

Fed, dressed and money in my pocket, I was ready to go. The start was always the most exciting. I would leave the house imagining what new adventures awaited me, I'd go to my local Chinese shop to buy tobacco and chewing gum and I'd happily make my way to Sol metro station. After a couple of seemingly unending stops, I'd get off at Noviciado or Bilbao, two minutes from Velarde Street and the rendezvous point.

What I liked most about Malasaña was that there was always someone I knew, someone I could sit with, chat with and start drinking.

The good thing about those times was that all my friends and acquaintances - who, in reality, were all the people at my school- had group cohesion from being of the same age, with the same tastes, worries and problems in life. Later I realised that the links uniting us were just circumstantial, and that life would carry us away along different paths, distancing us within a very short time. Sometimes fifty or more of us, friends and acquaintances, would meet up and spend hours sitting in the nearby squares, drinking and smoking like it was going out of fashion.

That day was no exception. I got off at Bilbao Station and walked down Fuencarral to the start of Velarde Street. It was about ten o'clock; a typical March Friday night in Malasaña. As the winter cold had mostly departed and the days were getting longer, there were more people on the streets at night. The barrio was full of kids in their urban tribe garb, carrying plastic bags, boxes of wine, drinks and other stuff. Some went up towards Fuencarral and others went down to the Plaza de Dos de Mayo, but most made themselves comfortable on the sides of the street, sitting on the ground or in the doorways, forming groups of happy drinkers and smokers. At that time this seemed entirely normal to me, but now I understand why the residents there complained so much.

Finally, having nearly reached Dos de Mayo, I met a group of familiar faces. They'd been there a while, so had already bought loads of Kalimocho, and were sitting round in a circle, drinking and chatting about their daily concerns - which generally meant studies and soft drugs. Basically, and despite the fact we were drinking alcohol, we were still children. In many parts of the World, eighteen year olds already have responsibilities, work and even kids; but we had none of that. Instead, we had progressive, understanding, solvent parents who financed our fun and our future university education. Of the fifteen or so people there, aged seventeen or eighteen, none of us had ever worked, and every single one of us aspired to go to university.

I asked them to make space for me, and I joined them. Gabo, Guti, Diego, Pedro and many others, everyone was there, but as we'd already spent the school day together we didn't bother with greetings. "Park your arse" was the sign of courtesy letting me know they were happy to see me.

From that point onwards the night played out as it ever did. There were fifteen of us, mostly guys, and we drank kalimocho, smoked and talked while passers-by milled up and down Velarde Street. Now and again other groups of people we knew would come by and stop for a chat, or would even sit down and join us. And so time passed, and when the drink ran out a couple of us would go up to the Chinese shop to buy more coke and cheap wine to elaborate kalimocho; and so the piss-up was refuelled. In the end, almost always one of us would end up making a scene; getting sick, vomiting or causing a racket. Sometimes we would all sing in unison; some song from underground local bands like *Extremoduro, Reincidentes, Ska P* or some similar. Usually I'd enjoy it at the start, but after a couple of hours I'd start getting nervous.

My problem was the alcohol mixing with my adolescent hormones, and I would be reminded that a part of my life was being somewhat neglected: my relationship with the opposite sex. This was a source of great frustration to me, as I understood that - sitting there on the pavement of Velarde Street - the probability of finding a girlfriend was rather remote. Of course, there were girls in the group, but they were from my year at college, and I already knew them. There were some among them I liked, but on the other hand I was resistant to the notion of inbreeding complications within the group. I was convinced, rightly or wrongly, that if we had gone to the Argüelles or Alonso Martínez areas, we would have met a load of new girls, and I felt hopeless seeing my mates hadn't the slightest intention of budging from their little corner anytime tonight. Some of them had their girlfriend with them, so why move? Others already had a girlfriend, so all they wanted to do was drink and hang with their mates. Others were just lazy, or had not yet awoken to romantic love, so for one reason or another, it was rare that I could ever convince anyone to go exploring. In my mind's eye I could see the streets and bars of Argüelles and Alonso, full of groups of girls, cute chicks and hard-bodied punkettes, half drunk and desperately looking for a bit with guys like me. Meanwhile, there I was in Velarde, wasting time, surrounded by drunks.

This paranoia was making me pretty unhappy, so I took a cigarette and went a little way up Velarde Street to sit in a doorway and be alone for a while. I lit the fag, took a drag and began ruminating on my frustration. "These guys." I thought "Going out like this it's impossible to pull."

A familiar voice took me out of my contemplation:

"Hey, Chencho, what you doing here sat all alone!"

It was Leo, one of my best mates at the time. Leo was a couple of years older than I, though due to problems at school he was in my course, though in the arts stream. Leo was a bit mad, no stranger to violence, and would dish it out on the flimsiest of pretexts. Even so, we had become good friends due to our shared hobby of getting into trouble. I think he saw himself as some kind of immortal kung fu champion, when in reality he was just a stoned adolescent. I couldn't tell him this for two reasons. The first was that he was my friend and I didn't want to damage his self-esteem. The second was that I too was a nobody, and he could easily beat me up.

"Those guys are down there with a load of drink," I told him, hoping he would move off without telling me about martial arts or one of his horror stories. The attempt failed and he sat down next to me and started talking animatedly.

"Mate, you know what? The other day I went to a martial arts shop near Argüelles. It's called 'Black Belt Tenth Dan'. D'you know it? No? Well it's fucking great. I was looking for some ninja nunchucks for kung fu, but found something I liked more."

"Look," he said, in an enigmatic tone, while retrieving a small extended object from his leather jacket pocket.

"What the heck is that?" I asked him, feigning interest and wondering to myself from what kind of enemies, fictitious or real, my lunatic friend would need to defend himself.

"This is a self-defence tear gas spray; the definitive urban weapon," he said, without concealing his enthusiasm, holding it out for me to take.

I weighed it in my right hand. It was no bigger than a thick marker pen, and was covered with insulating tape to hide its lethal identity. I carefully pointed it to a corner of the doorway, and not bothering about Leo I fired the weapon, intending to test its effectiveness.

Unfortunately, it wasn't - as I had expected - just a small squirt. Instead, out came a powerful discharge of tear-inducing, noxious, radioactive, pressurised gas which, after hitting the wall, formed a toxic cloud that came back fully into our faces.

"Son of a bitch! Idiot! What have you done?!" I could hear Leo's cries as we ran up the street, covering our eyes and face as best we could. "It is a Tear-inducing spray with a range of over five metres, contact with skin will fuck you up".

We escaped up Velarde Street until we felt safe from the cloud - not knowing it had drifted in the opposite direction - and we sat down in a doorway, trying to recover our breath. There Leo grabbed the spray from my hand and quickly made off, almost without saying bye. I decided to rest for another five minutes before telling my mates about my strange adventure.

By luck or bad aim, the spray didn't affect me too much, so I quickly returned down the street, anxious to recount this curious incident to all my mates. However, when I got to the corner of Velarde Street I couldn't find anyone. On the ground there were numerous plastic glasses and bottles, boxes of wine and bags of ice; all intact, as though their owners had been vaporised, leaving all this behind. I began to fear the worst as I moved on and came across people, searching among them for some familiar face that could tell me what had happened, or even confirm my fears.

In the end I found my friends on Dos de Mayo, just opposite to a bar called *The Antonia*. They were all shouting and blaspheming, stood in a compact circle like some sort of combat formation. A lad we called Juanito came forward and spoke to me, half amused, half pissed off:

"Chencho mate, we were attacked!"

"How? Who? When?" I asked, nervous as hell.

"Some Nazis attacked us, for sure, with tear gas," he replied. Juanito was a convinced and enthusiastic communist, so he saw the hand of Nazis everywhere.

"They've poisoned Gutierrez and all the others," he added.

With a quick glance I saw that Guti was collapsed on the ground, crying and trying to vomit, while being attended to by Gabo and some others.

"I should have stayed at home. Now what?" I decided the first thing to do was accept responsibility for what happened, and be truthful. In a word, confess. "Tell the truth though it hurts, but not right now, *mañana*!". Better to do it when they weren't quite so pissed off," I thought. And quite right too. I remember seeing a guy called Manolo brandishing a branch ripped from the hedge of a nearby garden, Davo with a broken bottle in his hand, and Juanito repeating his Nazi theory over and over. The hours of boozing had made them violent. Everyone was shouting and gesticulating, all apart from Guti, who looked like he was at death's door.

Time for a distraction. I approached a guy called Mateo, a friend of a friend, who was with us though I didn't know him too well; he wasn't even from our college. "Hey mate, for sure it was the neighbours. Pass it on," I whispered to him, and he discreetly moved off.

The lie didn't need long to take effect. Within a few seconds the most worked up of my mates shot off up to the doorway where we'd been drinking, and they began beating the door and insulting the neighbours or the occasional passing gossip who came to watch.

This gave me a breather to think what my next step would be. One option was to scarper amid the confusion, but I quickly discarded this idea. Fleeing would reveal my guilt and would make a coward of me. The other choices were:

Never confess my guilt, and act as if I knew nothing. The problem with this is that at least one person - Leo - knew I was the gasser of Velarde Street. Also I wasn't sure whether there were others who would know.

Confess once people's spirits had somewhat becalmed, and in a phased manner. In other words, first to one person, and then to another, starting with the most affected. Thus I would minimise the risk of being lynched by an angry mob. In short, we already know that humans are usually inoffensive on an individual basis, but very dangerous in a crowd.

Before doing anything I decided the best would be to talk with Leo to see whether anyone else knew my terrible secret. Strangely, I found Leo kicking up a fuss with the neighbours, as though he knew nothing of the matter. I took him to one side and said:

"Leo, mate, what should we do? How do I tell everyone it was me who did all this?

"Fuck, don't say anything. Let it pass, the damage is already done. Forget it and join in the shouting."

"But I feel bad, look at Guti, he looks wrecked."

"Fuck it. Leave me alone!"

And saying this he moved off and started kung fu kicking a rubbish bin in one of the doorways while the rest of the guys copied him and shouted at the neighbours.

Seeing Leo's lack of collaboration, I decided to wash my hands of him. At the end of the day, he was partly to blame, for being a fucking weapon-obsessed psychopath and for being irresponsible by putting the gas in inexpert hands. Even so, I knew he wouldn't say anything about who had caused this attack on public health. I looked around and saw that spirits were gradually calming down. That which, ten minutes ago, had seemed totally intolerable, an outrage and an assault, was slowly dissipating. First it changed from being pissed off, to simply being bothered, and a bit later it was just a curious anecdote that had given a bit of colour and emotion to another insubstantial part of a piss-up night.

Everyone's well, I thought. Fifteen minutes after the incident they hardly remembered it. Now the problem was to agree whose turn it was to go and buy more wine and how much money there was to do so. Well, everyone was fine except Gutierrez, who apparently still hadn't recovered. I went over and asked how he was. He told me he was really bad, and he coughed a couple of times to emphasise his words. Everyone had gone a way up Velarde Street, so there in Dos de Mayo there was only myself and Guti, who was being attended to by Diego and Gabo. Quickly, almost without thinking whether it was the right thing to do, I confessed to them that it was me who had done it, and I asked their forgiveness.

They seemed more surprised than angry. I carefully explained how it all happened, omitting details that would implicate Leo, so as to avoid any future problems with him. I told them a friend from the gym gave me the gas, and they believed me. Guti had a sudden and miraculous recovery, making me suspect he had been putting on something of an act over the gas, to attract attention. Whatever the case, he behaved like a true friend, he forgave me without hesitation and said nothing to anyone. Thanks to his discretion, and that of Gabo and Diego, I managed to keep my secret for the rest of the night, though not for ever.

After the incident, the night followed its usual course. We continued drinking in Malasaña, chatting, laughing and clowning about. In that phase of late adolescence, drinking for drinking's sake was still fun, not depressing like it is for adults. Though considering ourselves to be grown-ups, we had only been drinking for a couple of years, and it had a strange effect on us. It made us laugh, lose inhibitions, and offload the accumulated tensions of the week; but we didn't need to drink much to reach that state.

Later, at about two in the morning, members of the group started discreetly leaving. This because, at the time, everyone had a particular time they had to be home by. There were more tolerant parents, as well as the more intransigent variety, but usually, by three in the morning, there remained only a hard core group having a last drink in Velarde Street.

That night was no exception, so when the time arrived I also decided to make my way home. Normally I was among the last to leave, yet I was also among those who lived furthest away. Most of my friends lived five minutes from Malasaña, so when they tired of the piss-up they'd say bye and, hey *presto*, they were home in a trice. For me, though, a forty five minute hike lay ahead; and it wasn't always pleasant. The winter was cold, and I was usually drunk, tired or feeling down. On top of that the streets I was walking weren't the best in Madrid, particularly in the early hours, and alone.

I said bye to the group and went up Velarde Street to go via the Corredera de San Pedro by way of Calle de la Palma. Everywhere you could see the remains of a Malasaña night on the piss. Groups of youths had left the streets full of rubbish and plastic bags, to then move on to bars or go home. Now and again I'd come across some fight, some scene, some drunk being sick. Walking quickly through the narrow, dimly lit streets, I tried to pass by unnoticed. Occasionally some punks would ask you for money, twenty five *pesetas* for a bottle of *cerveza*, but they were usually harmless. Sometimes I would cross the street to let some dangerous-looking gang of skinheads pass through, even though their various badges clearly displayed to all that they were on the antifascist side.

Gradually I was leaving Malasaña, and the chaotic, youthful atmosphere of that area receded as I saw fewer drinking bars and more prostitute pick-up joints. At the end of the Corredera St. you entered the Gran Vía area. These streets were pretty sordid and there weren't so many young people, except for the Goths - who seemed to love the place. There was a lot of prostitution, and the old prostitutes of the *barrio* had been literally invaded by a new generation of foreign whores, particularly African girls. Suddenly the corners were populated by big, imposing black women, intimidating their potential clients with wild cries, and arguing amongst themselves over the best spots for hunting the drunken tourist.

Leaving those streets behind and arriving at Gran Vía, I felt relieved. Nothing's happened so far, I thought, while rummaging through my jean pockets for some change. Bingo; I had three coins, meaning I hadn't pissed all my money up the wall, and could get something to eat. In that area there were several places open twenty four hours, but what I liked most were the illegal Chinese food stalls. I approached one. In reality the stall was just a big cardboard box in the middle of Gran Vía, behind which was a little Chinese girl, no older than fourteen. "I'll have some rice," I told her, and she replied:

"No lice. Nooders." It looked like the native fauna of the area, the gays and ravers, had eaten my rice, so there was nothing to do except content myself with the 'nooders'. The Chinese girl got out a medium sized metallic container. I was amazed that it was still hot. "How do they manage it?" I thought, but resisted the urge to inquire, asking instead for a plastic fork and a serviette.

"Want something dlink?"

"No thanks, I've already 'dlunk' enough," and I kindly bid her farewell, though unable to help wondering whether she went to school during the day.

I didn't open the noodle carton until I'd left Gran Vía. Thanks to some kind of antisocial paranoia I didn't like to eat while surrounded by weirdos. For one thing, I thought some louts might throw my food to the ground, or even pinch it. Let's remember that with alcohol the human brain returns to the abyss of primitive instincts: get food, protect it. Plus there was always the possibility of meeting someone I knew in such a busy part of Madrid, and frankly I would have felt ashamed to be seen alone, drunk and pigging out on Chinese mess.

Once I had passed Callao square, I entered the street parallel with Preciados Street which, for some reason, is always empty, and there I began sating my hunger with the noodles and -who knows?- maybe meat from the Wong family's ancestors. The cartons were pretty big for the price, although I can't say anything about their quality since I only ever tasted the contents while drunk. Even so, due to the accumulated hunger, I finished them off in a few minutes. Once fed, I continued up Bordadores Street and crossed Arenal. In the streets near Plaza Mayor I found a quiet corner, and when there were no passers-by I had a much-needed leak. One of my friends once crapped in the street out of desperation. The guy got caught short in the early hours, far from home, and didn't think twice about it. He went between two cars, dropped his pants and laid an enormous, malodorous turd. However, that seemed a bit excessive to me. Pissing in the public highway is normal. Vomiting... what can you do? But to leave a recently defecated shit steaming on the cold tarmac, like some weekend gift, is a bit surplus to requirements.

Finally at my doorway, I got the key in the door without any trouble, the effects of the alcohol having worn off thanks to the food and the walk. Once inside I moved quietly to my room and, after undressing, got into bed.

For five minutes I resisted falling asleep, just enough to reflect on what happened that night. It was then that I became conscious of how the tear gas thing had been pretty dangerous. The consequences didn't amount to much, but they could have been much more serious if I hadn't been so lucky.

Firstly, only my friends were affected, but what would have happened if the gas had drifted onto others, or if someone had seen me and then identified me as the culprit? I think the first word that springs to mind is lynching.

It would have been worse if, from thoughtlessness or ignorance, I had fired the gas within an enclosed space, like a bar or the metro. When Leo gave me the gas, I squeezed the button without thinking about it, and I think I'd have done the same if I'd been in the *'Más Allí'* or *'La Vía Láctea'* nightclubs. If that had happened the upshot would have been dozens intoxicated, people injured trying to escape and perhaps someone killed. A ruined business, search and arrest warrants, violence, detention, charges, justice and rejection from family and friends. Thank God that didn't happen.

The next day I got up about twelve, grabbed some breakfast and set to studying like a man possessed. I would have to make up for the lost study time from the previous day, and try to make a bit of progress with the syllabus. After a couple of hours spent memorising drivel I felt I'd done enough, so set my books aside until Sunday. Some people are born more intelligent, some more stupid, some ugly, others good looking, but I'm afraid I was born carrying the laziness gene. "I've studied for two hours when I should have done four or five," I thought, "I'm a fucking layabout!"

However, I knew it was useless to try to force myself any further. Two hours was the maximum daily period I could concentrate for. Trying to do more was just self-deception, sitting in front of my notes, daydreaming. In any case, I had something else to do, I had to think how I would ask my mates' forgiveness that night, for having accidentally sprayed them with a toxic product.

The good thing was that on Saturdays usually far fewer people went out than on Fridays. Some went out of Madrid, others didn't fancy it, or they had to play football on the Sunday. I decided I would ask forgiveness in a sincere manner, while emphasising the fact that it was an accident. Anyway, lots of people already knew about it, and those that didn't know would surely find out on the Monday. So I thought the best defence would be a good attack, and I resolved to tell everyone as soon as I saw them.

The rest of the afternoon was spent with the usual preparations for going out, including a restorative nap. Then eat, crap, shower, dress and off to Malasaña again.

I arrived at Velarde street about half nine and started anxiously looking for my mates. I hadn't called anyone, so for a moment I was afraid they had all gone somewhere else without telling me, as a punishment for my misdeeds. Finally I found them sat in a doorway; there were about eight of them, most good friends. As soon as I arrived they all looked at me with unusual interest, and there was a silence that told me it was time to act. "Guys," I told them, "I have a confession to make..."

THE RIOT

And there my weekend finished. After carefully explaining to my friends how the incident from Friday happened, I bought them a few litres of Kalimocho. "I'll pay," I said "it's the least I can do." I stayed with them a couple hours more, but it was a boring sort of night, so we soon went home. I spent the Sunday trying to study, and pondering how I could best make myself invisible at school on Monday. I'd never liked being the centre of attention, and lately I was turning into the school's number one prick.

Fortunately, on Monday no one mentioned the weekend. I think we were all too busy with studying and exams to pay attention to our mates' various boozed up larks. We all wanted to go to University, and needed half decent marks to get onto our chosen course. I'd often heard that those university access tests were really easy, but such things were always said in hindsight. After getting a degree, doing interviews, and working forty or fifty hours a week one can look back at the pre-uni with some derision, but when you're a teenager, of average intelligence, and not given to studying, overcoming these academic hurdles seems difficult, to say the least. Especially if you add the pressure of being convinced that you're laying out your hand for your entire future.

So another week began. On Monday I got to college at nine, to endure six one hour lessons nestled between two ten minute breaks where you could grab a snack or exit the gates for a smoke. In even the best of cases the teachers' explanations bored me senseless, though it was quite normal to understand nothing. The mathematical demonstrations and formulae seemed like Chinese to me, so I limited myself to faithfully copying everything the teacher said, trying to decipher it at home.

The most difficult thing was trying to concentrate while being surrounded by your mates. These weren't just classmates, they were close friends and one's accomplices in nocturnal revels. I sat in the back row, which was like a bloody hen house, with all the class jokers and loons around me.

In the science class we were known as "The Crew". The honourable members were Gabo, Revuelta, Manu, Velao, Gordi, Florian, Lambea, Charly and Gonzalito. With such luminaries around me, concentration was not a simple matter. Lambea was the clown. He was a funny chap, and very much reminded me of a guy on the telly; one of those cheap humorists that was famous at that time. Lambea could really crack us up. For example, he once tried chatting up a girl in a bar in Argüelles, asking if she fancied a "roll" Spanish slang for casual realtionship. The poor girl said no whatever he meant with that, and he pulled out a toilet roll he'd nicked from the bog. He offered it to her, saying:

"Cause I don't need this roll anymore, I've just finished crapping."

Of course, there was an explosion of laughter from all the guys, and the young girl fled, totally humiliated.

The natural complement to Lambea was Gordi, who had a more primitive and visceral sense of humour. His repertoire of farts, snot and personal insults brought delight to us all. I particularly enjoyed how he would set about Freddie Pale-arse, the class swot, throwing peanuts, used tissues and other lovely things at him. And if he protested, well, Gordi had a black belt in judo and weighed nearly a hundred kilos. The other guys were all great friends of mine, though, like me, they were a little more discreet. We all wanted to lighten the tedious round of lessons with various jokes and pranks, but also pass the exams and get into University the following year.

Being part of The Crew put you under the direct gaze of Mr Chamorro, maths and chemistry teacher and studies supervisor. He was like a classic nineteenth century teacher, old-fashioned, getting on in years, big, fat, with a white beard and thunderous voice. To me he seemed a strange mixture of Father Christmas and Benito Mussolini. The guy always found some excuse to get one of the Crew up to the blackboard to solve some difficult chemistry problem or a calculus exercise, and due, in most cases, to us having no fucking clue how to solve it, this subjected us to a bit of public humiliation in front of the swots in the first rows: Alfredito, Woody, Juanito, Nico and all the members of the "Swot Club", our main rivals and friendly arch enemies in class.

Of course, in this matey atmosphere of constant kidding about it was impossible learning anything. So I would take full notes and try to decipher them in the peace and quiet of home, with generally unsatisfactory results. To cap it all, Mr. Chamorro decided to hold the second assessment revision exams for maths and chemistry just that week. This didn't surprise me, since there'd been rumours they would happen soon, but it didn't leave me many days to study. The chemistry exam would be on Thursday and maths on Friday, so I had Monday, Tuesday and Wednesday to study both, and Thursday to revise such painful subjects. On the positive side, it was in my favour that there had been exams just recently, so the knowledge I did have was quite fresh. I also had the original exams to draw on, along with all the notes conveniently summarised, as well as the solutions to exercises.

The rest of the week passed quickly. Mornings in class and afternoons at home, studying for exams. Three hours study per day was enough preparation for me. On this occasion I would do some quality studying before the usual blow out on facts. I stored all the important formulae in my brain, as well as scrawling them on the back of my calculator, and I made sure I knew how to do all the kinds of problems I'd seen in class. On Thursday, when the chemistry exam started, I saw that this preparation was more than enough. There were four problems in all, three taken from the previous exercise and a more difficult one which I didn't know how to solve. In the end, the mark I got was a seven out of ten. It wasn't at all bad, after three months of messing about and a failed exam in February; quite good in the end. Such are the advantages of a private education. On the Friday I got three quarters that mark in maths; another decent result from not having a fucking clue.

When the week finally ended I was quite content. The exam marks would take a couple of weeks to come out officially, but I more or less knew what I would get, because the answers to the exercises matched the ones I'd given, and those of other classmates. It had been a very productive week, I had not only successfully resat my two failed subjects from the second assessment, but the intense week of study would help me during University access tests. So I decided I would relax and enjoy my weekend, I'd go out and have fun, or failing that, laze about.

This time I arranged to meet my mates at ten on the corner of Velarde and Dos de Mayo, and went home. I got to the house at three in the afternoon, just as my parents were leaving. They had decided to spend the weekend in Toledo with friends, something I had not opposed, as I would have the house to myself. I remember being fifteen the first time they left me on my own for the weekend. At the time I realised that if everything went well then these weekend excursions would become a habit, and therefore I forced myself to have the house in pristine condition when they returned on the Sunday. Since then I would often be left on my own, and though I didn't throw any spectacular bashes, I hosted several parties, always with the consent of my little brothers who, for good or for bad, had never been interested in what I got up to.

I ate quickly and had a short nap. When I woke it was still early so I decided to go to the gym for a bit of training. Normally my training time was between nine and ten at night, but on Fridays I had started going from seven to eight, pissing off my trainer. The class at that time was for a lower grade of expertise, so according to him I'd just come to waste time. That was true, but it was also true that I liked going out on Friday night instead of being stuck in the gym with a bunch of meatheads. I should also say that taekwondo is a contact sport in which blows are not marked. It's true that many attacks are prohibited, for example, punches in the face, but the legitimate attacks can be done with maximum force. As a result, it's completely fine to knock out your opponent, and the same can happen to you if you aren't careful, both during competition and training.

The session went well and I won all the fights, though that didn't mean much seeing as it was a class of children. After showering, I hurried home to drop off my bag and get something to eat. I could have gone straight to Malasaña from the gym, but I didn't fancy going out carrying a backpack full of sweaty clothes. I had done it before, but every time I wanted to enter a club the bouncers would open it, looking for alcohol, weapons and God knows what, while asking me a load of stupid questions. Some would even pull out my sweaty underwear and have them on public show for the whole interrogation. That's pretty humiliating if it happens right in front of the whole queue, including the hot chicks.

At home I heated up a pizza and enjoyed the meal. I checked I had money and hurried off in the direction of Malasaña. I took the metro from Opera Station and got off at San Bernardo. While on the train I planned how the night should go. Maybe I could try bringing my friends home for a party, though that wouldn't be a great idea. In the first place, I doubted that the lazy bastards would want to move even a hundred metres from their neighbourhood. It's also a bit shit getting pissed while shut up in your house with ten other blokes. At least in the street there's always the possibility of coming across a nice girl, or, failing that, an unattractive one. Well, anyway, at least this weekend I didn't have the worry of getting home on time. My parents were quite tolerant and they had never imposed any set hour for returning, but there was still a tacit agreement between both parties not to lower the bar from three in the morning.

I was so lost in thought about all this that, on leaving the metro station, I barely noticed a discreet but considerable police presence at the Ruiz Jiménez Roundabout and surrounding streets. There must have been about eight or nine police vans, inside which the cops were awaiting orders, weighing up the situation. Must be to do with ETA, I thought innocently, unaware that *La Policía Nacional* had a load of riot control gear inside those awful vans, and that tonight it was destined to be used not on delinquents and murderers, but on unsuspecting, harmless adolescents who only wanted to have a drink and enjoy themselves.

I found my friends just as ever, installed on one side of Velarde Street in small groups. I quickly greeted everyone without bothering with hugs, handshakes or excessive cheek kissing, which was all very unnecessary. Then I went to the nearest corner shop for a packet of tobacco and some mint chewing gum.

Back with my mates I quickly got into conversation. The subject that night was an apparent demonstration by squatters and young anarchists through the Malasaña neighbourhood, which would be beginning soon. How interesting, I said to myself, without thinking for a moment about the kind of danger a violent demonstration can represent to someone with little experience in such matters. I had this in common with Gabo, who was already excited by the prospect of some street action, and we chatted superficially about it, focusing on the playful, troublemaking aspect of the demonstration.

Suddenly, a far off cry interrupted our conversation. Excited, we looked towards the back of the plaza, where it had come from, and we saw the demonstrators. It wasn't a big demonstration, though it was compact and quite heterogeneous. Among the tumult of people you could see that all the typical specimens from Madrid's far left were represented, in their classic uniforms. There were punks in ragged leathers, sporting colourful Mohicans, though the scabby types were more numerous, recognisable by their less outlandish appearance, despite being somewhat more militant. There was also a curious type of rural-ecological punk, close in ideology and attire to the Basque nationalist kids. Alongside them marched anti-fascist skinheads in their black bomber jackets and army boots, as well as various punk-skin hybrids, who added some punkoid fantasy adornments to skinhead sobriety. There were also some hardcore types, rappers, Rastafarians, and the unclassifiable. Strangely, the other half of the Malasaña crowd, the mods, the indies and the geeks had quickly disappeared, suspecting danger. Quite in keeping with their soft, pacifist nature.

This variegated band of urban subcultures was united by a common cause - squatting - although the demonstration wasn't making any specific demands. In reality, the only objective of most participants was to escape tedium and boredom in the only way they knew how. That is, by shouting, breaking things, looking for trouble and getting on ordinary people's nerves, and preferably doing this in a mob in order to dilute responsibility for any unjustified activity. Regrettably, I too would sometimes get bored in Malasaña, so when the demonstration passed in front of us I gladly joined it, followed by Gabo, who this time wouldn't be as sensible as he had been a couple of weeks ago.

Having united with the masses, we joined in, chanting the typical kind of slogans brayed at such events. "All coppers are bastards" and other things in Spanish, and even some *"Euskal Herria askatu"* which meant freedom for Country Basque, and was totally out of context. For a while, the demonstration proceeded on its route through the streets of Malasaña; Gabo and I fearlessly chanting and acting like wankers.

Deep down, we were intelligent enough to realise that the demonstrators' demands were highly inconsistent. In fact, I don't believe they actually had any. It was all a case of protesting for protesting's sake, against something ill-defined. The right wing government, the consumerist society, voracious capitalism, the universal laws of gravitation. The thing to do was complain and break things. Perhaps it was a two bit demo, but around us were some low IQ totally fanatical types who believed themselves to be in possession of the ultimate truth, and that this gave them the right to use violence against people and objects. Not for nothing did the bloodiest dictators of the twentieth century, Pol Pot, Hitler and Mao Ze Dong form their assault battalions using teenagers. The four dudes who'd arranged this demo, which was neither authorised or had any demand applicable to society, knew that to have scheduled it in the daytime and outside some public building wouldn't have mustered more than fifty people. Therefore they decided to hold it on a Friday night in a popular hangout area for kids. This made it look like thousands of young people supported their cause, and had enthusiastically joined the demo. The reality was that a few dozen idiots were ruining Friday for thousands of kids in Malasaña, Tribunal and Alonso Martínez, attracting riot police to the area.

Suddenly the march stopped, just before La Palma Street, as an undefined perception of menace spread through the demonstrators. It was just how a flock of sheep might stop and sniff the air, sensing the presence of a wild beast. At the end of the street we could see various hulking blue silhouettes, armed with shields and batons. Unblinking, waiting.

For a while everyone was silent, and it was the kind of silence that didn't bode well. The calm didn't last long, broken by the demo's more excitable vanguard, mainly punks. They had come with the single aim of confronting the police, so off they went into battle. Horrified, I watched the punks knocking over several bins and pieces of street furniture, laying them across the street to form a barricade. Meanwhile, others tore up paving stones or stole some from a nearby building site, to be used as projectiles. Someone even set a pair of bins alight to add a bit of atmosphere to the battlefield. The riot police, as usual, did nothing to improve the situation, but right from the start it was clear that for some demonstrators violence was not a means of self-defence or challenging injustice, but something they desired for their own purposes. Now I could see that the demo's ultimate aim was to create a full-on street brawl. In a way, it was like people staging a sit-in, or football hooliganism: people stupidly putting themselves in physical danger just to burn off some adrenaline and get a buzz.

On hearing the first shot I surprised myself by running off along with a mob of others, not to any specific place, just concentrating on not falling over, as falling would have meant being brutally trampled on by dozens or even hundreds of others. I wasn't enjoying the demo any more, I wanted to find some other barrio and get pissed in peace.

I felt better on reaching the corner of Velarde and seeing my friends there. They were already looking worried, having seen the turn of events. Some of them, myself included, felt it would be best to leave Malasaña for a while and continue the evening somewhere less dangerous. However, others thought things weren't so bad and that we could stay there so long as we kept out of trouble. We started arguing over what to do. My friends at the time, inexperienced and bemused teenagers, couldn't come to a decision. Some even started changing the subject, and I wasn't brave enough to leave on my own account. Those minutes of indecision and hesitation lost us precious time, and this was decisive to how the night would turn out.

While I was wasting time trying to convince my mates, the police were taking position, and the demonstrators were wrecking the streets. Passers-by fled and the bar owners shut up shop. Finally, we began moving towards Daoiz Street, to leave Malasaña, but then fresh shots rang out and a stampede of people started heading up Velarde, cutting us off, and forcing us to run in that direction. It's amazing how mass panic works. You see a crowd running in one direction and you follow them without thinking, assuming that if they're fleeing then it's for a good reason. You join them, thinking it'll save your butt. I went up Velarde as fast as I could, pushing those in front and elbowing anyone trying to get in my way. At the sides of the street the store owners locked their doors and lowered the steel shutters, each one just a moment before I could dive for cover inside. Unfortunately, the chance of finding refuge in some Velarde bar soon evaporated, and with all of them tight shut, me and all the other dicks had no choice but to continue up the street. I kept running, surrounded by strangers. I don't know how, but in all the turmoil I'd lost all my friends. Now I was alone, in a state of increasing anguish, thinking the situation was getting very ugly. Then, suddenly, I bumped into a familiar face.

It was Pedro, with his girlfriend - "Cockeyed" - and a friend of his called Rufo, who was known for smoking a disgusting form of tobacco. Basically, Pedro was one of my best friends as well as being a classmate, but he also had a strange ability to make me nervous with his involved and optimistic attitude to life. In contrast to what her affectionate nickname - secretly created by myself - would suggest, Cockeyed was a very good looking girl, even though one of her eyes had a slight strabismus. In a way, this gave her a very charming appearance and did nothing to discourage her many suitors, among whom had numbered Pedro, Rufo and many more. Later, Cockeyed would leave Pedro, have surgery on her eye, and end up going out with Rufo; but that's another story.

"Chencho, mate. What you doing here?"

"I'm running the bulls in Pamplona, stop fucking about," I said with a less than friendly face. "I'm getting out of here. You coming?"

"Wait on, mate, I have to let some friends know."

That was typical of Pedro. A person as sociable as him was always surrounded by friends, friends of friends, friends of acquaintances and acquaintances of friends. Fortunately I managed to convince him of the imminent danger before he could start recounting me one of his strange stories, and finally he, his girlfriend, Rufo and I went running up the street.

Increasingly scared we crossed Velarde, hoping to reach Fuencarral Street where, theoretically, we would have left Malasaña and therefore safety. When we arrived, the situation was very different to what we had expected. Quite the opposite, in fact. Fuencarral Street was the epicentre of the fight. Finally, and much to my chagrin, I got to see the police in action. Several vans puked out thick-set riot police, who attacked anyone they took to be a troublemaker, while the real demonstrators threw all manner of items at them and then ran off, shying away from any hand to hand combat with these uniformed blue beasts.

I froze for a moment, hesitating about which part of the street I should move to. Right or left, up or down, the decision seemed quite an arbitrary one since none of the options looked good. Finally I headed towards the Bilbao Roundabout, hoping to avoid the worst part of the fight, followed by Pedro and some stranger who didn't look well. Bad move, I thought, a second later when I saw the street cut off by a line of riot police. Even so, I hadn't done anything wrong, and to turn and run from the cops would have been like an implicit acknowledgment of being a demonstrator, so I kept walking towards them with a firm stride, avoiding running or making any sudden movements. "I've done nothing, I'm just a passer-by," I repeated to myself while approaching the police. There were several of them and they were deployed in a line which still left a couple of metres between one cop and the next. Armed with batons and shields, faces covered with ski masks, their strapping, heavy bodies gave them the appearance of hellish centurions from some video game that was too realistic for my liking.

Such an image impressed me somewhat, though it didn't seem to have the same effect on the guy who'd been following Pedro and me. Demonstrating a rare sort of stupidity, he apparently could think of nothing better to do than retrieve a glass bottle from God knows where and throw it hard in the direction of the cops. The bottle flew through the air and smashed barely a metre from the police, who reacted by leaping on the brainless bastard and, in the process, on Pedro and me, beating us with batons and pushing us violently against a wall.

So there I was. Ten o'clock on a Friday night, hands up against the wall... well, to be exact, up against the shop front of a haberdashery, and with a national policeman behind me, kicking my legs and howling threats at me. I had a quick, furtive glance behind me and got a close-up of an ugly looking riot cop with his baton raised, ready to strike. I tried to talk to them, offer an explanation and respectfully explain that as a citizen I had rights, but the negotiation process didn't go well.

"Speak and you'll get it!"

That was the only thing said in our brief conversation, so I decided the best thing I could do was keep quiet. Not allowed to look behind, I thought. So I carefully looked to my right and saw how another cop was frisking the bottle-throwing idiot. It started with the torso and continued down the legs, though it wasn't particularly exhaustive. Within a few seconds they found a big knife, a thick metal chain, and a carabiner (also known as poor man's brass knuckles) on him. As a defence, the guy had the audacity to say he was carrying all that because he was a professional climber. His reward for this was an instant slap for offering such a pathetic excuse.

I turned my head to the other side and saw Pedro in the same predicament as myself - against the wall, well, against the shop front, and wearing a certain nervous smile. "At least we can now admire the wonderful items in this shop," he said in an ironic tone, just prior to receiving a rap from the fuzz and being ordered to shut up. The fact that we still felt like joking showed we weren't taking the whole thing very seriously. I rather believed they would take our details and then let us go, leaving us time to go to a bar, get a drink, and discuss the whole set piece.

The "hands up against the wall" position went on for another ten minutes while *la policía* decided what to do with us. During all that time I entertained myself by observing the scene and even admiring the effectiveness of our security services against the demonstrators. Each time a cop rained down a blow it was one point for the national police, and every detention added another five points. The demonstrators, although they had come onto the pitch as the opposing team, couldn't score a single point, so it was no surprise that the fuzz were winning by an emphatic fifty seven points to nil. Around me people were fleeing from the melee. Some were young and weren't saying anything for fear of ending up like me. Other more senior types rebuked the police, calling them fascists, or criticised ourselves, calling us hooligans. Three of my mates turned up too, Gabo, Manolo and Mata, who, as soon as they saw my predicament carelessly approached to try to help me. First they addressed the cop guarding me, arguing I was innocent and hadn't been participating in the demonstration. The copper, a haughty, cocky type, told them to go to hell since he wasn't about to release his detainee just because a few kids demanded it. Once they've detained you they don't let you go, and if you're innocent you get to demonstrate that later, in court, and all that had nothing to do with them. My friends didn't understand this and started arguing with the cop in ever more heated tones. I begged them to leave but they ignored me. For a while there it seemed like Manolo, quite a big guy, was going to fight it out then and there with the cop. Mata and Gabo even had to separate them, which was pretty comical. In the end more police reinforcements arrived and surrounded my three mates, giving them an ultimatum, go peacefully or come down to the station as detainees. For a moment I was convinced that Gabo and Manolo would be accompanying me to the cop shop, but for my guard the high must have been wearing off a bit, or he simply didn't fancy the extra work, so that altercation went no further. My friends reluctantly acquiesced to the order and left the scene, though according to what they told me later, their night of violence and destruction had only just begun.

LUNA ST. POLICE STATION

Finally, it seemed the cops had tired of giving us a beating, either that or there was no more space in the vans for locking up thugs, so hurrying through the final blows they shut up shop, taking Pedro and me with them. Nevertheless, I have to admit that the journey in the van from Fuencarral to my next destination, the police station on Luna Street, wasn't bad. I never imagined that police vans would be so comfortable and spacious, with ergonomic seats and loads of legroom. Up front there were only two cops, driver and passenger. In the back Pedro and I looked out at Madrid's Gran Via by night, a rather unusual viewpoint. The only downside was that accompanying us in the van was the "friend" who caused our arrest, better known as "El Contreras", who was constantly bothering both ourselves and the cops with questions, cheeky comments, noises, and blowing his nose on a balaclava he found on one of the seats. "This guy is the pits," I thought, "there are people with no idea how to behave; even when arrested."

There's nothing more to say about this evening sojourn, apart from the great skill of the police driver who, despite all the chaos in the centre of Madrid, expertly dodged the cars and pedestrians, showing an unusual gift for driving.

When we arrived at Luna the welcoming committee was rather more pleasant than the riot police. These cops were just station pen pushers, not professional fighters, so they managed without violence, threats or insults. One by one we got out the van and found ourselves in a kind of garage inside the Luna station. As we made our way through the dank, shadowy corridors, I forced my eyes wide open to take in every detail of the building, the police and the prisoners, not only to get a good idea of where I was, but also out of curiosity. I think I'd been there before, to renew my ID card or passport, but now here I was as a detainee. It all seemed pretty unreal, a kind of bad dream you'd soon wake up from. The building was pretty old, with narrow passages, low ceilings and flaking pastel coloured paint. The offices were spartan, with tatty office chairs and furniture, the latter covered with papers, files and dossiers. It kind of reminded me of the school where I'd done my primary education years earlier.

The cop escorting me led me to a kind of counter when they asked me my name and some other stuff. I'm not sure why, because they didn't even bother listening to me. Then they gave me a form to fill out with all my personal details. Then I had to identify myself with my ID, which had been seized by one of the cops on the street. I told the desk policeman but he said this wasn't possible. "Well, your colleagues took my ID card," I answered, pretty worried. Now they couldn't identify me until the riot cops for that shift had the good grace to return my ID card. I wasn't too pleased about this, mainly because in all the chaos an ID card can easily go missing, and I didn't trust those cocaine-sniffing riot cops. It was quite likely they would sell it to the Bulgarian mafia in exchange for money, cocaine or sexual favours.

Then they asked me something I didn't know how to answer.

"You want a court-appointed lawyer?"

"Hmm? Well, I don't know," I answered quite doubtfully, to the cop's confused expression.

"Do you want a court-appointed lawyer, yes or no?"

How should I answer this? Do I want a court-appointed lawyer or not? I hadn't the slightest idea what would be the best answer in my case. They had taught me a lot of useful things at school, as well as a lot of tosh, but obviously nothing to help me get out of a situation like this. Okay, time to remember. Seventh part of the primary school: "Civil Rights", "The Spanish Constitution", "Modern Society". It didn't seem that any of these files stored in my brain a long time ago would help me in these circumstances.

"Think, for fuck's sake, think," I said to myself nervously. Got it! TV cops series, The A-Team. They were always ending up in jail.

"You have the right to remain silent. Fuck, not that, the next bit."

"You have the right to an attorney. If you cannot pay for one the United States government will provide a court-appointed one." Now I had it. "Thanks, American cop series, not only for all the entertainment, but for your wise teaching too. You give everything and ask nothing in return. The telly, pillar of western civilisation."

"We won't rush things," I thought, "I need to carefully analyse the necessary information, and then arrive at a conclusion". It seemed like the court-appointed lawyer thing was something you could always choose and freely use unless you were a big fish and already had your own, like the bad guys in "Knight Rider" and lots of other shows. From this I deduced that if the rich don't have a court-appointed lawyer and the poor do, then not having a court-appointed lawyer must be good...

"Court-appointed lawyer, yes or no?" interrupted the cop, really fed up.

"No, of course not!" I said, nodding vigorously. I wasn't sure how much a "non court-appointed" lawyer would cost, but supposed that my parents, convinced of my innocence, would hire one without question.

"Fine, tell me the name of your lawyer."

"The name?"

"Yes, the name of the lawyer you want to represent you."

"Well... I don't know yet, the one Mum and Dad will hire, I guess."

"So, for now, court-appointed lawyer."

"Yes," I said, giving in.

Having made it clear I was a rookie, I was taken to a cell to be locked up for an indefinite time. I could still faintly hear the cops' ridicule as I was led away "the one Mum and Dad hire", said one, as the others laughed.

The good news about the cell they locked me in was that it was very spacious. The bad news was that it was so packed with people you could hardly sit on the floor. It looked like the riot police had been going full pelt arresting guys in Malasaña and surrounding areas. Must have been about thirty of us and some were even standing because there wasn't space to sit down. Instead of listening to the complaints of those who had been standing for a long time, the cops just brought more detainees. I was quite close to the bars and could sit curled up in my half metre of space. Pedro was next to me, also sitting down and preoccupied with all kinds of gloomy thoughts.

"Pedro mate, at least we're together in this, imagine if you were here on your own," I told him, more to cheer myself up than him.

"Don't look, but I think that guy over there, the huge guy with the shaved head, is looking at you. Either he wants to beat you up, or he's a fag."

"Fuck me, Pep, you're the best at cheering people up."

After this conversation we were quiet for a while. The time was passing slowly and, little by little, the shock and excitement of the new gave way to a feeling of boredom and fatigue. For two hours the detention had been something new and even fun, which would make a great anecdote for our classmates the next day. My only experience comparable to this had been getting caught nicking stuff from a department store called *El Corte Inglés* when I was twelve, and in my innocence I was thinking an arrest would amount to more or less the same, involving only a move from the private to the public sector. A couple of hours locked up, they would take my details, send the fine to my house someday, and I'd be back on the street in time for a last drink before going home to sleep.

To kill time I entertained myself observing my cellmates. In the mere 6 by 6 metre area were crammed almost thirty people of all types and conditions. Several were ashamed like Pedro and myself; miserable downcast souls, curled in on ourselves in a vain attempt to insulate ourselves from the surroundings into which we had accidentally fallen. In contrast, many other detainees were no stranger to this kind of thing and you could even say they were loving it; laughing, joking, chatting animatedly, or meeting up with old friends. Many of the skinheads and almost all the punks were really enjoying themselves. The demonstrations, the brawls, and confronting the police were such an important part of their marginal lives that they felt right at home down at the station. Precisely the opposite of myself, like a fish out of water, I thought, huddling up to try and go unnoticed.

What worried me most at the time wasn't the fatigue or the discomfort, but the need to urinate, which, though still not urgent, I could see becoming a serious problem in the medium term. Luckily the early start of the demonstration and its subsequent suppression by the police had prevented me starting the piss-up, so when I was arrested I was sober, fed and without much need to piss. On the contrary, many of the guys around me didn't look so fortunate. Some smelt faintly of alcohol, cheap wine, suggesting they had been drinking before arrest. After downing *Kalimocho* in large quantities, the poor devils would have been surprised and possibly thrashed by the national police, before being invited to commence their hangover in a small and powerfully lit cell where the heat, humidity, and overcrowding only increased the already considerable feeling of anxiety before an uncertain future.

Finally the cops realised it was impossible to lock up twenty five people for the whole night in a cell designed for eight, so they started breaking up the community, dividing it up into different cells. I don't remember whether they extracted us by shouting our surnames, or simply in groups, but I was one of the first ones to leave. This seemed positive to me, given that it would be very difficult to be put anywhere worse than the previous cell, though much to my displeasure they didn't let me go to the toilet. Rather than being sent to another cell, the cop led me a long way through corridors. As we weren't getting anywhere specific I became nervous, imagining things. I hope this perv doesn't rape me in some dump, I thought, while my sphincter contracted at the threat of a not very promising future. Sodomised at eighteen, by a pig, just what I needed.

The cop must have seen the worry on my young face, and he reassured me, saying we were going to the floor above to complete an important and unavoidable jail ritual. Reading of suspect's rights, statement of the accused, and the ritual short phone call, courtesy of the boys in blue squad.

I entered a small, tatty office. Inside was a desk with a computer, several chairs, a few shelves full of files, and more papers and stuff stacked on the floor. There was hardly room to move, yet the cop sat behind the computer invited me to sit. "We'll now make the statement," he told me, "and then you can make one call."

I interpreted this as my big chance to demonstrate the great injustice they were committing against me, emphasising the fact that they still had time to correct the misunderstanding. Of course I hadn't been in any demonstration nor did I have any kind of ideological affinity with the demonstrators, or with anyone at all, because I had no friends and I spent all my time studying to pass my exams and make my parents very proud. What happened is that, as I was returning from the library, I was surprised by the tumult and had no chance to escape. And that was the misunderstanding, and although they had caused me some inconvenience, doing their jobs of course, I feel no resentment towards them and am willing to forget the whole thing and go home, and won't mention it again. I said all this to the cop in one go, without stopping to breathe, while adopting the expression of a humble, unintelligent but decent young man.

The policeman, a middle-aged man with an Andalusian accent, inspired some trust in me, so while he was writing my statement into the computer I continued:

"Please let me go home, what with all these people arrested one more or one less won't change things. What difference would it make to you?"

"We can't do that, my friend," he answered me frankly "once the process is underway we have to carry it through to the end."

As the cop seemed like a good person I wasn't going to give up, and I was ready to continue until I at least got some information, and suddenly a well-groomed, chubby individual came in and sat on the empty chair.

"They've assigned me to be your court-appointed lawyer, I advise you to say nothing and don't sign any statement until you're up before the judge."

"Fuck! I've already made a statement!" I said, while my right hand still held the pen with which I had just entered my name onto the printed copy of what the cop had written into the computer.

"My friend, I only want to help you, but if you want to make a statement it's up to you. Well, I have to go; see you at court. Bye."

And with that the bastard turned and went out, leaving me alone again with the cop who was shaking his head from side to side in disagreement. "Well that's one shitty legal representative," I thought, "If he does that well for me in court they'll sentence me to fire squad."

With the statement made, the policeman offered me the chance to make a phone call. I didn't want anyone to find out that I had been arrested, but as I didn't know how long I would be in this situation, I decided it was preferable to give my parents some short-lived displeasure rather than the fright of their lives when they arrived from Toledo and saw that I had disappeared. For a moment I thought about saying nothing, since they would arrive on Sunday afternoon, and if they let me go before then my parents wouldn't have to know anything. I remember that one of the squatters had mentioned that the detention time limit was 72 hours. Even then, it wouldn't work out, and it was possible there would be a later court hearing. Having seen the court-appointed lawyer it would probably be best to pay for a private one if they didn't want their offspring to end up in Alcalá Meco State Prison.

I called home and was lucky to catch my sister. In 1998 only the X-Files agents and some folks with more money than sense had mobile phones. I quickly told her everything and she assured me she would give the good news to my folks when they called to see if there was any news.

"Hi, it's Mum! Is everything all right?"

"Yes, everything's fine. Well, not everything. Don't be shocked but Chencho is in police detention."

"Chencho? Arrested? Why? We'll be right there."

I was sure the conversation would go something like that.

After making the statement and phone call I was unceremoniously returned to the dungeon with the rest of the detainees. Escorted by a less sympathetic cop than the previous one, I went down a long passageway lit with fluorescent lights and lined with closed doors, until the policeman ordered me to stop outside the last one. There, under the vigilant gaze of a couple of riot police armed with truncheons, my escort opened the half-wood half-bar door and invited me to enter the dismal hole where I'd spend the following hours.

Amid the shadows I could just make out the presence of other people who, for better or for worse, were now my cellmates. A familiar voice welcomed me on behalf of them all, and when my eyes finally adapted to the darkness I could see the face of my friend Pedro, as well as those of others, some from the previous cell and others completely new.

Pretty grateful to find that Pedro was also in this new cell, we started talking and sharing our respective experiences with the statement, the phone call, the reaction of parents and many other things. Gradually, other cellmates joined the conversation. With me being the last one to be put into the cell they started asking me a load of questions. How many people had been detained, what was going on on the floors above, had I seen this person or that person, and many other questions that forced me to answer fully, not out of solidarity, but more as a wise precaution of not making enemies among them. With my close-cropped hair, my sideburns, and my sober clothing, I could easily have been taken for a neo-nazi type, urban tribe arch-enemies of the punks/sharps. Luckily, or maybe due to the cell's darkness, no one thought anything was up and I managed to get by unnoticed for the moment.

There were eleven of us inside the cell, and the space was quite limited. The place must have been three metres long by three metres wide and behind the door was a cement bench which was the best place to be, away from the dampness of the floor and the puddle of piss which we were jointly contributing to in the far right corner. Pedro and I managed to install ourselves on the bench, and there we talked amongst ourselves, discreetly, observing the rest of our cellmates with concealed displeasure.

Apart from us two, the rest of the nine hooligans were of two categories. The first, larger group, were punks, who, thanks to their number, their experience and their group cohesion quickly took political control of the cell. The other group boiled down to two arseholes: a rapper who spoke to no-one and sat nearest the piss, as an unmistakable sign of his marginalisation, and a rich kid from Alonso Martínez. The latter was small, shy and a real cry baby who'd unintentionally got caught up in all this while waiting for the bus home.

Among the punks some quickly made themselves known, assuming some kind of cell spokesman status. The first was called Hugo, a more militant anti-capitalist and squatter kind of guy than your usual messy punk. Another notable figure was "lemonhead", a classic skinhead: huge, strong, shaven-headed, military boots and pretty thick. "Thirty-seven Thumps" was kind of the boss of all of them. He was an old punk, with a beard, a mohawk, and a very street kind of attitude. This bugger was as strong as an ox, as well as having a bad temper, by the looks of his wounds and scars. Thirty-seven Thumps was one of the few who'd managed to land a clean punch on the riot cops, and he boasted of still having a pending case for attempted homicide, "I was going down Alberto Aguilera Street and saw some fascists putting up posters," he told us, "I got one and hit him with my chain until he was done for."

The last, but not least important, was "Neanderthal", an affectionate nickname I secretly gave him. Neanderthal was a haggard, ugly, deformed sort of punk who wouldn't stop having a go at the police through the bars of the door. From the beginning, or at least since I arrived, he had been by the door, tightly grabbing the bars and hurling out all kinds of insults and invective against the police, politicians, and generally anyone who went by, while whistling, jumping and grunting like a complete chimpanzee.

"Son-of-a-bitch cop, I'm gonna burn your station down!"

"Bastard cop, when you leave have a look under your car!"

"Long live ETA!"

"Hey cop, cop, cop, d'you hear me, son-of-a-bitch?!"

"You're gonna die, copper."

"Bastard!"

And so he continued for a good while. Unfortunately the Neanderthal's compulsive behaviour ended up causing problems for the rest of us when the cops finally tired of hearing his unpleasant voice hurling out barbarities. Three helmeted, armed, enormous riot police arrived from the upper floors and asked the jailer to open the cell. Once inside they threatened us with their batons and told us that if they had to come again they'd really set about us. As if they hadn't messed us about enough they asked us each our names while the jailer made a list for God knows what reason. Finally, after a few more insults and threats, they left, slamming the door. "Good job, this time they let us off," I said to Pedro.

All Neanderthal's fault. Look at him: furtive expression, no chin, low brow, long arms, short legs, the twat looks like a monkey. This guy is the missing link, no doubt three chromosomes have gone walkabout.

After the riot cops' visit Neanderthal calmed down for a while, though it didn't take him long to return to his old tricks, but this time taking the wise precaution of shouting softly so as not to provoke the cops again. The rest of us tried to pass our time in the cell as best we could. The truth is there isn't much a young heterosexual male can do in a damp, hot, three by three cell full of strange guys. One of the punks, the intellectual of the group, started drawing on the wall. The others talked about the latest battles, perhaps repeating themselves. I would have liked to smoke a cigarette to release the stress. As they hadn't yet processed us we still had some tobacco. I didn't have any myself, but I knew Pedro had some. I was about to ask my friend for some when one of the punks exclaimed:

"What should we do with the stash!? I still have some."

"Should we get rid of it?" asked some other punks, turning to Thirty-seven Thumps, who was by far the most experienced in these matters.

"The fucking pigs will take it off us when they process us, let's have a few smokes while there's still time!"

Now I couldn't have a smoke because all the tobacco was collected to make the spliffs. It was ironic being in a police cell surrounded by cops, with eleven guys burning hash and dragging on it like men possessed. We managed to make several roaches before the tobacco ran out. I didn't smoke much because I didn't want my blood pressure to go down or have an anxiety attack while being locked up. Even so, I didn't blame the punks and I took a couple of timid drags. In the closed environment of the cell you hardly needed to smoke anyway. In a while we were all a bit high. I paid no attention to what the punks did with the rest of it, surely they chucked it in some corner, or who knows, maybe they tried to hide it in their smelly orifices.

As soon as the spliffs had unleashed the madness, laughs and howls travelled down the station corridors. I remember myself doing a handstand against one of the cell walls, and the frenetic Neanderthal jumping about like a monkey. One of the punks wanted to crap through the bars to annoy the jailer, but we stopped him because we'd be the ones having to smell his shit more than the cops.

Our biggest pastime was shouting to the guys in the neighbouring cells, and occasionally insulting the cops. As Luna police station was relatively small and very old the acoustics were excellent. At first everything was sporadic shouts and disconnected howls from other cells, which we responded to in kind. Soon, however, we developed a complex system of communications and information exchange between the different cells, which culminated in about fifty of the detainees singing happy birthday to one of our companions, who was celebrating his eighteenth birthday on that very day. We were also relieved that "La Puri", girlfriend of one of the detainees, had been well treated and that "Ox", one of the punks, was among those in the cells below.

Naturally though, the high spirits couldn't last all night. We had already spent four or five hours in detention and fatigue, overcrowding and the need to piss gradually started taking their toll, though some tried to keep up the good mood by swapping the latest news.

To avoid the chaos and trouble that surely had already taken over the other cells, the council of punks governing ours set out to lay down a few simple rules, of obligatory compliance. To allow all the cellmates to rest a while we would all be given twenty minute turns to sit on the stone bench. Also, the corner farthest from the bench was ratified as the designated area for those wanting a piss. For me personally, I found it very difficult to pee, having ten unknown guys invading my personal space. I guess it was the same for the others, but with no other option, we all ended up whipping it out in the corner and having a go, with differing results. My first go was something of a damp squib; except there was nothing damp about it. My second attempt was more fortunate and I managed to relieve my bladder a bit. It might seem silly, but later some of the other detainees who were in cells that had not taken the precaution of designating a specific area, or could not do it due to lack of space, told me that more than one guy just wet themselves. The third and final rule was not to smoke if you couldn't offer a drag to everyone else, but it didn't make much sense, since conscious of the fact that when they processed us they would take our smoking paraphernalia away from us, we had quickly puffed away everything we had.

All these measures, well-intentioned and useful, were nevertheless insufficient to alleviate our shameful predicament. Coming up to four in the morning we were all fed up, tired of standing in a dark, smelly cell; wanting to sleep, hungry, thirsty and bored. Fortunately, by then the cops had managed to organise things a bit better, and the senior officers decided that the detainees could not be kept in custody much longer, in the awful facilities of Luna street police station. Before doing anything, and due to our strong protests, they allowed us to go to the toilet, escorting us out mob-handed, one by one. With there being a load of us this operation took an age, though the cops finally arrived at our cell and we could use the facilities. I went just after Pedro, and the seconds seemed like hours before my turn came. Having a long piss in that cubicle was a great release, and along with a few gulps of water I was in heaven. After this process a strange kind of commotion began down among the cells. A few cops came by, opening the doors. They had a list and read out some people's names and took them away.

This alarmed me somewhat, mainly because when they came to our cell they only read out my name, and off I went with them. With an expression of resignation I said goodbye to Pedro and the other hooligans, and walked off into the unknown, escorted by the police. We walked through corridors, upstairs and finally exited into the street via a garage behind the station, where a police van was waiting for me, its doors open.

On breathing fresh air again I couldn't help thinking about it. Between the van door and the garage wall was a gap big enough for a little guy like me to get away. The cops didn't seem at all vigilant with me. For some reason - and they weren't wrong - they must have thought I was the least dangerous of the detainees. And if I escaped through the gap and ran down Libreros Street, would they catch me? I knew the area well, and I could easily hide in the alleyways.

Of course I didn't do it, not when I had already given them my details and signed my statement. It wouldn't have been difficult for them to find me later, and besides, I didn't fancy being a fugitive from justice. Even so, the fantasy of going home, quaffing a glass of wine-soda, smoking a cigg and going to bed, made me smile and dream of freedom and glory. Chencho, the only escapee from the Malasaña fifty. Total urban myth.

MORATALAZ DETENTION FACILITY

I was invited to enter the back of a police van and sat there reluctantly. The fact that I was inside a vehicle suggested that I was being transferred to another place, probably prison. The fact that the vehicle had not yet moved indicated that I would not be the only detainee to be transferred, because if I were, we would have already left, I deduced with a shrewd reasoning. I was caught up in such thoughts when I saw the first of my fellow passengers appear. I almost went into a state of shock.

I couldn't believe my eyes. A bird! A young, good-looking mulatto girl got into the van and sat down in front of me. What's a luscious *morena* like you doing in a van like this? I was tempted to ask, but instead I directed a neutral and harmless "Hello" as my eyes drifted hopelessly to some firm, round melons that could be guessed at under an Adidas cotton T-shirt.

She also said "Hello" to me, with a mixture of caution and prison solidarity. "Damn, this is not so bad", I said to myself while trying to start a conversation to get a little more intimate with the *mulata*. We started talking about the typical things that a man and a woman say when they meet in police custody.

"Where did they catch you? —I was arrested in blah, blah, blah... —Let's see if we get released soon blah, blah, blah..." —Our romantic conversation was interrupted by the arrival of another of the passengers in the van.

"Fuck, another chick!" I couldn't believe it. Another girl of about eighteen years of age and good looking, although this time white, got into the love van and sat down next to the *mulata*, who she seemed to know from before. "This has to be a joke, can't be happening" I thought to myself as I wondered if this was my lucky day. I had been surprised several times in the last few minutes, but when the van finally filled up with detainees and left, I was amazed. All the occupants of the van, except me, were girls aged between eighteen and twenty-something. All of them were good-looking, pretty and friendly.

"What a change, coming out of a cell full of piss and smelly guys and ending up here surrounded by young, fresh fanny and no chance of escape". For the first time I was happy to be in detention, life owed me this compensation after so many years without pulling. "At last justice was being done," I thought, and wished with all my strength that all the occupants of the van would be locked up in the same cell. "Fuck, five slappers and me locked up together, sleeping together, in the showers... If this is how prison is like, let them lock me up for life. I feel better already, I even feel in the mood for singing..."

I found love in a van

Property of the anti-riot unit

One cock, two balls

And five pairs of tits

(Sounded better in the original Spanish)

I continued to fantasize throughout the trip while chatting occasionally with all the babes. One thought that haunted me was the fact that sitting there was the closest I had ever been to a girl in all of 1998, and that was pretty pathetic. If I continued to be this clumsy with the beautiful sex, my chances of getting laid would be as slim as Real Madrid's chances of winning the European Cup again before the end of the millennium. Even so, the road was short and very pleasant surrounded by the girls until finally we arrived at Moratalaz Prison or something like that, and they invited us to come down from the van. It hurt a lot when they separated me from the girls, because I felt almost like the Sultan of Brunei with a harem and everything. "Shit, polygamy will have to wait," I lamented bitterly as they took me through the corridors and locked me in a cell with two other assholes, this time male.

I quickly made friends with my new fellow inmates, especially since you could tell from a mile that they were new in these environments just like me and were there by chance and not because they had done anything wrong. One of them was Alonso Martínez's little boy with whom I had already shared a cell. The other was a young law student, who wore a rather characteristic goatee that gave him a certain goat-like appearance, quite appropriate in this case as he was, just like me, another scapegoat in all this mess.

Mr Goatee was quite well aware of how the judicial world worked and I got a lot of interesting information from him. Apparently, we were not in prison itself, but in the Moratalaz Detention Facility, where they brought all the detainees from Madrid until the judges decided what to do with them. According to Mr. Goatee, the fauna in this police station was quite different from that in Luna St, not only teenage troublemakers but also real hardened criminals. This was not a tangible problem yet, as it was not contemplated that we would get out of the cell at all. As I said, it wasn't prison and therefore there was no yard where you could get beaten up or showers where you could get your ass raped, at least for now. I was more concerned when the Goatee told me that this was the stage where they would pull down your trousers, although he didn't give me any more details of what this meant. Panic set in and I spent the next few minutes trying to figure out what this could mean. Later I understood when they took me out of the cell for a moment and put me in a separate room. There they took away all my personal belongings and also my belt and the laces of my Adidas Samba. Then a copper searched me thoroughly and also ordered me to pull down my trousers and undies to check that I was not wearing anything there. I found this procedure quite humiliating, although I also felt sorry for the cop for being somehow condemned to see the cock and cojones of all the criminals and sonsofabitches in Madrid.

After the unpleasant experience of being obliged to show my dick to another man, I was returned to the cell without any more contemplation than receiving a mattress and a blanket at the entrance of the cell. This indicated that I would be there at least one more night. At first glance you could say that my situation had improved or at least not worsened. I was now in a larger, cleaner and better lit cell than the previous ones, which I shared with only two guys who, moreover, did not seem to be bad people. I had my own mattress to sleep on, a blanket to keep me warm and plenty of space. The only bad thing was that the cell had no bathroom, so it was not possible to pee, shit, drink water or jerk off.

I lay down on the mat, covered myself completely with the blanket and tried to get some sleep. As I was very tired I fell asleep right away, into a light and nervous doze. After a while I was woken up by someone shaking me and laughing. I opened my eyes in anger and found Pedro, who was to be my cellmate again.

"What's up mate? – Same cell again!"

"Yes, it looks like we're staying here for now."

"Cool!"

"I'm sure you weren't brought here in such pleasant company as I was."

Pedro was intrigued by my last comment. I tried to keep sleeping, but I couldn't. Apparently, my old chum was not the only newcomer and there were now eight of us in the cell. Because of this and the noise the newcomers made it was impossible for me to fall asleep, but anyway the lights came on at half past six and some policemen arrived to take us out to pee.

In Moratalaz the day starts when they take you out of your cell to urinate. Now I understood how our family dog *Piletus* felt. On the one hand you're half asleep and don't wanna get up, but on the other hand you know that if you don't take the opportunity to pee, you won't have another one until midday and you'll have to hold it in or wet your pants, which is also legal.

After peeing they brought us breakfast consisting of a 100 cl. container of milk and a few biscuits. I didn't like this breakfast at all, so I ate very little. Later, when they brought us the dinner, I understood that there could be worse things. Then nothing, just waiting. Time passes very slowly when you are locked up in a totally empty cell, diaphanous and powerfully lit by artificial light. Since you can't see the outside and don't have a watch, you don't know if it's five minutes or five hours until the next meal or until you can go to the bathroom. Half an hour after switching on the lights, they start to radiate a suffocating heat, and this stimulate the sweat glands of the crew in there, making us sweat like pigs and filling the cell with an unpleasant smell.

I can't say much about my colleagues either. The most remarkable thing is that none of them was older than twenty and that each and every one of them was innocent like me. In the previous cells, acknowledging that you had had nothing to do with the demonstration, or at least with the altercation, was like admitting that you were a fool. However, in this cell nobody wanted to lie and invent street-fighting rubbish anymore. We all knew that the guy immediately to your left was as dumb as the one immediately to your right, and both as dope as you. We liked this, it made us feel comfortable and it made us all equal, if not in brotherhood at least in partnership. In fact, I think we were all quite grateful not to have any punks, skinheads or recalcitrant thugs nagging around us. We were all victims there and knowing that helped us to make the ordeal a little more bearable.

Apart from Pedro, Goatee and Alonso's posh kid, there were four other people in the cell not including me. There was a fat farting boy who was very unhappy. There was also a bald guy from Rivas Vaciamadrid and there was also a boy called Jota, a very funny kid who reminded me a lot of one of the members of a famous comedy act, quite popular those years in Spain. Finally, there was a guy we called

Echeverría[7] who had it very hard during the time he was detained because in fact Echeverría is a typical, and stereotypical, Basque surname. Apparently, it had been rumoured over the last few months that militants belonging to the Basque Separatist Kale Borroka guerrilla group had gradually infiltrated the squatters and other anti-establishment movements in Madrid. Politicians and police argued that these young ETA supporters provided training and advice on urban guerrilla tactics to the squatters, as they were too well organised lately. Faced with this, the government delegate decided to act harshly against the squatters, arresting as many suspects as possible in order to maximise the chances that at least some of the alleged Basque extremists would also fall into the police nets and thus be able to prove that the Basque connection existed. In time it would become clear that all these suspicions were unfounded, but for a few days the police top dogs thought they had found what they were looking for in the person of poor Echeverría (I never knew what his first name was, as everybody addressed him by his surname), who was in fact only an eighteen-year-old bricklayer who had never set foot in the Basque Country in his fucking life and who was drinking kalimocho with his mates in the street that Friday when he was arrested.

At a time, 1998, when the terrorist organization ETA was killing politicians, journalists and innocent people day in and day out, the struggle not only against armed wing of the organization but also against their supporters had intensified and both Madrid Mayor Mr Manzano and government delegate Mr Morgades vowed not to let the Kale Borroka urban guerrilla to spread to Madrid as well. I, for my part, thanked the heavens for not having a Basque surname, because while we were hardly bothered, Echeve was taken out of his cell four or five times for interrogations, identity checks, confrontations with the officials and God knows what else. Of all those of us who were there, the poor kid had every chance of being one of those not to be released after seventy-two hours of detention. Apparently, there were already four or five policemen who testified that they had been attacked by him, five huge agents almost two metres tall, equipped with helmets, shields and riot gear, claiming they'd been brutalized by a skinny, 5 feet 8 inches tall, eighteen-year-old cocksucker. Ridiculous. They were not going to let the prey escape so easily, and thank God that fundamentalist terrorism was not in fashion at that time, or else they would have checked the poor boy's dick to see if he was circumcised.

---

[7] Means "New house" in Basque Language.

Morning passed slowly. From half past six when the lights went on until two in the afternoon when we were given something to eat, nothing of any consequence happened, apart from the fact that we were bored to death in that room. The only one who didn't get bored was Echeverria, who was taken out of his cell every few minutes. The boy was not discouraged at first and decided to fight back legally. –I told my lawyer to apply for an *"habeas corpus*," he said with some seriousness. What is that shit?" asked one of the others. I didn't have a fucking clue what that little Latin phrase meant either, but Mr. Goatee quickly illustrated. –It means that you go to court immediately without waiting for the seventy-two hours of detention–. From then on, we all began to repeat "habeas corpus" as if it were magic words. We all wanted habeas corpus too and to get the hell out of there as soon as possible.

Little by little, we started to invent ways to pass the time. The first one was to talk to our colleagues about our difficult situation, to complain about everything and to speculate about when coppers would let us out of there. Soon other leisure alternatives emerged, such as spitting contests, and we even officially designated one of the corners as a place to spit. More important was the making of a small ball with pieces of rag torn from the blankets and tied together. This gave us the possibility to practice the beautiful game in a new form of mini football invented by us and called cell football. We quickly formed four teams of two players each and started the World Cup. I teamed up with Pedro, who has always been very good at footie, and I must say with pride that thanks to his dribbling and goals, but also to my tenacious defence, we were the fair winners of the first championship.

At mid-day it was time for our first meal. In the morning I had hardly been hungry, the sleepless night had turned my stomach and I didn't feel like eating. Some old workers brought a metal cart to the cell and the police started to distribute the food. The first and only dish came in plastic containers: fish cooked with potatoes and no salt heated in the microwave. I took the cutlery they gave me, also made of plastic, and set out to eat something. I started with the fish, but I didn't get past the first bite. It tasted atrocious, a mixture of plastic, bleach and sewage. In the end I only ate a couple of slices of potato.

"Look at them bastards," I said to the Goatee. "The food they give us is so fucking rubbish. At least they could have put some salt in it for flavour."

"No, they don't add salt on purpose. Salt can cause you a hypertension attack in here and drive you bananas."

"Fuck, I had no idea salt could do that." –Watch out for this Goatee guy, he has a fucking answer for everything.

After eating, time continued to pass just as slowly as in the morning. There came a time when neither the football nor the talk with the other detainees reassured me. All I did was walk my anxiety attack continuously through the cell. Ten steps up and ten steps down, from one wall to another in that room. It was as if the only thing that calmed me down was walking, so I did it like if I was swimming laps in a pool. My only obsession was that I wanted to get out of there desperately. It's not that I was treated badly physically, my problems were more psychological. If I was at least a habitual offender, I would have had time to digest the fact that one day I would have ended up like that, but I wasn't. All I knew was that the minute before I was having a drink with my mates and suddenly I was in a cell. "The maximum time you can be detained is seventy-two hours," I kept repeating to myself. How many hours would have passed by now, thirty? Forty? I had no idea. Then, apparently, I had to see a judge, who would decide whether to release me on charges or send me to prison. The arrival of this moment also made me uneasy. I imagined an unpleasant fascist with a black moustache and opaque sunglasses asking me questions and judging me without knowing me, because that is what judges do, isn't it?... they judge people.

In the late afternoon there was an unusual movement of police officers that reminded me of the transfer from Luna Street. Some cops arrived and opened the door of the cell. They called my comrades by name until they gathered four of them and took them away without saying anything. -I asked aloud, but Mr. Goatee had parted with the others, so I was left wondering what was going on. About fifteen minutes or two hours passed, I can't say for sure, and finally the comrades came back. I wanted to ask them what was going on, but they were already taking us with them. "Pictures, footprints," said Pedro in a whisper as I left. I could already imagine what was going to happen.

We went through some white tile corridors, clear and clean, until we reached a door that said: Scientific Police. "I hope they don't give us a seminar on science," I said, making a joke that nobody understood. Long faces and disapproving looks told me that we weren't mean to open our mouth there, much less to say anything stupid. Inside, besides coppers, there were people dressed in white lab coats, like the one my dod used to wear when he was a professor at University.

The process began with a check on the identity of the detainee followed by a small questionnaire about physical data, occupation and a few other things. Name and surname: Chencho blah, blah, blah. Born in Mad-drill, age eighteen, medium height, slim build, dark hair, light eyes, occupation student... And many more questions. We were weighed, measured and explored in search of tattoos, scars or identifying marks. Then came the black and white photograph, irrefutable proof that you have been in detention. One of the "whitecoats", the one who was driving the photo booth, told me to lean against a kind of metal headrest and took the picture. I tried to smile and look casual. You never know when these photos might come out and fuck up a brilliant career as a film star, so I took the pose of the sexy rebel and let myself be loved by the camera.

"Next!" shouted the nearest pig, screwing up my Marlon Brando-style teenage glamour moment. "Anyway, it's done, I'm officially a criminal now," I thought as another man in a lab gown smeared each and every one of my fingers with black ink and stamped the prints on white cardboard. "You don't need the toes too, do you?" I said to the officer on duty in a fit of defiance, but he ignored me completely. In general, I found the process interesting but also humiliating. I, a future university student from an upper middle-class background, locked up and booked like a chav. Well, it will serve as a lesson to keep me out of trouble in the future.

Back in the cell we had a pleasant surprise. Relatives of some of the detainees had dropped by the Moratalaz Facility to ask about the kids and also brought some food, sandwiches, drinks, biscuits and so on. Needless to say, as good companions we shared everything, fortunately for this poor soul, because my folks didn't bring me anything. Pedro managed to see his parents for a few minutes thanks to a *Guardia Civil* family member with contacts among the National Police Force, and the good work of his lawyer. As well as two wonderful *serrano*-ham baguette rolls, he got a lot of information from this meeting which he later transferred to us. The most important thing was that his parents had contacted my parents and together they had agreed to hire a competent lawyer to defend both of us. We also learned that outside there had been a lot of commotion about the Malasaña incidents and that we had even been in the news. I ate half of one of Pedro's rolls as we talked about all this.

"How did you see your parents, were they angry with you?"

"Not really. I guess they know I'm not into this kind of stuff and that it was all a misunderstanding. Oh, by the way, they've been talking to yours."

"And what did they say?"

"That they shouldn't worry. Our lawyer is ace, you'll see that in a few hours we'll be out of here."

"I hope so, because I've had enough of this situation. I could kill for a can of Coke."

"Fuck, Chencho, we've only been locked up for a day."

"Well, it's taking forever for me."

Pedro became good friends with the other detainees, or at least more than I did. With his more open and friendly personality it took him a short time to joke around with Jota and the other kids, to make plans to meet up some night in the future or chat about totally unimportant things with them. I, for my part, kept a little more distant from my colleagues and my conversation was often limited to issues related to our detention and especially our future release. "I wish they would release me before the end of the weekend, so that I would have at least one day to relax and disconnect from all this crap", I thought as I tried to decide if what I most wanted in the world was a glass of Coke or a cigarette. "Definitely, the first thing I'll do is to have a Coke and then we'll see. That's if they let us go. These bastards are capable of sending us to prison without us having done anything wrong". And so I spent my time, talking to myself and taking walks around the cell to release some anxiety.

I was also not happy about spending a second night there. I was sure that once again it would be impossible for me to sleep surrounded by so many strangers. If only I had been alone in the cell, I would have been able to get some rest, but with all the fuss, it was impossible. Having company was fine, but eight guys in the same cell was too much for me, I just wasn't used to having so many people around me for so long, and this seemed exhausting.

As the evening progressed I got the idea that I was waiting for another night in the cell. The hopes of getting out were high at first, but they were dashed when the workers from the police station showed up in the cell with the food cart. The sterilised plastic jars that were to serve as dinner were once again carried in the trolley and once again I could not taste a bite of how bad it was. In fact, I didn't even bother to take one from the cart. On our last visit to the toilet that day I took the empty juice box that had been brought to one of our colleagues and filled it with water, at least that night we would not be thirsty. Once we all went to the bathroom, they turned off the light in the cell, although it was still lit through the bars. The outside wall of the cell was all bars, so there was enough light to even read a book. That would be great, books in the cells to read and pass the time. That way you could even learn something while waiting to be put on trial. Well, maybe it's not such a good idea, the inmates could use the books to attack each other, slit their wrists with the sharp sheets or even try to smoke them.

Once in the semi-darkness, we all stood around talking for a while until we finally got out of it one after the other. I lay down on the mat, covered myself with the blanket and closed my eyes. I knew it was useless, that I wasn't going to fall asleep that night. Not because of the light or the noise, but rather because of the certainty of being surrounded by strangers. I suppose that if I had to be like this for days or weeks I would eventually get used to it, but that night I knew that all effort would be in vain. The other kids kept talking for a while, but little by little we heard less whispering and more snoring. After an interval of time that would be impossible for me to quantify, everyone was asleep, all except me who was getting more and more nervous. After a while I couldn't take it anymore, the simple fact of having my eyes closed made me fall into sinister thoughts and lying down increased my anxiety. I almost had a small panic attack, so I got up and started walking around the cell again, from one end to the other and counting the steps compulsively. One, two, three... I realised that I was not counting steps but seconds, one second less locked up (I hoped). Now I think it was anxiety, and even after I went to the doctor sometime to talk about it, but then I didn't know what it was. It was like a very strange feeling of discomfort. You feel very bad and you don't know why. It's like you're upset for the fact that you exist.

"Could it be that I have claustrophobia? Can't be, my room at home is tiny and I've never felt so bad or so nervous in it. Maybe it's the tobacco cold turkey that makes me so restless. Maybe it's the evil eye that's been cast on me... No, Chencho, no, that's rubbish; what's wrong with you is that you're a nervous wreck because you want to get out of here".

I kept walking for what seemed like hours, until little by little I calmed down. "That's right, to walk and walk until we get tired and then sleep, yes, sleep and not to think about anything". Soon I got up the courage to lie down on the mat again. Pedro, who was next to me, woke up and we talked a little until he fell asleep again. I stayed a while longer with my eyes open and I had almost decided to try and close them when I noticed an uncomfortable feeling of pressure down below. "Fuck, that's all I needed, now I'm not going to sleep at all. Let's see, they will take me out around seven in the morning to the bathroom. What time could it be? Maybe it's not even one o'clock. What shall I do? Call the cops, no, they won't listen to us during the day, much less at night".

I got up slowly and saw that everyone was sleeping and outside everything was quiet. No copper was walking around in the corridors, so I went to the bars that were the wall of the cell. They were square and very thick, you could hardly be seen from the outside, and what was more important, just below them along the whole length of the cell was a metal grid, like a kind of sewer to drain liquids. "I'm sorry, guys, but I have to pee," I thought as I drew my gun and aimed at the corner formed by the bars and the wall. Just as I thought, the piss escaped perfectly through the grate, staining the minimum and making little noise. "I'm sure they've done worse things in these cells, I'm sure many junkies have peed, pooped, vomited and even died here. This cell is perfectly designed to drain a little pee". The operation lasted thirty seconds, but it allowed me to spend a much more acceptable night. Nobody noticed my piss, so it was the perfect crime. After this I went to bed again and miraculously managed to get some rest.

I spent the rest of the night sleeping an unrefreshing sleep, waking up every few minutes and having strange dreams. In one of them I saw myself making love by candlelight with Daughter of Satan, a nickname for one of the girls in my class, who was not considered very attractive and had a rather bad reputation. "Fuck, I'm going bloody bonkers," I thought as I woke up. "If the sex drought continues for much longer, I might end up like this tho."

When the lights came on at half past six in the morning, I couldn't lie down for another second. I had woken up an hour ago, but I hadn't got up because I obviously couldn't go anywhere. Slowly, my companions woke up and started talking to each other. Some were still reluctant to leave the mattress, but the police not only turned on the lights but forced everyone to get up to go to the toilet, whether they wanted to or not.

The dweller in the cage opposite protested bitterly when the policemen made him get up. This was a rather shattered heroin addict whom we had never seen before, but whom we knew well from his cracked voice. The man on duty turned on the light in his cell and barked, "Here every fucking animal goes to the loo at half past six whether he feels like it or not, damn it. You have three seconds to get up". Apparently, the junkie got up, left his cell, but instead of going to the bathroom he turned off the light and went back to bed to continue with his cold turkey business. That's what my mates told me while they were laughing their heads off. The move had been quite comical and we all found it quite funny, but the laughter stopped when we heard first a swearing, then stronger and stronger blows and finally a weak and pitiful whimpering that would go on for a few more minutes. We all remained silent with a strange feeling of discomfort and shame. The junkie had been beaten up quite gratuitously, but none of us came to his defence even if it was in a testimonial way, as we were simply afraid to interfere in the course of justice.

After the macabre episode we went out one by one to the bathroom without complaining and looked down so as not to witness the humiliation that followed the beating. "You smell like shit, you bastard! Don't you know that you have to wash up every now and then, you filthy soap dodger," said a National copper to a bearded, skeletal man who was making serious efforts to stay on his feet. I didn't want to know any more and hurried to the bathroom, pissed and went back to the cell where breakfast was already waiting for me. I ate a couple of biscuits, saved the rest for later and sat down to wait. Today had to be the day, today they would let us go home or else they would send us to prison, wouldn't they? "Let's see," I said to myself, "we were arrested on Friday night, so tonight would be the forty-eight hour detention. Fuck, they can still keep me in the police station until Monday to serve the maximum of seventy-two hours. I hate this fucking place, I hate all this fucking situation; if I don't get out of this hole soon, I'm gonna go mental!"

PLAZA DE CASTILLA COURT

It finally looked like we were going to leave the Moratalaz Detention Facility and go to see the judge. Around noon some *nacionales* arrived and took us out of the cell in two batches. In the first batch, I was with Pedro, Echeverría and El Gordo. Again, we marched through the corridors of the police facility until we reached a kind of courtyard where there was a van ready to leave.

The cops organised a small group of prisoners to get into the van. Apart from the four of us, there were two Moroccans, one young and one in his thirties. They both looked very dodgy, with scars on their faces and fierce eyes. "For now, they seem calm," I thought, "but I hope they don't put me in the next cell with them." Finally, an old fat guy who was totally groggy came along. The man had an absent gaze, could not speak and could hardly stand up straight. But he wasn't drunk or high on anything, it was more as if he had been lobotomized, and we even had to help him get into the van. Once upstairs he sat down and fell heavily to the side on one of the Moroccans, who pushed him violently towards the other side. In the end, we all managed to keep him balanced while the van was stopped, but once it started to move, the poor bastard was falling all the way down and we had to hold him down until we got to our destination.

"What a difference between going and coming," I said to Pedro as I wondered what had become of the girls. Apparently, my outward journey had been a rather serious irregularity on the part of the police. Locking men and women together in a cell, or even in a van, is illegal and against "human rights". I thought it was great at the time, but I can understand that the girls might not have been so happy about being locked up with a man, even if it was with an incredibly attractive one like myself, I must say.

It took us about fifteen minutes to get to the courts in Plaza de Castilla. That was our destination and the place where a judge would decide whether to release me or send me to prison. Once there, we were put back through some corridors and ended up in a cell, Echeverría, el Gordo and I. I don't know where they took Pedro, but after a while, they brought another fellow in. The new one was a young punk with a mohawk and stuff. I didn't ask his name or introduce ourselves, but I called him *El Indio* (the Indian) in my internal forum, because his brown and beardless face, together with his hair, reminded me of the villain from The Last of the Mohicans.

This new cell was relatively large and had the advantage of having a toilet and a tap, although it was older and more deteriorated than the one in Moratalaz. On the walls, there were hundreds of graffiti and handcrafted prints, as if everyone who had passed by had followed the sacred ritual of giving expression to his name, his motto or his deepest desires, from "Viva Romania" to "Death to Capitalism" or "They're All Whores". Our first mission in the cell was clear, we had to record our passage there, so we set out with enthusiasm. The Indian found a piece of plaster, which we divided in two and started to paint on the smooth surface of the stone bench. The Indian painted "Oi! Long live punks & skinheads union", while I, more individualistic and less sectarian, wrote a "Chencho was here, March 98". When we finished our work we looked at it. The Indian seemed satisfied with his unitary plea, but to me, it seemed too little for my ego: "How ephemeral!" I thought. The first son of a bitch who sits on the bench will erase my glorious seal with his fat ass." So I began to search the floor of the cell for some object of a harder nature, with which I could engrave on a wall the trace of my passage through that filthy place. After a few minutes, I found a small piece of tile with which I was able to imprint my name on the plaster wall at a respectable height.

Echeverría and *El Gordo* did not join in our ritual. Echeve was like a big child and was content to watch in amazement what we were doing, while he was the happiest person in the world committing some small damage or spitting out some unusually gross phlegm on the floor. I think El Gordo was depressed because he hadn't spoken or done anything since we got there. When we finished painting, the Indian and I, he simply picked up the chalk and wrote it on the wall: "Everything will be fine", I suppose that was dedicated to us and to all the unfortunates who would hit their bones there in the future. "Now I've seen everything, a sensitive, feeling fat bastard giving us lessons in humanity. God bless this mess!"

Once we got bored of doing graffiti we started talking to *El Indio* about how he had been arrested. As we already knew the stories of our previous cellmates by heart, we were delighted to hear a new version of the fateful Friday night when we all had been screwed up. Surprisingly, *El Indio* was innocent too, he told us. The guy had been drinking kalimocho sitting in a doorway in Dos de Mayo, accompanied by a Skinhead friend and several girls, and although he was tempted to intervene when he heard the racket, the possibility of hitting on one of the girls took him away from the violence momentarily. Unfortunately, his Mohican hairstyle and chains attracted the attention of the cops a few minutes later, and he was arrested without the slightest consideration by the law enforcement officers.

Despite his innocence, Indio was pessimistic about his expectations when he was brought to justice. "I'm fucked up cause I've been locked up a few times," he said in an attack of sincerity. "As soon as I get in front of him, the judge will start asking me 'if you're innocent what were you doing there' he'll notice my looks, see my record and send me to prison for good."

"Have you been in the nick before?" asked Echeverria.

"I got close once. A *guardia civil* beat up a friend of mine in my *pueblo*, so we all went after him. I was arrested, but I was released on charges. This time I don't think I'll get away with it."

This thing about prison and being locked up in a cell was quite funny. Until now, all the kids I had met seemed like good people to me and so did El Indio. It must be that there was a kind of prison solidarity between us, or maybe it was that once you see yourself in the situation, you don't judge so quickly. Personally, I didn't judge anyone at all, I just wanted the judge on duty to be benevolent and let me go home.

The conversations we had over the next few hours focused on just that. At the height of the arrest, we would have to stand in front of a judge and convince him that we had done nothing wrong. If we did it well, the prize would be to go home, and if we did it badly, the punishment would be a prison where there were real criminals, for whom a young lad would be the closest thing to a woman they had seen in years. In principle, I assumed that they would let me go home after the 72 hours of legal confinement, but after some conversations with my mates, and some things I had seen, I was not so sure. Moreover, I had not spoken to any lawyer who could reassure and encourage me, only to unfortunate people who painted the situation darker than it really was. Apparently, it was enough that a riot police officer said that you had assaulted him, or your name was randomly written on a list, to tip the scales in favour of pre-trial detention.

We kept talking and talking, fearing a moment that was taking forever to come and imagining how to face it. Several hours must have passed, maybe even five or six, without anyone coming to request our presence. Since they locked us in that cell with a solid door and no windows, we had never heard anything from the outside world, not even a sound. In a way, it was as if we had been forsaken there and forgotten.

"How strange," I said to the others, "shouldn't we have seen the judge already? That's why we came. Am I right?" The others remained silent. You could see how doubts and nervousness had begun to gnaw away at their morale too. We remained silent for longer, in an attitude of "let's not get hysterical" that we all respected. The minutes passed, or perhaps three hours, and still, nothing happened.

"Man, they have forgotten about us- -the Indian said to me."

"Don't fuck with me, how's that possible?"

"Fuck, they got so many blokes here, they been filling up the cells with idiots and now they don't remember which ones have people in it and which ones don't."

"Besides, from the outside, it doesn't look like a cell because it doesn't have bars," said Echeverria, who was quite nervous.

"The three of us looked at each other and without thinking twice we went to the door. We put our ears close to it to find out if we could hear anything, but nothing."

"Maybe it's already night time and they've all gone home."

"And they left us here until tomorrow."

"Or until they remember."

We looked at each other again and there was no need to say anything. A second later we were screaming like possessed lunatics and pounding on the door in desperation. Fat Man in the corner was about to cry.

"We are here, get us out of here!" we shouted. After a while, we stopped pounding. The noise got louder as we ran and kicked the metal door. Here the Indian made good use of his military boots, but I especially shone with my repertoire of taekwondo kicks. I made them lateral, circular, frontal..., and they all ended in a thunderous blow to the door. Little by little, we got tired and began to assimilate that we had been abandoned.

Finally, when we were already thinking that we would eat the Fat Man first to survive, the door opened and two national police officers appeared. "You and you!" they said, pointing at the Indian and the Fat Man. "Come with us," and they took them away without giving us time to say anything. Well, at least we knew that they had not forgotten us in the cell. After a while, they opened the door again, but this time not to take anyone, but to bring two new tenants into the cell. Our new companions were two guys who were closer to their thirties than their twenties. About the first one, I deduced by his old-fashioned tracksuit, his traveller hairstyle and his faulty diction that he might be a heroin addict. With the second one, it was not so clear. He also had a shady but somewhat more modern look, with a bomber jacket and Panama Jack boots, which was the quintessential youth uniform in the second half of the nineties. The guys sat down without saying a word, and so we remained in uncomfortable silence for quite some time.

In the end, the boredom overcame the caution and little by little we started to have a conversation. First, it commenced with a declaration of good intentions between the newcomers and us, we were all legit people and we didn't want any problems. Later we started to be interested in the stories of the two newcomers and them in ours. It soon became clear that the older junkie was the one with the most experience with the system, so we started asking him all sorts of questions related to the procedure of seeing the judge. The second newcomer was also a heroin addict, but he had never been in prison before, so he also asked him quite a lot about how life was like there, mostly to get an idea of what was in store for him.

"Jail is not so bad, a bed, three meals a day and it is not difficult to score some horse, although it would be better for you to quit if you have no one helping you from outside."

"Can you score inside then?"

"Yes you can, but it ain't safe. Moroccan gangs control drugs inside. As soon as they find out you got the habit, they start pestering you for money and horse, and then you´re fucked up. Now it's the Moroccans who rule prisons. Gipsies don't move a fucking thing no more."

"Which one do you think they will send us to?"

"Maybe *Alcalá Meco* Prison, but I'm not sure."

And so they spent a long time talking about their things. Echeve and I just remained silent and listened to the voice of experience. Some things about the prison also affected us, but ninety per cent of the conversation between our two new friends revolved around a single topic: Heroin. At one point they told each other what substances they were taking, how often, how much, with whom, and many other stories from Madrid's shantytowns that made us sick. The two guys had been shooting heroin for years and, although they weren't too badly off compared to the skeletons we had seen before, they realised that in addition to ruining their lives they had also become obsolete.

"So, what you young folks up to now? How do you get high?" asked the old man.

"Booze and joints they do", replied the young junkie as he turned to us and said, "That's great lads, if you don't go any further than reefers you'll be fine!"

"Problem is you get a bit carried away and try to start *La Revolución*, don't you? That's why you here, innit?"

And so we continued to talk more and more animatedly. The old man told us that when he was arrested he had heroin on him and had to eat it to avoid having possession added to his charges. I, of course, didn't have enough knowledge about the subject to say if that was possible or not, so I just nodded when he told us that the taste of horse was horrible. The other one was arrested when he had just stolen a car and he was about to escape from Madrid, according to him, to get away from the streets.

"Heroin is fucking hell, it has fucked my life up. I used to have a job, a girl, mates, but then I started shooting that shit up my veins, and you see how I have ended up".

"I know it's not my problem, but... How did you start?"

"In my neighbourhood, with my mates, we all did it just like you do alcohol and joints, I got hooked and that's how I have ended up. I'm twenty-eight years old, I'm HIV positive and I'm going to go to prison."

"And why don't you quit in prison." The two junkies laughed at this silly question."

"Giving heroin up isn't that easy. There are almost as many drugs in prison as there is on the street."

"And how do they get it in? I can't imagine how you can get a whole load of heroin in there, with security and everything."

"They don't put in a load, they only get small amounts in. Besides, in prison there are not only drug addicts, but there are also dealers, and they keep on dealing."

"I would never have imagined this."

Little by little I became friends with the youngest junkie and our conversation got more and more fluid. I asked him a lot of questions about heroin, drugs in general and his tragic personal situation. He answered everything with sincerity and without giving many detours. The truth is that I found his situation so terrible that for a while my own problems were almost laughable compared to the ordeal my new colleague had gone through, and what he still had left. During his years of heroin addiction, he had lived in a constant and crazy race to get his next fix. Once he got it, the relief and peace it brought lasted until chills and a horrific sense of pain and discomfort drove him onto the streets to get another dose, starting the cycle all over again. In the process, he had gradually lost his job, his friends, his girlfriend and the support of his family. "It would have been wonderful to be able to combine work and addiction, this is every junkie's dream," he said, "but in the end, you have to choose one of the two. I also stopped seeing my friends to be with other addicts, but there are no friends in this world. My girlfriend left me when she found out that I was HIV positive, she told me a million times to quit, but I didn't listen."

Now I understood a little better why it would be so difficult for him to give up heroin in prison. If when he was free he preferred heroin to his family, mates, girlfriend and job, now that he would be locked up in a horrible and depressing place, while sentenced to suffer an incurable and fatal disease, he would try to find some comfort in the habit. After these revealing talks, I came to two conclusions, the first was that I did not want to go to prison, the second was that I should consider myself lucky in life. For the time being.

The talk lasted until the junkies started feeling sicker and sicker. I asked them when they would get the withdrawal syndrome and they answered that they already had it before they arrived at the cell. This scared me a lot, being locked up with no way out with two heroin addicts in the throes of withdrawal. My idea of this, probably fed by popular literature, was that those who suffered from it went mad with rage and fury at not being able to take their dose. The syndrome gave them superhuman strength and they were capable of anything to get a bit of a drug. I almost imagined the junkies taking us hostage and shouting at the guards: "If you don't give us methadone, we'll kill these two suckers right now!"

I got a little scared and moved away to a corner of the cell while I was studying my two future opponents. At first glance they were not badly damaged, almost healthy and stringy, not to mention the alleged superhuman strength of the junkie and his blind desperation, and, on top of that, his wounds could give me the dreaded HIV virus. I was definitely screwed. Luckily, my paranoia was far from what a withdrawal syndrome really is. The two junkies lay on the stone benches and plunged into a kind of feverish drowsiness with sudden chills and cold sweats. From time to time they became more active and sometimes more sleepy, but at no time did they pose a threat to Echeverría or me.

I was also quite tired and hardly felt like talking to anyone. "No wonder," I thought, "I've been without food or sleep for two days now. I hope they bring us something to eat soon."

It almost seemed as if they had read my mind when they opened the door and a couple of officials brought us food in a metal cart, like the ones we had already seen at the Moratalaz Facility. This time, however, we were in luck; it wasn't microwave-heated containers, but a proper meal itself. Traditional pork and chickpeas stew, *cocido Madrileño* with its soup, chickpeas and even some decent *chorizo* sausage, and on a glass plate with a metal spoon and everything.

Before starting to eat came the inevitable round of bartering. The junkies didn't seem to want to trade, but Echeverría didn't like chickpeas, so he suggested I trade them for my soup. –"No problem" –I told him, "I don't like soup". I ate the two portions of grub quickly, although I tasted them with delight. This stew was the best food I ever had in my life, the most exquisite and delicious. It had been prepared with a special ingredient, hunger. There is no better condiment for a dish than leaving the diner two days without eating before tasting it, I would have eaten the whole tray if they had given it to me.

After eating we piled the plates all together on the stone bench. The junkies might have the syndrome and whatever, but they left their plates clean, and even one of them ate three pears, that was the dessert, one after another. Personally, eating helped me to regain my strength, but it also depressed me because I deduced that the coppers wouldn't give us any food if our liberation was imminent.

After a while, some officials arrived and took the trays away, and on the way they also took Echeverria. "What would it be this time," I asked myself. "A line-up, another statement, a visit to the judge..."

It didn't take long for them to bring him back to the cell and then he explained that he had had to confirm his statement and that in ten minutes they were taking him to see the prosecutor. As the procedure seemed important, if not decisive for his future, he asked me to lend him my plaid shirt to make him look more presentable in front of the prosecutor. Apparently, he had been subjected to a rather harsh interrogation, in which he had already been formally accused of being a member of the kale borroka urban guerrilla. The alleged evidence of this was a fine gravel that had been found at the bottom of his backpack and that would be the remains of the stones he had used as projectiles in the urban guerrilla actions. This evidence was not worth a damn when the accused was a bricklayer and had been working that very afternoon, but the police top dogs, or top pigs, did not care, they just wanted to find a Basque name to accuse him of terrorism.

Once he put on his shirt, he went to the toilet in our cell and combed his hair with a little bit of water. "How do I look?" he asked.

"You're fine," I said and was glad there was no mirror in the cell because the shirt and hairstyle gave him a certain prisoner look. "You'll see how everything works out great for you," I encouraged him a little. "Lord have mercy," I thought.

When they took him away again, it was as if I had been left alone, because the two junkies were in such a bad state that didn't want to talk. Since I was bored, I spent my time drawing with one of the pieces of plaster on the walls. After about ten minutes they opened the cell door again and Echeverría came in. The poor boy was pale and had a face like the world had fallen on him.

"Man, the prosecutor has asked for two years in prison. Two fucking years!"

Then, murmuring an excuse, he went to the small toilet in the room, pulled his trousers down and started to crap without caring at all that there were other people present. Then I understood the expression "shit yourself with fear" better, and at the same time, I regretted the fact that life had forced me to watch a grown man pooping. I turned around to avoid seeing the spectacle, although I couldn't isolate myself from the sound of his farts and the noise the turds were making as they dipped into the toilet water. The worst thing was that, apart from being unpleasant in itself, it set a precedent and soon the two junkies would also be depositing their shit in the small toilet of the cell. I refrained from taking a dump, not because I was ashamed or didn't want to, but because I didn't want my buttocks to touch the toilet where they had taken a shit a few moments before. I suppose this sounds unsupportive, politically incorrect and even a bit ignorant, but it's the truth. The last thing I needed was to catch some of the opportunistic infections that these people usually suffer from, so I kept my shit in my ass until I saw myself in circumstances more conducive to expelling it.

After the round of shitting it looked like another visit to the prosecutor was imminent, so we all got a little nervous. I was quite worried that it was my turn, but the junkies were rather excited at the prospect of going to jail. The youngest one told me that he was really looking forward to it because there you could score horse, or at least some other kind of drug, hash or even tobacco. The boy had managed to hide a thousand pesetas note during the interrogation and was now eager to use it in prison to get a fix. "If I had a shot or at least a smoke of smack, I wouldn't care, I'd even sleep here so happy." The old junkie was attentive to the conversation and couldn't stop intervening.

"What really works in prison is tobacco," he said slowly. "There you can exchange cigarettes for anything you want."

The other junkie was very interested in this, so they started talking to each other. I was quite nervous at the prospect of a son-of-a-bitch prosecutor asking for six months in jail for me when I couldn't stand another day locked up. For that reason, I didn't follow the conversation and stayed out of it, but it seems that the junkies were negotiating seriously. Every time the officer entered the cell the old druggie had been asking him for a cigarette or a cigarette butt that he had seen on the floor. The official, reluctant at first, had promised the junkie that he would buy him a pack when he took him out of the cell to testify, provided he gave him the money. So the old addict was allowed to buy tobacco, but he had nothing to do it with.

I don't know how it happened, but in the end, they both agreed that the young druggie would lend the old one the money to buy a pack of cigarettes during the time he was taken to testify before the prosecutor, with the cooperation and permission of the official, of course. Later they took the old junkie to testify, but instead of returning him to the cell, they sent him directly to prison, taking the young junkie's ciggies and cash with him. It seems that the old man had taken advantage of his knowledge of the justice procedures to swindle the other junkie out of his money. As scared as I was about my next visit to the prosecutor, I couldn't help but feel sorry for the poor devil. The guy had been deluding himself that he was going to score something in prison with his roughly ten-pound worth note, but the other manipulator had swindled it like a master. It must be true that there are no friends among those in heroin. "Fucking hell," shouted the young junkie, crying in desperation.

The rest of the time I spent in that cell I tried to isolate myself as much as I could from the various human dramas and miseries taking place within those walls until finally the time to see the judge finally came. Some officials from the courts in Plaza de Castilla opened the door of the cell and called my name. I said goodbye to Echeverría and to the naïve junkie and followed the officials to a small room where a middle-aged man with a bushy moustache was waiting. "You must be Chencho, right?" he told me, "I'm Pedro's legal representative and will also represent you this time". After the introductions, the lawyer explained to me a little about the procedure we would follow to see the judge and also gave me a series of recommendations of what to do and what not to do. The procedure was simple, enter the room where the judge was and shut my mouth until someone asked me something. The recommendations were basically to be polite, to put on an imbecile face and to deny, very respectfully, any participation in the squatting movement or any other. Needless to say, when I finally entered the judge's chambers, I tried to fulfil all these premises as if my life was in it.

The judge's office was quite large and reasonably luxurious for the shitty place that was the courts of Plaza de Castilla. We entered it accompanied by two judicial assistants, who encouraged me a little. "Be calm," they told me, "we all know that the Police have arrested mostly innocent kids just having a drink in Malasaña." This gave me some confidence to face up to the bad moment.

I imagined the judge as a nasty geezer, so I was quite surprised that it was a middle-aged woman whose kind face denoted intelligence, and not an angry, unibrowed fascist. What's more, the judge reminded me a lot of *Ana Rosa*, a famous TV presenter those days in Spain, and this gave the story a little more surrealism. After being arrested and locked up among squatters and junkies for two days, barely eating or sleeping, the time had come to be judged by Ana Rosa. It was almost enough to make you laugh.

But instead of laughing or making some strange move, I stood very still and silent while the lawyer addressed the judge with the utmost courtesy to inform her of my condition as a young man unjustly detained. The judge listened patiently to the lawyer, sometimes interrupting him with some technical questions. After this came the long-awaited moment when I was finally allowed to say something in my defence. When the judge asked me about my participation in the events, I strongly denied having been in any demonstration or having participated in any violent act. I was very surprised when she asked me about a balaclava that the police had supposedly seized from me. For the first time in two days, I squirmed with indignation and frustration against the fucking cops. It was one thing to have been arrested in a ruckus for being stupid and quite another to be accused of something that both they and I knew was false. Yet I disguised my anger and measured my tone of voice to the millimetre to be respectful, I told the judge in a closing argument:

"Look madam, I have not been in any demonstration or I am a militant in any political or anti-system movement. I am just a secondary school student. I was having a few drinks with my friends last Friday evening when I was unjustly detained by the police."

The judge looked at me carefully and she seemed convinced of what I had told her. In a way, I felt that her silence encouraged me to keep talking.

"Moreover, it's quite normal for a young lad like me to socialize and have a few drinks in an area of *ambiente* like Malasaña."

"*Ambiente* area did I just say?" I thought, "Oh no, that sounds very queer, isn't that what they call gay districts?" Of course, I had nothing against gay people but this was 1998 Spain and homosexuality was not so well accepted by the most conservative types, so I didn't want to be mistaken for a gay man, just in case.

"I'm sorry milady" I set out to fix it, "I meant that Malasaña is more of an area, you know…, full of nightclubs."

"Holy shit, now I've fixed it!" In many parts of Spain they still use the word *nightclub* to describe brothels and whorehouses, rather than normal dance clubs. "Now this chick sends me to jail for being a libertine." I started to get very nervous and I think the lawyer made serious efforts to keep his composure and not to grab me by the neck and strangle me. Fortunately, the judge was an intelligent woman and understood perfectly what, despite my clumsiness, I had tried to explain to her.

"Don't worry," she told me, "I know that young people gather in Malasaña and Bilbao districts to socialize and have a few drinks." Then she turned to the lawyer and gave him a string of technicalities that I thought would get me off.

I could hardly believe my eyes when the officials escorted me to another cell where there were already a lot of people. Apparently, we were the ones who were going to be released. There was Pedro, whom I hugged and thanked for putting up with me the whole time, and many other kids, among whom were most of my cellmates from Moratalaz. There was also Echeverría, who I wouldn't have given a penny for minutes before. Our lawyer had defended him for free and saved him "in extremis" from being sent to prison. Inexplicably, the young junkie was also there. "How was that possible," I thought. Of course, the officials had mistaken him for one of the squatters. "Man, God gives you a second chance; if it works out, take advantage of it to quit heroin."

The negative side was that they had taken the fat man to prison. "Don't fuck with me, *El Gordo*, the most innocent and sensitive guy in all the fucking courts." Well, the poor guy spent a whole month in prison just because the fucking riot police were so creative in making things up.

I said goodbye to all those kids, involuntary companions of an experience in life that had been unpleasant but enriching. I only frowned a little and avoided shaking hands with *El Contreras*, the villain who caused our arrest. Finally, it seemed that the judge's verdict for all of us, except three who would go to prison, had been free with charges. This meant that we still owed a debt to justice, and that the shadow of a future trial was still on the horizon, but that we were free for now. The charges were disorderly conduct, destruction of public furniture and resistance to authority, but all I cared about at that point was going home to rest.

"I'm free on charges, that doesn't sound bad at all when it comes to impressing some hippie girl," I thought as we were led through the corridors to the exit of the courthouse. As we got closer we started to see that it was already dark outside, but that despite this many people were waiting for our release. We started to hear shouts against police, conservative politicians, and in favour of squatting. Some clairvoyant mind had had the brilliant idea that we detainees should form a human chain to denounce torture and God knows what else. Personally, I was not up to bullshit and just wanted to go home to my family. Fortunately, our lawyer persuaded the imbeciles of the chain to leave us alone, and he also prevented the detainees from having to appear in court every fortnight to sign a form and attest that they did not intend to escape. A good guy the lawyer, although in the end, he kept for himself the provision of funds that my parents gave him to face a trial that would never take place. Well, nobody is perfect.

We finally went out on the street and all the people waiting for us went crazy and made us a kind of corridor as if we were heroes or something. Amongst all those around me were, besides family and friends of detainees, many of the people who had been mounting a fight in Malasaña on Friday. "Bastards", I thought, "you should be in jail and not the poor Fatboy!" I quickly lost sight of all the other detainees and found myself walking through a crowd of frantic people until I finally saw my mother's crying face. When she saw me she pounced on me and held me tightly as she started crying again. "For God's sake, mother, I'm not coming back from the eastern front." My father was also there with her and seemed satisfied with my release. Being a man of great temper, I had feared that he would be angry with me for the huge mess I had gotten myself into, but it didn't seem to be so. Apparently, he had already released tensions by dispatching himself in front of the television cameras, calling public officials such as Mr Manzano, Mr Morgades et al, fascists.

After the reunion, we went with Pedro's parents to have a drink at a nearby cafeteria, where I finally enjoyed some ice-cold Coca Cola. Then we said goodbye to Pedro and went home in a taxi. Once there I had two fried eggs with *chorizo* and something else and took a much-needed shower. Paradoxically, it was once there that I started to feel sick again. I really had no reason, I had finally been released, but after dinner, I began to experience a very strange feeling, as if I could not recognize my own home. Again anxiety and nerves appeared, I was panicky to stay in a room of the house for more than ten seconds and I started to walk around. As I didn't want to scare my parents, who had had enough, I took this episode by myself. Again, just like in Moratalaz's cell, I felt very bad and very strange, but I didn't know why. A vague feeling of threat and uneasiness tormented me and all I wanted was time to pass as quickly as possible. In the end, I managed to calm down by reading some childhood comics, after trying to watch TV and play a bit with family dog *Piletus*. I'm not a psychologist, so I can't say what it was, maybe it was post-traumatic stress, anxiety or whatever. After a while, it passed and I was able to go to sleep.

PARQUE DEL OESTE

The next day I got up late and skipped all my classes even though it was Monday. All I wanted to do was to be at home and get my strength back for the interrogation that awaited me on Tuesday at school. In the afternoon I got a bit cheerful and went for a walk around my house with the dog. In a way, I took Piletus with me because I thought that no copper would stop me if I had a dog with me, and I also took care to go properly documented with my ID. After the walk, I spent some time tidying up and preparing notes and other school materials until it was time for dinner. After dinner I watched some TV, I think it was "X-Files", then I smoked a cigarette in the bathroom and went to sleep.

My parents woke me up around half-past seven in the morning. I didn't feel like going anywhere at all, but I knew I had to go back to school if I didn't want to get into trouble with my university access test. I got into the shower still groggy and dressed up in the clothes I had prepared the day before. Then I shaved, combed my hair a little, took my things and went out to the street without having breakfast. While I was going to the Sol Underground Station I was trying to figure out how people would react to seeing me, since I had become, together with Pedro, the undisputed protagonist of the weekend, and I was also planning my performance in front of all of them. "I wish they left me alone," I thought, but I knew very well that they would not. I went through all the possible and probable questions they were going to ask me and thought about how to answer them without giving too many details or trying to sound cool. I also decided to stick to the version of the story in which I was completely innocent, so I wouldn't get into trouble with the teachers and school management. I took the metro at Sol Central and got off at Moncloa Station, at the end of line three. As I walked up the street to the private school where I was taking the A-levels Spanish equivalent, my steps became shorter and shorter and my desire to turn around and go home increased. I finally summoned up my courage, crossed the green painted doors and headed for the stairs to get to the floor where my class was. There were few people in the corridors, as I had arrived a bit late deliberately to avoid the crowd at the entrance, but I was not spared the talk of the janitors. As soon as they saw me, they approached me, asked me all sorts of questions and assured me that if necessary, they would even testify on my behalf in a future trial. "Thank you very much," I told them, "but for now, I'm fine."

Then came the dreaded moment of entering the classroom covered in glory and being the target of all eyes. "There he goes, that's the convict, what a dodgy face..." I imagined all the classmates commenting quietly and making accusatory gestures. I entered the door when almost everyone was already seated and paraded, with all the dignity I could muster, to the place where I usually sat. The three seconds from the door to my place took forever with all the boys and girls looking at me, although fortunately, no one made any comments or jokes. The years of taekwondo and the fights in the courtyard had given me a reputation as a guy, generally friendly, although fickle and unpredictable, so no one dared to touch my balls. When I sat down, I waved and talked a bit with the crew members around, but avoided the obvious issue. Then the class started and we all started taking notes like maniacs.

For the rest of the day, hardly anyone bothered me about my detention, except for some girls who asked me a little bit how I was doing. At "recess" I surrounded myself with my best friends and more than telling them anything, they were the ones who told me everything that had happened while I was in detention. After the last class, I went home quickly to avoid the typical chit chat groups that formed on the way out. Once there I ate something and took a nap. The rest of the afternoon was spent studying as best I could and then the daily routine: dinner, getting ready for the next day and going to sleep.

The rest of the week was similar to Monday, except that I opened up a little more to my mates and told them about some of the episodes that had happened to me while I was behind bars. Fortunately, teenagers are quite self-centred and nobody seemed to be too interested in my story. After all, we all had our little problems and exams to pass, so everyone minded their own business.

What I did find amazing was all the commotion caused by the Malasaña incidents and the arrests. There was still something on the news in the middle of the following week, and I even saw my own father on telly calling Mr Manzano fascist, which made me very happy. Apparently, the police action had been disproportionate and many of the arrests quite irregular. When the weekend came, the matter was still hot, so the squatting movement organised a demonstration to protest against the brutality and arrests under the slogan "Occupy the space".

On the advice of the lawyer, my parents and because I didn't want more problems, I, not only didn't go to that demonstration, but also stayed at home all weekend. The rally was called in the centre of Madrid, very close to my house, so I could see part of it from the window with mixed feelings. On the one hand, I had sympathy for the squatters, my former fellow prisoners, but on the other hand, I was apprehensive about how this sort of legitimate social movement was sometimes kidnapped by violent groups. Squatting is about finding public spaces that are not being used and turning them as social centres to help people, as well as claiming the right of every human being to have a decent home. Squatting has nothing to do with getting drunk and razing a neighbourhood of poor people and immigrants like Malasaña, even though some kids see it that way.

Fortunately, the demonstration had a festive and peaceful air that made it very different from the previous week, so there were no incidents. It can be said that both sides learned from their mistakes and did not fall into provocation. The squatters claimed themselves as a non-violent, supportive and constructive collective, and the authorities sent only some local police patrols to watch from a distance and not the riot national police to create a stir.

After that weekend of voluntary confinement in the tranquillity of my home came another week, a repeat of the previous one, where the only thing that really changed was the syllabus explained by the teachers in class. It was not in vain that we were already advancing inexorably towards the final baccalaureate exams at the end of May and then the dreaded university access test in June, and we had to hurry to cover all the subjects. The weeks went by more and more quickly and at the end of each one came a weekend in which the temptation to go out at night were slowly taking over from the caution and apprehension caused by my detention. In the beginning, I started going around Malasaña, very carefully, and at the end of April, I started to go out at night almost normally.

For me, Malasaña had died in March 1998 with my arrest, but even if I did not enjoy going out there as I used to, I could not prevent this neighbourhood from being the meeting point for my mates. Many times I had to choose between going back to Velarde or staying at home without going out because all the troupe was still hanging about there. In general, it wasn't bad, but now any threat of a fight, the appearance of the police or a demonstration caused me such a panic attack that I would end up leaving the neighbourhood or going into a bar until the storm passed. This wasn't a bad idea on a couple of occasions when there was trouble like the one where I was arrested, and from which I escaped without any problem this time. This attitude may seem exaggerated, but to be arrested a second time in a riot, having also a record, could have ruined my access to university the following year. It was also on these post-arrest Malasaña outings that I met several of my cellmates, who updated me on all the developments in our case. On Dos de Mayo square I met *El Gordo*, who I was happy to greet and see that, although he was still a bit green, he looked good in general. I also met *Indio* once and the whole Rivas Vaciamadrid crew. The hottest encounter was with Neanderthal late at night, and drunk when the two of us were going home. The guy told me that our trial was suspended or something like that, but that he had two more trials to worry about. I kept talking to him for a while more until I got tired of his bullshit and chose another path to go home.

The weeks passed quickly once I calmed down a bit and got used to the routine of going to class in the mornings and studying in the afternoons. I organized my weekends in such a way that I went out on Friday nights, rested in the mornings and studied, without much enthusiasm, on Saturday and Sunday afternoons. I chose to organise my time in this way because experience showed me that Friday was a totally sterile day for studying, but, on the contrary, Saturday and Sunday afternoons could be used to review whether Friday had been enjoyed out sufficiently and I no longer felt like partying. This strategy worked well, so the last days in April and the first ones in May I went out a bit for Malasaña while I managed to make good use of my time.

As the final exams approached, we became increasingly nervous. These were in the middle of May to leave us almost a month after to review for the university test. If I managed to pass them, I would have completed at least part of the task, which was to finish higher secondary education. These exams would be like a mock exam of the University Access Test, with exercises taken from previous years, and would take place in the same time frame as those, i.e. three days. The subjects would be the same, obviously: English language, which was mastered thanks to a couple of summer courses that I did in the UK previous summers; Spanish Language and Philosophy, which seemed affordable. The science branch was where my real problems were, with Physics, Chemistry, Mathematics and Technical Drawing. Of these last two I have to say that no matter how much I studied, I could not understand them and much less solve the exercises that they presented to me.

When the fateful week of the school exams finally arrived, I had managed to do a more or less exhaustive revision of all the subjects, except Drawing, but I did not know how to solve more than the tasks that we had already done in class, which were the typical exercises that one ends up knowing by heart. Luckily, or rather, as was to be expected in a private school, the teachers were indulgent and gave us easy and predictable exams. Throughout the year they had been very demanding, but now the school management had suggested they lower the level shamelessly to inflate the students' final grades to give them more options to get to university. There was a reason why our parents paid thirty thousand *pesetas* every month to a privately owned school instead of sending us to the state high school. Many of my classmates were very bright boys, but the proportion of A's was much higher than it should have been. Even I got a few, but my grades were more like those of normal intellect.

When the week of school exams was over and I saw that it had not been so hard, I understood that it had only been a formality, training for the University Access Tests. I still didn't know my grades, but what I did know for sure was that no one was going to fail, no matter how badly they did it. For years we had been taught more or less fiercely, but they were always preparing us for the moment when we were going to take our University Access Tests, so there was no point in giving us bad marks. In a way, it would be like a boxing coach giving his pupil a beating the day before the title fight or like Madrid not showing up for the European Cup final which they were surprisingly due to play in a few days. The real and only test would be the Official University Access Tests, but that was in a month, so all of us kids decided unanimously that before studying to death and facing our destiny, we would go on a monumental spree that weekend.

That Friday we showed up for class more than anything else to get to know some exam results from the teachers, and also to meet up and plan what we would do with that parenthesis of freedom in the form of a Friday that we had before facing the most serious month of our young lives. Due to the good weather and the fact that the days were already very long, we decided that that Friday we would meet up in the afternoon to have a *botellón* drinking session together in *Parque del Oeste*. This park was one of our favourite drinking spots when it was hot, due to its shiny meadows and its proximity to the school. For these reasons, we decided that we would meet at seven at school and walk there all together. This would allow us to go home to eat and take a little nap and then start with renewed strength.

Once I was clear about the plan I decided to go home early instead of staying with my classmates chatting on the benches outside the school. I had a lot to do and I didn't want to waste time, because for me the pre-party ritual was something very serious and I wanted to make sure I could carry it out calmly. So I got home around three o'clock in the afternoon, ate something and went to bed to take a *siesta*. When I woke up it was already five o'clock, so I was a bit short of time. It took me about twenty minutes to fully wake up and get in the shower. Once I finished I quickly got dressed and prepared something as a snack-dinner, which was important considering how much we were going to drink that night.

It was about quarter-past six when I was ready to go out, although I had to wait a little longer to hear my parents' warnings. Be careful, son, don't get into trouble, you know you have a record and other stories. For my part, I countered by telling them that I was the most interested in staying out of trouble while putting on a beatific face and telling them I was going to be good. Although I was still technically a teenager, I was past the age of outright rebellion against my parents, and I just felt a little sorry for them, for all the worries I had given them lately. Despite this, they gave me all the freedom in the world and all the money I could possibly need, contenting me with the occasional lecture in return. Before leaving the house I assured them that nothing bad would happen again and I took to the streets bound for the Sol underground station.

This time we had arranged to meet outside the school at seven o'clock in the evening so I was already a little short of time. To make matters worse, the metro took a long time to start and also stopped for an eternity between the stations of Argüelles and Moncloa. In the end, I was a bit late, but my friends hadn't left without me as I feared. There they were still deciding where they would buy the alcohol while waiting for the stragglers. At half-past seven we decided that we wouldn't wait for anyone else, so we started to go down from school to *Parque del Oeste*, stopping at a supermarket to buy the alcohol. Before, we used to drink kalimocho and beer, but lately, we were getting pickier and we only bought whisky and vodka, although the cheapest brands and therefore of worse quality. We went into the supermarket a few of us and came out loaded with all kinds of alcohol bottles, soft drinks and ice packs. We distributed the load among everyone and happily went down the streets and parks of the area until we reached the *Coruña* Motorway at the height of Franco's arch. From there we crossed the street and in five minutes we were all sitting on our favourite meadow, opening the bottles and preparing the drinks.

There must have been about thirty of us, most of us guys but there were also quite a few girls. It was possible that as time went by someone else would join us in the session because it was not difficult to find us as we always made the *botellones* in the same place. Our meadow was almost at the beginning of the park and you could see it from the path as well as from the main road that went down to the depths of Ciudad Universitaria.

A few years ago, when we were not of legal drinking age, we would go deeper into the bush to hide from the police, but once we were all of the legal age we preferred to stay more on the periphery as it was safer. After all, a park at night is not the best place to get lost drunk and although nothing had ever really happened, many urban legends were circulating about neo-Nazi aggressions, perverts in search of young flesh and other dangers. The one that impressed me the most was the story of a boy named Yuri. Of course, nobody knew Yuri, being this the friend of a friend, but it was rumoured that the guy in question went missing in the park drunk and stoned and that his friends found him unconscious with his trousers down and a trickle of blood flowing from his backside. When he was taken to hospital, doctors confirmed that he had been raped, according to DNA analysis of semen extracted from his rectum, by at least three different men.

Today I doubt the veracity of this story, but then we were quite shocked. Parque del Oeste is huge and there is only public lighting at the beginning, so when we no longer had to hide from the police, we decided tacitly not to tempt fate and to stay in the illuminated areas close to the street. Fortunately, after the first *cubalibre* I was no longer tormented by strange stories. It was Friday, I was surrounded by all my friends and there were no squatters or riot police in Parque del Oeste, so nothing could go wrong.

Our *botellón* drinking sessions were always similar and resembled a kind of metaphorical roller coaster. In the beginning, we were climbing slowly, but there came a moment when the booze suddenly hit our brain cells and we fell into the abysses of drunkenness at a rate of one thousand miles per hour. Time accelerated, people drank and talked faster and faster and inevitably someone would end up getting sick and throwing up. In a way, it was like an unpleasant lottery in which we all participated, although some had more ballots than others. Needless to say, most of us went through the unpleasant trance at one time or another, but also through the funny moments of taking the piss out of the unfortunate.

That afternoon we were already close to that state when suddenly the people started to feel uncomfortable. A vague feeling of threat and uneasiness hung in the air. Some began to act strange and nervous when two kids from our school joined us bringing disturbing news. A little further down the park, all the third graders were having a drink when a gang of neo-Nazis had started to harass them with insults and threats. The mere mention of the word "Nazis" made us all quite apprehensive and we began to discuss what to do about it. Most of us thought it would be best to set up the camp in an orderly fashion and head together to somewhere safer. It didn't even cross our minds to confront the Nazis for control of the park. If they wanted it, they could shove it up to their asses, we were not going to risk fighting those savages if we could avoid it.

Since the early nineties, the words skinhead and neo-Nazi became sadly infamous in the streets of Madrid when bands of skinheads took the relay from the 70s and 80s old fashioned fascists and started to beat up people who they thought deserved it. Among their targets were foreigners, homosexuals and especially young people who they believed to be left-wing. These were punks, anti-fascist skinheads, but also any young lad who simply wore long hair, a beard or was informally dressed. Thus, Nazi skinheads were feared for their aggressiveness and hated to death by other urban tribes and generally by anyone with a bit of a brain. As we were not tough people by any means, but only middle-class school children, the fear of Nazi-skins was stronger than our contempt for them. So, it is not surprising that when we saw all the third graders arrive where we were, we panicked and decided to go up to Moncloa together. The poor lads had been forced to give up all their drinking in the face of the growing hostility of the Nazis, coming to our position both to warn us of the danger and to seek protection in numbers by adding their forces to ours.

The situation became dangerous when the Nazis finally made their appearance. Several silhouettes emerged from the bushes and we quickly identified them as skinheads by their bomber jackets and shaved hairstyles. They must have been around ten and seemed to be armed with sticks, chains and possibly also knives. The bastards were quite motivated and soon began to harass us while throwing stones and other objects that fortunately did not impact on anyone. "Well," I thought, "now it's clear what will happen. They are few but very cohesive and willing to do anything, and we are like a flock of sheep. Soon they will charge at us and everyone will run away, that's how it happens. They take advantage of the fear and shock to provoke the scatter and then hunt down one or two stragglers and beat them to death. In fact, they call this *hunting*, and they make them of foreigners, faggots and, as in this case, of lefties, which is us".

I slowly grabbed a glass bottle and started walking faster and faster with my companions towards Moncloa. "I don't think they'll catch me," I thought, "there are fat lads and girls in our group, but if this happens at least the first one will get a good blow in his fucking face". The Nazis started to come after us, but for some reason, they were not determined to launch the final attack. After a hundred meters, the orderly escape turned into a crazy run towards the entrance of the park.

It was at this point when we were most vulnerable. While I was running I was concentrating on not falling and I was tormented by the idea that some of my friends could be already under the military boots of those bastards, but what could I do by myself, more than running away and saving my ass?

The climb to Moncloa took forever. Halfway up, some of us were already tired and flabby, let's not forget that we had been drinking and smoking the time before and that we were in no way expecting such an attack. The Nazis followed us the whole time as we fled, but they were content with barking at us like dogs do at sheep, rather than throwing themselves at our necks as wolves do.

We finally arrived at Moncloa and stopped to catch our breath at the bus station. It took the Nazis a while to get on, so while we were recovering from the race, we had a quick assembly to decide what to do. Surprisingly, the girls didn't realise how close we had all come to being beaten and suggested that we forgot about the altercation and got on with the party. I think women can be smarter than men in most things, but definitely not when it comes to issues related to violence. Women have no fucking clue about these things, they just don't have the instinct from nature to do so and don't know when a situation is really bad. They couldn't be more wrong if they thought that neo-Nazis didn't hit girls. Lucrecia Pérez, whose only crime was being a Dominican girl, was killed by Nazis. They are not neighbourhood thugs who beat up the boys to impress the girls, they are would-be murderers, racist and evil.

What worried us most was whether we were all okay. To the cries of "Are we all here?" others answered "I don't see this guy!", or "we couldn't find this other person". As the skins didn't come up, we were very afraid that this was because they had hunted someone. As the shock stopped clouding our reason and courage, and our guts dropped from our throats to the usual position, we began to feel anger and indignation. We were just having drinks in the park without messing with anyone and those infective clowns had attacked us for no reason. Some of our course kids gathered around Manolo, who was the biggest guy and the only one who was a decent fighter. Next to him, stood Leo and me, but also my friend Gabo, Florian, Guti, Davo, Manu and some others. The third graders also chose their battle leader, a lad they called *the Killer*. He was also a dealer and hard as nails, but then he turned out to be a quite friendly chap when I got to know him better. Ten or twelve guys gathered around him who, despite being from our school, were known to be kind of dodgy.

When the Nazis appeared smiling at the end of the road, the little smile of triumph lasted just as long as it took them to realise that the tables had turned. The Killer sent two of his friends to the Argüelles area to gather more people and get some baseball bats. He then harangued us all with a battle cry "We're twenty now, let's get them boys!" to which we all responded with more shouts and ran to where the enemy was.

The Nazis fled like chickens into the park being chased by a mob of angry guys, but once we got them on the run we stopped chasing them. The bastards probably thought that we were already getting scared, that we were content with that and that deep down we were just a bunch of shits. For us, it wasn't over yet, but we didn't want to rush into the park where we didn't know how many Nazis there were or if they were armed or not.

We quickly climbed back to our exchanger headquarters to see how the recruitment of reinforcements had gone. It was a bit weak, only about five more blokes had come from Arguelles to help us, but they had brought two baseball bats that we could use to scare them and also to distribute some pain if necessary. We unanimously agreed that Manolo should carry one and the other should go to the Killer. The rest were armed with what they could find on the spot, as we did not know if they had knives. Most of us took glass bottles, some steel pipes that we found around and some sticks. Then we decided that only those of us who were willing to enter the fight seriously would go to the brawl.

Some tried to talk me out of it. My mate Ray was quite insistent on the fact that I had a record, but I didn't listen to him. In the end, we didn't make it to twenty-five, but we were willing to look for the Nazis and beat them up well. We all went out into the park in a kind of light trot, but without running. We were silent, almost tiptoeing to avoid making noise, and were led by the Manolo and the Killer, who each wielded a baseball bat. As we advanced it became darker and there was not a soul in the vicinity, neither passers-by nor youths or dog walkers, everything was deserted. As we rounded a bend in the road, we saw a group of about five people coming quietly. There was a second of doubt "that looks like bomber jackets, soccer shoes, is that them? Yes, that's them!

It was worth it to be there just to see the face the fucking Nazis made when they saw twenty-five guys running towards them to beat the shit out of them. They immediately ran in the opposite direction while we shouted and chased after them. In a desperate decision, they chose to head right and cross La Coruña Motorway. We fell on them just as they were crossing this road and we started to whack them like crazy, to the Nazis and even to an innocent citizen whom we took for one of them. The poor man had the courage to shout: "Let me go, I have nothing to do with it!" -And this made us realize the mistake in time and not beat him as well.

The Nazis were brutalized in the way they usually do with their victims, that is, six or seven to one. The poor bastards did not defend themselves, but they tried to turn and run away at all costs, and you could tell they were terrified. Between us all we organised an impressive brawl, twenty guys hitting some suckers between the moving cars. It was a miracle that no one was run over that night. Some drivers would stop and scold us: "You hooligans, leave the poor kids alone!" -And yet, their solidarity ended there, because they accelerated passing by when the Nazis begged them to let them in and tried to open the doors of the cars.

All the Nazis were beaten up with wild joy on our part, but between the ruckus and the cars, four managed to escape. The fifth Nazi, more unfortunate, could not get away and continued to be beaten until some of us started to protect him instead of assaulting him so that the rest would not kill him. I personally did not feel any satisfaction in attacking a defenceless person, yet not an innocent one, and I joined the side of the protectors. Finally, the Manolo and the Killer took him one on each side and got serious with the most exalted. No harassments until we had interrogated him and even then we would most probably hand him over to the police. Although the guy had just been beaten up, he hadn't been seriously injured.

I was curious because I had not seen many Nazis as close as this one. In a way, he looked like me physically and although he was a little taller than me, he was light years away from being remotely similar to what was considered an Aryan in National Socialist Germany. Arian Boys, we took out of him the name of the band that had attacked us. That made me laugh because the little shit in front of us wouldn't be considered Aryan even in Baluchistan. I was a bit more worried about his clothes, the guy was dressed almost like me. Indoor football shoes, tight jeans, black cotton shirt and a black bomber jacket without any badge now seemed to be the uniform of the Madrid fascists. "Fuck, I'll have to change my style if I don't want to get confused with one of them", I thought worried.

A guy called Florian chose himself as an interrogator in the cause and the rest of us agreed for his outstanding role in the fight. The first thing was to make sure that the Nazi was not seriously injured, but as we saw that he only had a few blows and the fright, we quickly started bombarding him with questions. The bastard strongly denied that he was a Nazi and explained to us that he was actually Antifa because he enjoyed listening to Metallica. That seemed to be the worst and most absurd justification in history and of course, nobody believed him. In contrast, we were disappointed that the guy didn't wear any Nazi paraphernalia to rub his face in it. Very clever these Nazis, when they started to be harassed by the Police and all the people who hated them, they let their hair grow and refrained from wearing identifying signs or military boots. Even so, it was clear that he was a son of a bitch and that just half an hour ago would have had no mercy on any of us in the park.

"Please, let me go, please!"

"No fucking way. We're going to lynch you, you son of a bitch, as you usually do with lefties…, don't you? We're gonna beat the crap outta you!"

"Twenty to one, that's what you do, right? Well, now you're going to meet your fucking master Hitler in hell, you son of a bitch, you Nazi scum."

The guy was about to cry when we hadn't decided what to do with him yet. Of course, we weren't going to do anything drastic or inhumane, but we were enjoying the beauty of scaring him and making him suffer. We knew we were incapable of it, but he wasn't, so we performed the comedy to the end.

"We're going to kick his ass!" said one of us in the background, and we all laughed. "No!" said another, "let's take his clothes off and leave him tied to a tree in the park all night". "I'm sure some immigrant bloke will rape you and you'll like it," said a third man as he put his fist an inch from his face.

Other ideas were to throw him on the ground and dance a pogo on him or to have fun watching him fight a death match against the beast Manolo, but after several more minutes tormenting him, we decided that we would let him go, although with two conditions. The first was that we would keep his ID and phone number as hostages to ensure that he would not attempt revenge. The second was that we would take him to a phone box in Moncloa (in 1998 only Agent Mulder had a mobile) to call his parents and confess that he was a neo-Nazi.

After he spoke, Florian picked up the phone and explained to the Nazi's folks everything that had happened. The parents, he later told us, were defiant at first, but then they began to break down and ended up being ashamed as well. Goal accomplished, the Nazi was totally humiliated and defeated. So we let him go home to think about what he had done, although that's not where it ended. Some of the third graders were not happy with our magnanimity and decided to apply their own punishment, so they slipped away from the bulk of the group and started to beat him up again in the middle of Moncloa. A riot quickly broke out and the local Police arrived to put the situation in order. This time I told myself that they would not catch me, so I mixed among the people and left for Malasaña where I had nothing to fear from any Nazi.

Once there, we gave up the botellón in the street and went to our official drinking station, the *"Más Allí"*. We liked this boozer so much because of the price of the drinks, which were terribly cheap, although the hangover was devastating the next day. We spent some time there among our classmates commenting on the Nazis' incident. After two hours of drinking beast mode, we went out like thunder to spread out through the bars of Malasaña. As the night progressed, we started losing some of our crew, but I was enjoying the bars too much and had even talked to some of the girls there. In the end, Gutierrez, Nico and I ended up in a legendary nightclub in Gran Vía, the famous Morocco, accompanied by some chicks of our class that we all knew as the grunges. These girls were a bit special and sometimes acted as divas, but that night they were quite friendly, so we had a great time.

After we had finished setting up the place and said goodbye to the grunges at seven in the morning, Gutierrez and I couldn't resist the temptation. Drunk as a skunk, we went to a phone box on Gran Via and took out the little piece of paper on which we had the Nazi's number written down.

UNIVERSITY ACCESS TEST

The next day the books were waiting for me to start my last and desperate review for the official University Access Test, better known in Spanish as *La Selectividad.* The return to this reality was hard but necessary, so I spent the whole Saturday gathering and preparing my notes for the month of study ahead of me, and I also planned how to distribute the time between subjects. On Sunday I made a tepid attempt to start studying and on Monday we resumed classes again at school.

These revision classes for the selectividad exams were quite different from the exhausting note-taking sessions that we were used to and focused more on practical issues that might come up in the exams. This was a lot of text commentary in Spanish Language and Philosophy and a lot of exercises in the other subjects. Some of my classmates had already mastered this completely, but I was pretty much a disaster in almost every subject.

Every day I would come back from class with a set of corrected exercises from various subjects and cram them home in the hope that these questions would fall in my exams. I also made some ultra-summarized notes for each subject, containing only the essential information for passing. I did this because I found myself unable to memorize long, leaden texts in the short time available to me, so I decided to study to pass rather than showing off by getting good marks. The subject I had the worst was Technical Drawing, so much so that I decided to leave the exam blank when the time came, except for one of the questions which were always the same every year and I already knew it by heart. So I took a whole subject out of my head and was able to spend the time studying other subjects where I was more likely to do something. The two points that the only kind of exercise I knew how to do would be a good reward, considering that the effort invested in the subject would be zero.

So I divided my time between six subjects and tried to study as best I could during those days. When the weekend before the University access exams finally arrived, I was so nervous that I couldn't even learn my way around the Complutense Law School, where the dreaded test was to take place. Luckily, I managed to convince my friend Nico, a sensible and studious young man, to meet me at the Sol Underground Station and go to the exams together. So, when the fateful Monday morning arrived, we met at eight o'clock where we had agreed.

Nico was calm and confident about the exams, unlike me, who was a nervous wreck. In a way, I think that if I hadn't had someone to take me almost by the hand to the Law School, I would have been unable to find it on my own. While we were going on the metro in the direction of the University campus, we were killing time trying to predict the questions for the exams we would take that day. These were no more and no less than four. Mathematics, at nine o'clock; Physics, at twelve; and in the afternoon, Philosophy and English Language. I, who like problems to come one at a time, had a pretty hard time the days before just deciding which subject to review the last one or which parts were more important.

After the metro, we took a little walk around the University campus and arrived at the Law School around a quarter to nine, where the official exams were going to take place for us. All our classmates were already there and also some teachers who had come to give us moral support, and who knows if secretly to gloat over our suffering.

At nine o'clock the doors of the classroom where we were going to take the maths exam were opened and we were called in alphabetical order to enter and take our seats. This process went on for almost half an hour, crushing my already altered nerves. I don't think it was too hot, and it might have been even cool, but I remember sweating like a pig and feeling considerably overwhelmed while waiting for my name to be called. Once I was called, I showed my ID and went to class, where it was even worse. Once there, they had us sitting for another twenty minutes before they started handing out the leaves. You couldn't say I was nervous anymore, now I was directly sick, dizzy and felt like throwing up and shitting at the same time. When I finally got the exam, the situation didn't get any better either.

I read the questions of both options and realized that I didn't know how to answer the exercises in them. I had seen the same exercises solved thousands of times in class, but I was so nervous that I didn't even know how to start doing them, the only thing I knew was that I had to get out of that classroom as soon as possible or I was going to faint. I raised my hand and one of the exam supervisors approached me. "I've finished," I said as I offered him the exam, "I have to get out of here". The supervisor explained that they had to wait half an hour to take in any exam in case a student was late. "Fucking late," I thought, "Why can't they arrive on time like all the rest. I have to get out of here or I'll get sick". I insisted again to the teacher saying that I was not feeling well, but he was adamant. "If you leave now," he told me, "you'll give up your exams and you won't be able to enter university until next year".

He also suggested I Should try to do at least some of the exercises and not to leave the exam blank.

As I had no other choice but to be there for half an hour, I read the statement of the first problem of option A. While I was doing it, a feeling of anguish was taking hold of me and I noticed how a knot was forming in my throat. I had done thousands of these exercises and yet I had no idea how to start solving that one. In the end, I had to choose between writing or crying right there, so I decided to go for the former, even though I knew for sure that everything was wrong while I was writing. After doing the first exercise, I attacked a system of linear equations that came in the fourth problem. In class, I had been given a series of techniques to solve them, which I had studied ad nauseam, but strangely enough, I could not remember them at that precise moment. Again I started to write meaningless numbers on the sheet at full speed until I came up with an impossible solution. The *Selectividad* University Access Test was supposed to be a proof of maturity, but apparently, I was still an immature kid. In just half an hour I smashed the exam and left the classroom as soon as I was allowed to hand it in.

As soon as I got out, I went to the bathroom and I threw a fit. Then I washed my hands and face and looked at myself in the mirror. I had been the first to leave and it was barely ten o'clock when the exam was due to finish around half-past eleven. I didn't need to wait twelve days to know my math results; I already knew it would be a big, obscene zero over ten that would haunt me for the rest of my life. "Chencho, the guy who got a zero on the math test". It took me a few minutes to accept that the grade of the first of the exams in which my future was at stake, would be that one. Then, I came down a bit and started to lament my bad luck and kick the doors and walls of the toilets. A few minutes later, I regained my composure and said to myself: "Okay, Chencho, you screwed up on the Math exam, but there are still three more exams today. If we do well in these exams we can make up for the zero and it's even possible that we'll pass our exams and become a university student."

I went to the faculty cafeteria and bought a chocolate croissant to get my strength back. Then I looked for a quiet corner away from the rest of my classmates and started studying for my physics exam at twelve o'clock. Once I went through the whole syllabus calmly and then sat down quietly to wait. What I hadn't learned I wasn't going to do it an hour earlier, so while I was trying to relax a bit it occurred to me that success or failure in this type of exam does not depend so much on knowledge, but on keeping calm and knowing how to apply it.

In Selectividad grades of all the exams counted the same and were added up to make an average, which would be the final grade and should be higher than four over ten to pass. For this reason, it was not so serious to fail but to get a zero that would dramatically lower the arithmetic mean of all the subjects as a whole. That was exactly what I just had done and that was also what I had to avoid doing in the following exams. If I didn't know how to solve them, I should at least try to scratch a few points and not sink into the depths of despair.

At twelve o'clock we entered the classroom again to face the Physics exam. This time I was much calmer, so I went through the whole process with much more dignity and courage than in the previous exam. When I finally had the paper in my hands, I was glad that at least things sounded a bit more familiar than in Math. I took a few minutes to decide which exam option I would take, the A or the B. In the end, I decided on B because A had a thermodynamics exercise and I had left this part unstudied.

This time I started to answer the questions wisely. First I answered the ones I knew best but in strict order. I started by making a small and very summarized theoretical introduction and then the approach of the exercise and the techniques I would use to solve it. The purpose of this was that if I made a mistake in the operations and solved the exercise badly, at least the teacher would take into account the effort and give me half a point. In this way, I managed to successfully complete three of the four exercises. The fourth one I had no idea how to solve it, but I still wrote down some theory on paper to try and scratch a few more tenths. When I handed in the physics exam, I couldn't help but be satisfied with myself. I wish I had been this calm in Math, the damage would have been much less.

Once the morning exams were over, I breathed a sigh of relief as at least two of the more difficult ones had finally passed. I went to lunch with the rest of my classmates in the faculty cafeteria, taking care not to fill up too much so that I would be in full force in the afternoon.

At four o'clock we had English, which was mastered; and two hours later, Philosophy. In this last subject, the exam consisted of a topic on a famous philosopher and a text commentary. As I was not too bad at writing, the success of the exam would depend on how well I had memorized the lives and theories of some famous philosophers. Fortunately, there were several tricks here that allowed us to get a certain advantage, such as that of all the Greek philosophers who entered the COU curriculum, Aristotle or Plato were usually asked, so at the stroke of a pen, we would get rid of the rest of the Greeks.

Moreover, everyone knew that only a handful of authors normally fell into the examinations and even if there were any surprises, these could be avoided thanks to the two options in the examination. In the end, I only studied six typical authors: Aristotle, Saint Thomas, Descartes, Kant, Karl Marx and Friedrich motherfucking Nietzsche.

At four o'clock we started taking the English exam and by six o'clock I had answered all the questions quite confidently, so it was clear that the marks would be good. I had always been one of those typical Spaniards who didn't know a damn thing about English even though they had studied it all their lives, but that changed when I went to the UK for a couple of summers to do some immersion courses. This didn't turn me into a Hugh Grant overnight, but I improved a lot. Being in the country and feeling the need to communicate to get the most basic stuff like food, things or sex was much better than all the assholes who taught us grammar at school for so many years.

Finally came the Philosophy exam, where they asked me about Plato and Sartre, plus two other more predictable ones. This was quite annoying, but I didn't let these clever ass philosophers defeat me, so with a lot of imagination and a few looks at other people's examinations I managed to reconstruct Plato's life and work acceptably and wrote an excellent essay on Nietzsche.

After finishing this last exam we all went home quickly to review a little before going to bed. The next day two difficult exams awaited us. Technical drawing, of which I could only solve one exercise, and Chemistry. Drawing developed as I expected. I took the exam, completed the only exercise I knew how to do in ten minutes, waited another twenty minutes without doing anything and handed it in. With Chemistry, I had much more fight and it took me almost two hours and a half to finish all the exercises, although I wasn't sure at all that they would have the correct answers. Once the exams were over, we went home to make the last effort reviewing Spanish Language and Text Commentary for Wednesday.

This last day of exams I woke up much happier than the previous ones with the perspective that the torture was nearing its end and I went directly to the *Complutense University* without meeting my chum Nico first. As I knew the way, I spent the underground trip going through the Spanish syllabus, and occasionally looking at the young chicks who I shared the metro car with. One more little effort and I would be a university student, after three glorious months of holidays in which I could make up for all the troubles I had experienced during the winter. When I arrived at the university they were already calling to enter the classroom, so I didn't have time to study anymore. When they called my name I entered the classroom and took my seat.

The Spanish language exam was not as easy as I had hoped. Some of the questions were quite far-fetched and none of the classic subjects from other years were in the exam. Anyway, I suppose that every language teacher will always have a resentful son of a bitch inside, willing to take revenge on the students for the disdain with the subject is treated by some. Then came the text commentary, of which I could not say whether it was easy or difficult. I just started writing like crazy until I filled in the two pages and then handed it in thinking more about the kalimochos we were going to drink in a few minutes than about the exam I had just taken.

I left the classroom door with great excitement and started to run through the faculty corridors looking for my classmates who had already finished the exam. For a moment I thought about flushing my language notes down the toilet, but then I thought about it and decided that I wouldn't do it until I was sure that I had passed. I met a small group of my colleagues at the end of the corridor and had a lively chat with them until all our friends had left the examination room. Once we were all reunited again, we went outside the college and sat down on the lawn in the gardens. Surprisingly, the area around the Law School was full of little clandestine stalls, run by university students, selling plastic glass filled with kalimocho, beer, and to a lesser extent *cubalibres*. "Who said that the youth did not have an entrepreneurial spirit?" We thought this was fantastic because we could already see ourselves having to go up to Moncloa to buy drinks. We went to one of them and bought the guy a few drinks to start a celebration that would last all afternoon. After those drinks came others and more, and we ended up getting all wet on the lawn sprinklers to celebrate that the exams were finally over. So much alcohol and wet T-shirt made me lose track of time and when I realized how late it was, I found out that I had forgotten to call my parents and even to eat.

I arrived home around seven in the evening and found my old folks a bit upset. They had been worried because I hadn't called to say how I had done or even to give any signs of life. I didn't mean to do this, but when you're a teenager your parents are the last of your priorities, and I just forgot about them completely. After a little discussion, I went back to the streets to continue drinking with my mates. Let's not forget that I hadn't been out for almost a month and I wanted to make up for the lost time. That night we all met in Malasaña to have a drink and, even though it was Wednesday, we partied until the crack of the down.

From that day onwards, a period of laziness and milling began in which the only thing I had to do was wait for the results of the *Selectividad* examinations because it didn't even make sense to decide what course or university I wanted to study at. Not until I knew my average marks and which degrees I could apply for. The days passed slowly and there were no noteworthy events. In the morning I slept until quite late and spent my afternoons playing computer games or watching the 1998 World Cup on telly. At night, as usual, I stayed with people in Malasaña, drank kalimocho and tried to pick up girls with little success. Finally, at the end of June, the big day came when he had to go to school to receive our University Access Exam results. For a long time, I had thought that it would be better to fail than to pass with marks too low for anything decent, but now I wanted to pass at all costs, not only because I was terrified of going through all the trouble of studying and taking the exams again, but also because of the humiliation of still being a schoolboy when all your friends were already university students.

The exam results were given to us personally by Mr Chamorro, our incombustible head of studies. As soon as he saw me entering his office he reprimanded me paternally.

"Well well, who we got here… Mr Charlie. I really wanted to talk to you son. "

"My name is Chencho, sir." The bastard never remembered my name.

"Well, Chencho, the truth is that things didn't go very well. How is it possible that you got zero out of ten in Mathematics? What a disaster!"

"Yes sir, you're right. I got nervous, you know, and in the end, it turned out to be a bit of a bum. "

"That's no excuse. At university you have to study much more…, so don't be a fool and get your act together. "

"Of course, sir."

"Of course what?"

"Of course not."

"Of course, you're not going to study more!"

"No, I meant no to the fool's bit; to study, yes, that's for sure."

"Ah, well!"

So he continued to scold me a little more, but without much enthusiasm, as he was aware that all the damage had already been done. From then on, the responsibility for educating me would no longer be his but someone else's, because, yes! I had passed my exams, albeit by the skin of my teeth. Then he gave me the results for all the subjects:

Mathematics: a pathetic zero out of ten

Technical drawing: two point five

Chemistry: three

Physics: seven

Spanish language: four points out of ten in my fucking native language.

Text Commentary: six and a half

Philosophy: eight

English language: eight point seven

These grades added together and prorated, gave me an average of almost five on the University access test, which when added to the high school average, put my cut-off grade for choosing a university degree at a modest, though not too bad, six-point something. I finally knew which degrees I could apply to and which universities. The list was quite long, but I only had a few days to decide until I submitted my application to the Head Office of Madrid Central University authority. Among the options were Physics, Chemistry, some low-demand engineering courses and, of course, Business and Economics. All of them, in my home-town Madrid, and in a state-funded, affordable-for-normal-people Public University, so my folks wouldn't have to pay more than the equivalent of five hundred UK pound a year in fees.

It took me some time to draw up the list, but in the end, I put Civil Engineering in the first place, followed by two other engineering degrees, I don't remember which ones. In my innocence, I thought that studying a little harder than at school I would not have a problem in getting ahead. When the day came to hand the form in at the Head Office, I met some of my classmates at school and we went to the campus all together. On the way, I had a revealing conversation with Gutierrez.

"Listen buster, you and I are rather lazy people and the sooner we accept this fact, the more suffering we will be spared in the future," he suddenly said.

"What's that supposed to mean, man?"

"It means you're crazy signing up for an engineering degree. It's too hard for someone like you."

"What do you mean, someone like me?"

"Well, you're not exactly the best thing to come out of our school, and it's not that you don't try to, but you can't polish a turd, no offence."

"I know that if I set my mind to it, I can get it. Why not?"

"Because you're a fucking bum and in Maths, you don't hit the nail on the head. Besides, to become an engineer you have to study your ass off every day as if it was the day before the final exam. Honestly, I don't see you capable of that."

"Well, it's my life and I'll join an engineering degree if I want to."

"Well, that's up to you, what do I care? You'll tell me about it."

So we continued discussing for a while more and I have to admit that if at the beginning the Guti's raw sincerity touched my balls, little by little his arguments became more convincing. I have always been a very persuadable person and after a few minutes, the idea of engineering seemed crazy to me. Within a quarter of an hour, I was totally convinced and happy to be surrounded by people who told me the truth without any hindrance.

"So, what course were you gonna take, Guti?"

"Me, Business Studies; I wanna be in the money."

"Do you think it's very difficult?"

"Nay, it's a bloody joke!"

"Business doesn't sound bad," I said as I crossed out all the engineering fields on my application form and wrote it in big letters. Then, I handed it in at the secretariat and went off with the others for a few beers.

"Peasants, workers, students join the ranks of the Communist Party! No, man, that's a joke. Let's all drink Pepsi, buy a PlayStation and listen to the Spice Girls, which is much more fun. Also, this summer there is the World Cup and the favourites to win it are Nike and Adidas". At the end of the nineties, it became clear that capitalism had won by a landslide and parents forgot about May 68 and hurriedly sent their children to learn English in expensive British schools or to summer courses abroad. So little by little, we all become bilingual Spanish-English, which is the language of the Empire, and later monolingual in English only. The world becomes a great melting pot dominated by the Internet and low-cost flights and Ronald McDonald is appointed Galactic Emperor. "What a strange dream man, I'll never have half acid in my fucking life again!"

The day after receiving my *Selectividad* scores I woke up with a hangover from the celebration that followed the exams, and I realised that summer had just begun. I had almost four months of holidays until I started classes at University in October and no idea what to do with so much free time. Well, I had a lot of ideas, but ideas that could be put into practice, not so much anymore. The aim was to have fun and make the most of the summer, and for this, I not only needed time off but also money, the approval of my parents and some mates. Three and a half months on holiday when you're eighteen is something too precious to waste by doing nothing decent.

My two basic options were staying in Madrid, or going to the little town in the countryside where my parents always spent their summers, as they had relatives there. Staying in Madrid was okay but I didn't like the second option because I've always found little town life very boring. I had no friends in that hole and I could not connect with local youths in any way. We simply belonged to different worlds and had nothing in common, apart from the natural distrust of the rural peasant towards city dwellers.

So it was all right-ish to stay in Madrid, but I didn't want to go to Little-town no matter what, and my schoolmates weren't going to offer me any solutions to my problem either. A few of them, including Diego, Gabo and Pedro, were going to Paris and Amsterdam for ten days. I was sure that this trip was going to be a unique experience and that they were going to have a great time together drinking, smoking joints and going to museums, but this was not what I was looking for. I wanted a plan that would cover most, if not all, of my summer and not a ten-day trip, after which I would be hopelessly doomed to be bored in town with my folks.

Some girls from school, the notorious grunges, had invited me to go to *Costa del Sol* during the summer to the house owned by the parents of one of them. This invitation surprised me a lot and also made me create the typical expectations that any heterosexual male would have. The problem was that when I asked them to be a bit specific about what dates and how to get there, they kind of ignored me, so I came to the conclusion that the invitation was just one of those typical plans that people make when they have had one too many. On top of that, I met with the strong opposition of my parents, who refused to finance such a cheeky plan, fearing that I might make one of the girls pregnant.

Moreover, my parents also opposed that I stayed in Madrid during my holidays. To make one long and very complex story short, when they went to the last interview with my teachers at school, they told them "Get him out of the streets during the summer. He has already been arrested once, and there are many rumours at school that you haven't heard of, drugs, gangs, fights… get the lad out of Madrid or he will get into trouble again, or worse…"

So my parents decided that I had to spend all the summer in Little-Town, rural Spain, with our relatives, and although I was 18 there was nothing that I could do to prevent that. Even if I was an adult now, I was financially dependent on my parents and until the day I finished my education, got a job and moved out, I had to obey their orders. The only decent alternative they gave me to escape my fate was to enrol in a language course abroad, just like the ones I had done previous years.

As the other option I had was awful, I decided that the best thing I could do would be to repeat the experience of previous years and go for the language course. This had been my salvation in 1996 and 1997, and so far the only successful way to avoid the boring family holidays. Despite having to work a bit, the course it had been quite fun, as I was surrounded by people of my own age all day and added to that was the excitement of being in a foreign country living with local people.

Still hungover, I started looking for the phone number of the guy who organized the courses. His name was Bill Palmer and he was a super friendly Gibraltarian, as well as a teacher and the owner of a Language school. As June was almost over, I knew it was useless to start looking for courses and comparing prices or offers. I was sure that all the places would be taken and I could only hope that my friendship and good relationship with Bill would help me to find a place at the last minute. After several unsuccessful attempts, I managed to contact him and asked him straight out if there were still places on his course for me. He replied that there was still time, but that the list of students would be closed in a couple of days, so I should confirm attendance and above all pay the amount as soon as possible.

Apparently, Bill must not have had enough students that year, so the arrival of one more was always welcome and also meant more financial benefit for him. Now that I knew that there was no problem of places, I only had to convince my parents to release the three hundred thousand pesetas that it cost to send me to a small town in England for a month to improve my English. This was not difficult. My parents were willing to give me all the money I needed, as long as the purpose was educational, legal and morally correct. The next day I had both the blessing of my parents and a bank cheque, so I decided to go and see Bill immediately to formalise my participation in the course. The course would run throughout July and would include English classes in the mornings, various activities in the afternoons, as well as accommodation with a local family for the duration.

As Bill's school was in Leganés, I had to take a train at the nearby Atocha Train Station and it took me almost an hour to get there. During all this time I was thinking that Bill's course was a good way to spend the month of July, but it didn't solve my problem in August or September, nor did it represent any kind of challenge or novelty for me. I had already done the same course the previous two years in the same town, the same school, the same host family and probably even the same teachers and classmates. In a manner of speaking, the course didn't mean much to me, but between the stations of Zarzaquemada and Leganés I came up with an idea that could make my stay in England much more interesting.

"What if, now that I'm an adult, and I would be already in the UK, I stayed there and worked until the end of September? I'm sure this would be more useful than going with my parents on holidays," I thought as I fell prey to the excitement and started planning everything mentally.

"Let's see, Bill will be back in Spain with the group of students at the beginning of August. Here I have two options, the first is simply not to go back with them and miss my flight. If this happens I can always buy a ticket there, on the condition that I return before September 29th to register for university. The second option would be to see if Bill could get me a flight with an open return date. This would be cheaper for me and would save me the money for one flight and the trouble of getting another. As far as accommodation is concerned, I don't think the family I'll be living with will have any problem keeping me with them for a few more weeks. That is, of course, religiously paying the seventy pounds a week for rent and food. I know that Bill pays them this amount and they are very happy and besides they're already familiar with me and know that I won't create problems, or in other words, they don't know me enough and think that I won't create problems."

With these two points resolved to spend the summer in England was beginning to be feasible, but I still had one more issue to consider. I needed to find something to devote my time to during those two months, and also to have people I knew to go out with and do things because when the Spaniards left I was going to be on my own. To occupy my time I thought it would be best to find a job and to meet people I could use the month of July when I would be a bit more sheltered by the other kids. Anyway, I decided not to move forward until I had talked to Bill about my plan and seen what his opinion was. After all, he had lived in the UK for thirty years before coming to Madrid and setting up his English language school.

When I arrived at the academy Bill's welcome was very warm. The guy was very happy that I signed up at the last minute, not only because of the benefit of having one more student but also because Bill appreciated me so much. He quickly showed me pictures of all the girls who were going to the course while telling me if they had a boyfriend, were nice and some other curiosity. Then he invited me for a coffee and showed me some hot chick's photos that he had taken from the Internet, which was something very new in 1998. "Wow Bill, this Internet thing is great, innit!" I told him without hiding my amazement, and he answered that besides being an excellent pornography supplier, it was also used to buy flights and many other things. In fact, he told me that thanks to the Internet I had no problem getting my flight at the last minute and that the return trip to Spain, unlike the other students, was open, so I only had to call the airline the day before I wanted to return. "What a great invention this Internet is," I said, "this is going to be real useful to people, not like that new bullshit of mobile phones. You'll see how in a couple of years nobody will even remember them."

After giving me all the details of the course and formalising my registration, we started to look back at the best moments of the previous summers. We talked about the girls we had met, the nights out and also the fun times in class. Bill was the organizer, head of studies and only responsible for the course, but with us, he behaved as if he were just another kid. Despite being around fifty, Bill was the first one to go to the pub with us and have a laugh, and he was also very talkative with women, with whom he was always surrounded. Bill always gave us the utmost confidence, but on condition that we behaved in a minimally responsible manner and did not take risks. Sometimes, he was even the cheekiest of us all, but he was such a good teacher that we learned so much from him, being English only a small part of it.

Regarding my idea of staying alone in England and work, Bill warned me that it was hard, although if I made the most of it, it could be something quite positive in terms of life experience, money and even sex. He also promised me that he would talk to the family I would be staying with to see if they wouldn't mind renting me a room for a couple more months.

Once we had tied up all the loose ends and when I had nothing left to ask him, we agreed to meet at the airport on the 5th of July when our flight to London was leaving. With nothing more to say, I said goodbye to him until then. I only had four days to pack my suitcase and everything I needed for the trip, so I immediately set to work preparing everything.

When making preparations for anything, I always like to be extremely meticulous, farsighted, and perfectionist, i.e. I leave nothing to chance and consider every detail with military precision. This time it was no less, so when I got home I took a notebook and decided it would be best to start by making a list.

Preparations England 1998

Time available: four working days.

Budget: about ten thousand *pesetas* plus what the old folks give me.

Areas to be covered:

1 Documentation.

2 Clothes and shoes.

3 Hygiene.

4 Drugs and sex.

5 Gifts and other stuff.

This original list was broken down into several sub-lists, each belonging to a different area. The documentation list was to be the easiest to make but also the most important. I wouldn't be the first one to stay on land for not having the right permits to travel. The most important document was undoubtedly the passport because without it I wouldn't be going anywhere. That's where I was already starting to cock it up because mine was expired and to renew it I would have to go, ironically, to the fucking Luna police station.

"We really got off to a good start," I thought as I put the list aside momentarily to smoke a cigarette and try to master the anxiety that had suddenly set in. A quarter of an hour later, when I had calmed down, I realised that there was no other option in this situation. To fly I needed my passport and to get my passport I had to go back to the police station from which I had such fond memories.

Well, as there was no other choice, I decided to fix this passport thing before anything else, because if I didn't do it, everything else would be useless. Somewhere I had heard that in theory, you could travel to other European Union countries just by carrying your National Identity Card. Of course, in theory, you can do many things, but I didn't want to risk it. I took my ID card, my expired passport and some ID photos that I, fortunately, had at home and I headed for Luna Street without much enthusiasm. While I was walking, it occurred to me that maybe if I applied for a renewed passport I could be refused and forbidden to leave the country because of my outstanding debts to the judicial system.

I stopped and reproached myself for not having thought of this before. "What a disaster" I said to myself as I debated whether to travel alone with my ID or risk applying for a passport. I hesitated for a while between one thing and the other, but in the end, I decided to renew my passport, not only because of the flight but also because if I wanted to find a job it would be best to have a reliable document in addition to my ID, which does not exist as such in the UK.

The good thing about renewing your passport was that it was done in a little over an hour, so I thought that in such a short time they shouldn't have much time to do checks and investigations. Still, I decided that to avoid being recognised I would make funny faces for as long as I was there and speak in a whispered voice. When I arrived at the police station there was a huge queue to renew my passport, so I had to wait patiently for an hour until it was my turn. All around me people were complaining loudly and some were trying to jump the queue with little success. When I finally got to the window, I was helped by an official, who looked quite miserable. The woman asked me for all my personal details and made a photocopy of my ID. Then she kept everything and told me to come back and pick up my passport in the afternoon. The first part of the procedure was completed, but I still couldn't sing victory until I had the passport in my hands.

As I couldn't do anything else, I went home for lunch and then spent time collecting the rest of the documents that I might need during my stay on the British mainland. In a large paper envelope I put my ID, Spanish NHS card and a debit card. I hardly had any dosh in my bank account, but in case of emergency, my parents could always make a deposit into the account so that I could take it out there, paying, of course, an astronomical fee.

Now all I needed was my passport and a few pounds that my father had ordered from the bank, which I had to pick up the next day. That same day in the afternoon I went to Luna and picked up my new passport. No one seemed to notice me at all, but I still decided to pick it up as soon as possible so as not to tempt fate. Then I continued to work on my packing lists.

Organising the clothes list was quite easy, as I already had almost everything I needed at home. I put all my luggage in a big rucksack that I already had. I would take two pairs of jeans, several cotton T-shirts, a few shirts and some sports clothes. For the cold, I only had my Lonsdale bomber jacket and for shoes, my irreplaceable Adidas retro. After taking inventory I decided to buy just a pair of sunglasses and some underwear. For my toiletries, I had almost everything I needed, which wasn't much. With a deodorant, a shampoo, my toothbrush, a razor and the aftershave I had been given for Christmas two years before, I had more than enough. If I needed something else I would buy it there on the spot.

The list of drugs and sex was the one that gave me the most trouble. Regarding drugs, I decided that I would take two bottles of red wine, a bottle of whisky, a whole carton with two hundred cigs, some bromazepam that I stole from mum's medicine box, aspirin, a little bit of hash that I had bought from a friend on one of my last nights out and, if possible, half a gram of white powder. To be honest, I wasn't that much into drugs, but I thought it would always be useful to bring supplies just in case I had to exchange them for the attention of some native girl. On the subject of sex, I decided that I needed some condoms in case I was lucky and also some pornography, in case I wasn't. Finally, on top of all this, I would need a Swiss Army pocket knife to defend myself in case of getting into conflict with some hooligans. I wasn't actually going to stab anyone with it, but only use it to scare attackers out if that was necessary.

Getting all these things meant different degrees of difficulty for me. Alcohol and tobacco were very easy, as I was already eighteen. Condoms were not so easy, because I was so embarrassed to ask for them at the pharmacy. The hash was already in my possession, as well as a couple of videotapes with pornography that I camouflaged inside the boxes of Trainspotting and A Clockwork Orange, my favourite films at the time. Getting the white stuff was impossible because the friend who I was going to get it from, failed at the last minute and I wasn't going to go around the shanti-towns looking for it. It was better that way since coke was already a too serious subject to mess around with. Finally, the wine bottles were given to me by my father and although they were a gift for my adopted native family, I decided that if the time came they could be used to make kalimocho.

I dedicated the last days in Madrid to prepare my luggage and get everything I needed for my stay abroad, and also to follow with special interest the World Cup matches during those days. The elimination of Spain in the first round was disappointing, although it also had its positive side because this way we would never play England and attract the wrath of the locals if we won. A few days later they also eliminated the English, which made me very happy. I didn't care which country won the World Cup, but I didn't want to be in the UK on the day they kicked the English team out of the competition. I knew from my own experience that it was not good to be a foreigner in England on that day, with all the hooligans in the country trying to get revenge for the affront of being eliminated from the World Cup.

The day Bill set for the start of the course finally arrived. On Sunday 5th July at 9am I showed up with all my luggage at terminal one in Barajas Airport and sat in front of the British Airways counters, which was the agreed place for all the course participants to meet. By half-past nine no one had turned up yet, so I started to get nervous there on my own. My parents asked if I wish they came with me, but I told them that it was not necessary because I wanted to start the adventure on my own from the beginning.

Finally, Bill appeared after a while, escorted by two sturdy ladies, probably mothers of some of my companions. Little by little the students of the course appeared and Bill introduced them to me as he went along. It's possible that I was a brainless teenager, but there's one thing I've never done in my life and that's judge or disregard. However, as I was introduced to the kids, the word "geek" appeared in bright red letters in my mind. What a pathetic crowd they were, scrawny, gangly youthful bodies, bottle-ass glasses, braces, acetate sweatpants and tennis rackets. All that was missing was the guitar and the Vatican flag. Going with this troupe to England was like flying the flag of "Kick my ass" right from the first day. "Actually, it wasn't their fault; they all looked super young," I thought. "I'm sure some of these guys will get beaten up by the local chavs before they go back to Spain. I hope it's not me." The girl thing was a little better. There were three of them: Pili, Maria and Vanessa. From the beginning, I thought they were nice, and also pretty, but the problem was that once in England I wasn't very interested in the Spanish ones. I preferred the English ones by far, which were cheekier and hotter. The only one of my comrades that inspired me to trust was Mario, aka Mario the Battle Ram, who I knew from previous years. Mario was two years older than me and was destined to be the natural leader of the group, not only because of his age but because he was a guy with balls and very self-confident. Besides, the boy was a physical beast. With same height as me, he weighed more than a hundred kilos, mostly muscle, and held a black belt in Jiu-Jitsu.

So after meeting the group I started to sketch out my role in it. Bill was the undisputed leader by divine grace, but on the field, Mario would be the alpha male and I would be like his lieutenant as the second in age and bad temper. Together we should lead and protect a group of young students through the English countryside, especially outside College. Once this mission was accomplished, we would both go out into the night to try and collect a few pieces to fuck. He had already wet the *churro* a year earlier and I was left with a zero score. As for the girls, it is possible that they came with us too because all three of them were older than eighteen. This could be good as a cover and also help us to make friends and allies among the natives. The rest of the kids, the ones under eighteen, better go home early and don't fuck up with our night fun.

After the presentations, we checked the bags and lined up the corridor to the security control. This was for me the most delicate moment of the whole trip because I was a carrier of illicit substances. As I said before, my relationship with Bill was very good, but I still knew that he would not hesitate for a second to throw me out of the course if I was caught even with a little bit of hashish. I don't think I would have been put in jail for the little amount I was carrying, because it was very clear that it was personal consumption, but even so, the scare, the fine and probably the hours arrested would be inevitable.

For a moment I was tempted to go into the bathroom and flush the thing down the toilet, but then I remembered how useful it could be for me in UK and decided that since there were no dogs in sight the risk was not very high. As I passed the checkpoint I tried to stay calm and approach my younger companions, those who looked more like geeks. After a bad moment, I passed the checkpoint without any problems and the journey continued without any further incidents.

I thought, "How nice! This is the kind of situation that the minute you throw away or finish the stuff foolishly you meet a hot girl who shags you in exchange for a couple of joints."

I spent the next few hours dividing my time between memorizing all the paperwork for driving myself to the airport on the way back, and also getting to know my fellow students a little better. The flight went by without any more problems than the typical excitement of the youngsters, constantly swapping seats, and an insipid lunch served to us by the cabin crew.

At around 3pm we landed at Stansted airport and after collecting our bags, we went through the security checkpoint before leaving the airport. This was another sensitive moment for me, but the agents were more concerned with controlling the entry of illegal people than substances. Fortunately, the procedure went quickly and soon we were all outside, sitting on the bus that Bill had hired to take the whole troop from the airport to the town where we would live.

Our destination was called Danetree and it was a town of about thirty thousand inhabitants, located right in the centre of England. The word town refers to a settlement too big to be called a village, but not big enough to be considered a city. The site in question consisted of an urban centre with pubs, shops and supermarkets, surrounded by a large residential district of small detached houses and green areas. On the outskirts, there was some industry and a little less agriculture. The town also had several schools, a health centre and a high school where we would take our classes in the morning, as the locals were on their summer holidays break. To go out at night there were several pubs, two discotheques and a Turkish fast food shop, something we had never seen in Spain.

We arrived at Danetree around 5pm and the coach dropped us all off at the school where we would have four hours of English lessons every day. There, the native families who would welcome us into their homes during our stay in the country were waiting for us. I already knew the family I would be staying with because they were the same as in previous years. The first thing I have to say about them is that they were good people and always treated me as if I were their own son. Their names were Janet and Danny Stevenson, and they were two older people who lived in a semi-detached little house outside Danetree. Although their house was not exactly the Palace of Versailles and was full of cats, I always felt comfortable with them. The best thing was that they didn't interfere with my nightlife; on the first day they gave me a key and I could arrive whenever I wanted, and that for me was paramount.

After the greetings and the excitement of the reunion I got on their old Ford and they took me home while they told me all the news in town, which was not much. Once at their house I could see that everything was still the same, a lot of mess and cats everywhere. Once there, Danny got on his favourite armchair with a beer in his hand and I think he never got up from there again in all the time I lived with them. Janet went to the kitchen and prepared something to eat. I talked a bit with Danny, about the trip, about Spain and also about the new cable TV they had. After some dinner, I went up to the room and went to bed early.

DANETREE

My first day in England began when Janet woke me up at eight to go to my classes at Tertiary College. This didn't sit well with me because I had just finished my A levels and was didn't really want to go back to class. I still knew that this was part of the deal and an inevitable procedure within my stay there. I quickly got dressed in a tracksuit and went down to the kitchen to see if I could eat anything, and also to pick up the Tupperware with my lunch from the fridge. Janet offered to drive me the first day, but I told her not to worry. As I already knew the way, I decided it would be better not to bother her and walk there.

After a twenty-minute walk through deserted streets and residential areas, I finally arrived at the College. All the kids were already there, so after the presentations of the teachers, whom I already knew, we got into class and started with the work. Fortunately, the classes were not too boring, as they were more about conversation in English and role-playing than grammar explanations. The secret to getting through it was to do whatever you could get your hands on, but always keeping your composure and pretending to be interested. There were days when I did absolutely nothing, but still, always pretending to be interested and saying "Yes, of course" to everything with a smile on my face. Sometimes I even made an effort to learn, aware that knowledge of English could help me during my stay in the country and even provide me with pleasant rewards.

The classes went quick on the first day and then it was time for lunch. As it was a bit cold outside we stayed in the College cafeteria. There the kids began to discover that in England they were not going to eat as well as they did at home. I opened my Tupper and found two ham and cucumber sandwiches, a blackberry juice sort of thing called Ribena, some salt and vinegar chips and some fruit. This was no problem for me. I had eaten out since I was a child because my mother worked all day, so I was used to eating any kind of junk. I was happy with a piece of hard bread, but the other kids, used to mum's home cooking, the British ranch was a very hard thing to digest. Like every year, I took advantage of the situation and kept the food that the others didn't like. When I had gathered a lot, I simply threw away the most disgusting and ate what I felt like eating. This was not the best solution, but at least I could always choose between several options.

After lunch, the daily routine that Bill had designed for us took us to a sports hall near College where we could and should play sports from three to five in the afternoon. The kids quickly started playing basketball, badminton and other time-wasters. I used this first day to snoop around the sports centre looking for something to steal and also to see if there were any chicks around.

Apparently, the facility itself was soon to be dismantled, so it was quite empty of equipment and staff. Next to the basketball court, there was a large storage room with sports equipment inside, which I assumed nobody would miss if something was lost. At first, I thought I could keep some of the basketballs, but then I asked myself what I would do with them if I didn't like basketball. Of all the things I saw, the one I found most useful was a bucket with several hockey sticks, cricket bats, etc. After weighing them all I decided that I would keep a small cricket bat that would fit perfectly in my backpack. This would serve me as a self-defence weapon at least during the day, in case we had problems with the local chavs like other years. I still chose not to take it with me yet and continued my round of inspections. Right next to the room I found a small gym, which although it was quite dilapidated could be used to train a bit daily instead of wasting time playing ping pong. The most interesting find was a room that was once the bar at the sports centre. The bar was closed with a kind of metal curtain, but behind it, there were surely still alcoholic drinks waiting for some smart ass to find a way to get around the blind and access them. Besides, the room was very far away, there was never anybody there and what is better, it had several sofas and armchairs quite comfortable and little light. This could be perfect for taking a nap after lunch and who knows if it would be a place to do dirty things in case a candidate for such honours showed up.

After my little inspection of the site, I spent the rest of the afternoon talking with my colleagues to foster friendship between all of us and make ours a cohesive and welcoming group despite our individual differences. First I was talking to Mario and Bill about previous years, about our pub crawls and the girls we met. We both had little stories to tell, but we always listened with reverence to those told by Bill, who in his thirty years working as a paramedic in London had them in all colours and for all audiences. I was very amused by the story of a drunk woman who took a dump while making love to him, especially as Bill used to explain to us all the details in a very amusing way. In between old stories, Mario and I made plans about how to face the weekends, what to do and where to go because despite our particularities, we both had as a supreme objective of our stay in England to have a great time and shag, if possible, some local/student girl.

But I didn't make the mistake of leaving out the younger kids, because they were going to play an important part in my adventures too. Of course, on weekends I would go to the disco with Mario and the girls, but during the week the experience told me that it was much more practical to wander around the parks doing *botellón* than to try to find luck in the empty pubs. Of course, these days the hotties are working and not going out at night, but the underage girls do, and since they can't go to the pub they wander around the centre looking for something to occupy their summer holidays. As I was only eighteen, and even if I tried to hook up with some chick in a disco, the most likely thing would be not to neglect the sixteen and seventeen-year-old age group, which realistically was where I had the best chance of pulling.

So, with all these preparations, all my expectations and all the excitement of the world for meeting hot chicks, my first afternoon in England passed without anything worth mentioning. At six o'clock in the evening we each went home for dinner with different results. I didn't eat badly, roast beef with potatoes, vegetables and some cat hair, but many of my colleagues would later tell me that they were not so good. After dinner, we arranged to meet at eight o'clock in the evening in a centrally located pub called Friday's. In theory, minors were not allowed to enter, but Bill managed to convince the owner to let them in on condition that they did not consume alcohol. There we sat down at a table, and the older ones asked for a pint of beer.

As it was Monday the place was empty, and the younger kids were getting a bit bored. Not that they were the biggest party animals in the world, but they also wanted to have a good time. This group was made up of about seven or eight kids between the ages of fifteen and sixteen. Among them, the ones I got along with best were two boys from Alcorcón, Henry and Xavier. I knew these kids since 1996 when they were actually children. Now, in 1998, you could tell they were becoming teenagers, although they were still a bit nerdy.

As these kids were also on an important mission, I went out with them outside the pub and told them to wait for me in front of the nearby Anglican Church. I then went to the supermarket and bought eight half-litre cans of lager, which we drank right behind the church, between the gravestones in the local cemetery. That's when I told them that they had the duty to find and try to get hold of the local girls who were hanging around the village because they would have it pretty bad to get into the pubs and discos as they controlled the entrance of minors quite a lot. After this little drinking session and some more talking, we all went back to the pub. We stayed until ten o'clock and then, as we were not used to having dinner so bloody early, we got hungry and paid a visit to the Turkish kebab shop for something to eat.

The next morning the whole cycle started again. Quick breakfast, walk to the College, four hours of class and lunch at one o'clock. In sports, we went outside to play football because the weather was nice. In the evening, the same routine, with Friday's as our headquarters and a bench in the cemetery as our secret place to drink beer cans. So the week went on and little by little we were making progress and some approaching to some chicks. Thursday was quite boring because we all went to a pub called The Peppermill which was quite far away. Although there was a certain atmosphere, in the end, everything ended up being the night among Spaniards. Not that I disliked it, because the people were very nice, but I had come to practice my English and not to chat with people from Madrid's outskirts.

On Friday afternoon we made the first contact with a group of English girls. I was already half excited about the weekend, so I went with Henry, Xavi and some other kids for a walk around the village and maybe drink a few cans of beer on the way. Bill was at Friday's with Mario and the rest, but I thought it was a bit early to be in the pub, and I was not wrong. Lurking in a park we saw a group of local girls doing the same thing as us, drinking alcohol and looking for trouble. So we decided to go over there and the girls, who were not shy at all, called us right away and started joking with us. They were seven girls about sixteen-years-old sitting on the grass in a circle. Some were pretty and some were not, but they all drank from a big bottle of cider while smoking cigarettes, laughing and talking loudly. We quickly started telling them the typical bullshit that we were from Spain, that we didn't know the town and other stories. They seemed receptive to our presence, mostly out of curiosity, and we were more than willing to take advantage of the good vibes that had been created at one point.

Unfortunately, so much movement attracted competition. When we were about to sit down with the girls, a small group of local yobs suddenly appeared. A quick glance confirmed that they were about seven or eight, that they were quite drunk and, moreover, that they were bigger and stronger than us. I could still handle one or two, but Xavi and Henry were definitely not up to it and, besides, they were too many. They approached us and the girls shouting and showing a rather aggressive body language, with fast and abrupt movements. When the yobs got to where we were, they started talking to the chicks, deliberately breaking up our conversation with them, although still showing some misgivings. On hearing our voices and discovering from our accent that we were foreigners, their excitement increased and those who seemed to be the leaders of the group began to insult us, although still not seeking direct confrontation.

Big fucking foreign pigs - shouted at us an energetic shaven-haired kid, quickly followed by the rest. I knew at that moment that everything was lost, that we had to take advantage of those seconds of indecision that precede all fights to make a withdrawal fast enough to avoid problems, and subtle enough not to attract the attention of the hooligans and encourage them to chase us.

"Xavi, Henry listen to me. You have to leave right now! Go, go, go!" I said to them as I started to talk to the girl who had given us most of the attention before.

"It was really nice to see you again, I got to go now, see ya!" I told her as if she were an old acquaintance. Then I run off, following in the footsteps of Henry and Xavi. Luckily, the yobs stayed with the girls and forgot about me.

After this, we met near Friday's, the kids and I, and we started to comment on the incident while I got out my little rock of hash and started to roll a reefer. I could trust the Henry and the Xavi, as well as the other kid, Dieguito. I knew that they were legit and that sometimes they smoked. Not that I really wanted to smoke, but I did it to make us more cohesive as a group within the group. We were going to be like a reconnaissance squad within the Spanish, always behind the chicks and ahead of the chavs. A group of which I would be the leader, as Mario was already too old for this nonsense. It could be that when the time came to go to the disco I would abandon them and join Mario, but the rest of the time I would command them, if they wanted to follow me, in our little guerrilla war.

They seemed delighted, commenting on the incident and making plans for the future. I already had three soldiers for my cause, not because I had convinced them, but because their goals and mine were in complete agreement. Of course, the four of us, Henry, Xavi, Dieguito and I, were equals, but they implicitly recognised my leadership as being older and more rogue. Both the Xavi and the Henry were sixteen and Dieguito was seventeen. All three were very cool boys, but still a bit geeky and rather weak compared to the English lads we were up against. Well, we might not be top boys, but we tried hard.

After talking a while longer we went into Friday's, ordered a pint of beer for myself and bought another from them, taking advantage of the happy hour buzz. There I learned with indignation that Mario and the girls had decided that they would not go to the disco that Friday's because they were tired. "Fuck, what a bloody waste of time, we've only got eight disco days to try to get laid and we're already flushing one down the toilet," I said to myself. Bill seemed happy and even relieved with the decision, so, in a clear minority, I had no other option than to swallow my malcontent and pretend indifference.

When the pub closed at eleven o'clock and we were thrown out, we went to eat some chips at the Turkish restaurant. This was not a great idea, with all the drunks coming out of the pubs at once and bothering us in a more or less threatening way. Fortunately, nothing happened and after a while, we went home to rest. This was a really good idea because on Saturdays we had to go on a trip and we had to report to the College at nine in the morning to be picked up by a coach. The first excursion was to Cambridge, the famous University in the centre of England. I had been there in previous years, so I knew what to expect from the day, a tour around the colleges and perhaps a boat trip on the River Cam, where usually some naughty kid would fall into the water.

During the trip, I slept all the way through until the little ones woke me up with the typical fuss of bus tours. The little darlings had painted my face with a lipstick that they stole from Pili, as if I were an Indian, and they had a good laugh until I found out and wiped myself with a tissue. Once in Cambridge me and the gang had a lot of fun and eyed all the girls, giving them marks according to their degree of hotness, and even tried to chat up to some of them. As Cambridge is a university city, there were lots of young girls on the streets and we always tried to talk to some of the ones who came like us in small groups of foreign students, especially if they were Italian or Spanish. This was in a way a waste of time because in any case, we would leave the city soon, but we still took it as a training and a fun trick.

During the whole excursion, we did nothing else but to go around with the radar on, classifying the women according to two criteria simultaneously, beautiful-looking and accessible-impossible. Blonde, slender, tall women scored high on the first, but dishearteningly low on the second; while chubby teenagers scored just the opposite. For a second I even wondered whether such an obsession with the opposite sex would be normal or whether I should seek out a psychologist, but then, since my peers' behaviour was very similar to my own, I opted for the former.

On the return trip I sat next to Mario, apparently to have a relaxed conversation, but in reality to subtly suggest him to go to the nightclub at night. Mario was one of those quiet guys who knows what he wants and won't lift a finger if it doesn't suit him. My suggestion became more and more obvious as we talked and I couldn't get a committed response from the king of "we'll see". In the end, I implored him: "Mario, please, let's go to the disco tonight, I want to pull some of those hot girls out there." And after that, I said to him "What the hell is wrong with you, you don't want to be on the pull tonight, why? Are you gay now or something?" But both the frontal attack and the lowering of myself to pleading didn't work. I think the guy enjoyed watching me suffer and that's why he didn't give me a clear answer.

We arrived at Danetree in just the right time to have a quick dinner and take a shower. I usually liked to spend time with my old man at home and dinner time was when we talked the most, but that day we had arranged to meet at eight o'clock in the centre and there was not a second to lose. Almost with the food still in my mouth, I left the house looking forward to partying like a maniac and a twenty-pound note in my pocket. This amount was the equivalent of five thousand pesetas, a much higher figure than I used to spend at home, but I wasn't going to be a cheapskate the only time I got out of Madrid. Each pint of beer was two pounds and the entrance to the disco another five. Besides, you had to set aside at least another three pounds to eat something on the way back and mitigate the effects of a hangover.

At eight o'clock in the evening, we were all together at Friday's having a pint. The joint was still quite empty, but you could see that they had set up some lights and removed some chairs to improvise a small dance floor and turn the traditional sober pub into a discotheque. As usual, Mario would sit with the girls and start chatting with them over a pint. For a macho type, this Mario was quite a gossiper and also enjoyed this kind of light talk about nothing in particular that our girls liked so much. Later Bill arrived with the little ones, who he also sat at the table with strict orders not to move much, and joined the conversation with Mario and the girls. As the pub was still very quiet, some of the kids decided to go outside to drink some beer cans in the cemetery. They were not allowed to drink in the pub as they were minors, so they had to go outside if they wanted to indulge themselves with booze and take shelter between the gravestones to avoid the police. I went out with them to buy the drinks, and also to drink myself at more affordable prices.

Each of them gave me a pound, and then they went behind the church while I bought eight cans of beer for six pounds at a nearby supermarket. After we sat down on a bench and started drinking. Then, some of the local girls we met on Friday appeared and sat on the next bench with a bottle of white wine. The alcohol did the rest and soon we were all together drinking and joking. Later on, we were also joined by one of the English kids we almost had a fight with the other day. Now he was the one in the minority, so he posed no threat. Still, we thought it would be best to have as many allies as possible, so we gave him a beer and invited him to stay with us.

For an hour and a half, we were drinking beer and talking to the girls in a rather casual tone. As the alcohol kicked in, the conversations, looks and body language made more reference to sex. We all gradually got rid of our Judaeo-Christian prejudices and transformed ourselves into primates on heat, so that after a while we were not only talking, but also playing silly games, shouting, howling and chasing one another around the bench amidst laughter and adolescent roaring.

I was having a great time, but when half-past nine came along I decided it would be best to go back to the pub to see how Mario was doing and to try to convince him to go to the nightclub. This was a pity because having a piss up with the English girls didn't look bad at all. They were already drunk and although they were a bit young, they were not so innocent. For a moment I was tempted to stay there and try my luck, but then I decided that I had to aim for something more than fifteen-sixteen-year-old girls. Before I left, I talked to the kids a bit and told them that I was leaving, but that they had a good chance with the girls. -The most important thing," I said to Henry, "is that you tell them to meet with us some other day so that we can gradually become a group of friends. Having stated that, I said goodbye to everyone and headed to Friday's Pub to join the party.

Mario was still there drinking beers, but he was no longer chatting up the girls, but surprisingly was talking to a group of English people. The girls on the other hand were still sitting at a table with Bill and a couple of Spanish guys, Albert and Frank, who were rather quiet. The younger ones had been sent home by Bill without further ado because their presence in the pub was already too outrageous.

I bought a pint and approached Mario to remind him of our nightclub business. Then I discovered that I also knew the locals Mario was talking with. There was Matty and his brother Chris, also a big guy called Mark and the girlfriend of one of them, I couldn't tell which one, whose name was Lindsey. I was very happy to find out that they remembered me, and also because they had already convinced Mario to go to the disco that night. I, of course, extended the invitation to go to the disco to myself and started drinking pints of beer to warm up, while talking to the English guys and remembering old times with them. I will always remember how I met these three guys. It was the year 96 and my first night in England. At sixteen I hadn't been out much at night in

Spain either. I don't know how, but we started drinking together at Friday's and then we went to a nightclub. There we had a fight with some hooligans in the middle of the dance floor and, besides, we picked up some girls who then took us to their house. In the house, Mario snogged two of them and me none because I was too inexperienced and didn't take advantage of the opportunities when I had them. Even so, it was an unforgettable night followed by many others in the company of our English friends.

Excited to repeat a memorable night in England, I convinced Pili and the other girls to come with so we wouldn't give the impression of being a hunting horde, but rather of a well-adjusted group of friends. At eleven o'clock they closed Friday's, so we left, Mario, the chicks, the English and me to the nightclub. This one was called Freddy's and was not far away. As a disco, it left a lot to be desired because it was very small and rather shabby, but, nevertheless, the boy-girl ratio was quite balanced. In addition, the birds there looked all hot and willing to have fun. As the town was rather small, almost a hundred per cent of the people belonged to the English ethnic group and unfortunately, there weren't any exotic chicks like in the bigger cities. All the girls were of the rubicund blondish type and quite tallish, a rather Nordic phenotype with which I, by the way, had never had any success either. Unfortunately, the Nordic girls never liked me, although I never understood why. "Wasn't it that the average José was flirting a lot with German tourists back in the *Costas*? If they did, why can't I? Could it be because of my short stature compared to the locals or because of an ancestral but hidden racism of the people of Northern Europe towards Mediterranean folks?"

Anyway, that night I didn't find the answer to all those questions and although I tried to interact with the opposite sex, I didn't manage to get too close to any of those blondes who were wiggling their asses around the dance floor either. Mario also made his attempt with a tall, skinny but hot girl. The poor guy got gobsmacked when this chick told him that she was actually married, had two kids and didn't want anything. What a culture shock, a girl of no more than eighteen wearing a miniskirt and out of step in the disco and it turns out that she is a mother. Apparently, life went faster there than in Spain.

I made up for the lack of attention on the part of the natives by drinking beers and talking to our own girls, thus avoiding looking like a pathetic loser and at the same time providing the Pili and the other two with some cover so the locals would leave them a little bit alone. Matty and Mark were very friendly to us and I was really happy to see them, not only because they were decent chaps, but also because it meant that

I would have some acquaintances in Danetree when the Spanish left. The colourful moment of the evening was when two local lads standing next to us started throwing blows to each other in the middle of the dance floor for no apparent reason. This is quite typical in the British Isles, where working-class culture irrevocably associates leisure with drinking alcohol and the latter with violence.

The fight right next to us and the subsequent intervention of the bouncers to bring order was the signal we needed to understand that the night would not give more of itself. There was only half an hour left to close and a quick glance at the place, where there were only drunk guys, confirmed that it was time to make a withdrawal. Matty and the other ones decided to stay a bit longer, but they were in their home-town, so they knew the people and how to deal with them. Mario, the girls and I left Freddy's with the feeling that we still had time to avoid the last-minute troublemakers, and decided to buy ourselves something to eat in a kebab van that parked outside the venue. I found this invention most curious and while the Turkish man in charge of the business was serving us the chips, I couldn't help but admire how cleverly that travelling restaurant was set up.

Once we were served, we ate our food while we accompanied the girls to their houses. At that time there was nobody on the street and some of the revellers could become quite dangerous when they came back from a drinking binge. After making sure that they were already very close home, we went to sleep. Luckily, Mario lived close to my house, so we went almost all the way together, which for me was a guarantee of safety, as we commented on the best moments of the night. Even though neither of us had hit on anything, we had tried, we had gotten moderately drunk, and we had also enjoyed the crowd of solid blondes that had paraded in front of us all night long with their provocative attitude.

When I woke up on Sunday morning, I was surprised to find that my hosts, Janet and Danny, had taken the trouble to organise the day's activities for me so that I would not be bored. On the one hand, I would have liked to be on my own and get some rest, but on the other hand, I could understand them. They were retired, with children already emancipated, and they had gotten into this business of bringing in a foreign student to distract themselves a bit. As they had hardly seen me all week, they had decided that they would dedicate Sunday morning exclusively to me. Janet had set to work in the kitchen and had prepared a hearty British breakfast for me. In general, connoisseurs think that English cuisine is bad, as bad as the cuisine of any Protestant country. When Luther and Calvin tried to reform the Church in the West, they outlawed sensual pleasures and thus culinary refinements. As a result, the English, a people of many virtues, lacked a decent national cuisine and indulged in filthy dishes or foods borrowed from other countries. The only dish that has any appeal to me was the traditional British breakfast, consisting of two fried eggs with bacon, sausages, ham and beans in tomato sauce. All very strong and very industrial, the perfect start to a hard day's work, as required by the Protestant ethic.

After breakfast, we got in the car and Janet drove us downtown, leaving us at Freddy's, the same joint where eight hours ago I had been drinking and trying to pick up girls and which had now returned to its natural state as a traditional British pub. Danny and I got inside and ordered a pint of beer. Danny's main, if not only, hobby was drinking alcohol in large quantities. I barely managed to follow him until the third pint of Lager, although I had to stand up and tell him I didn't want to drink any more. Not that three pints, a litre and a half, is much, but when you're hungover and the British breakfast is still in your stomach, the last thing you want to do is swell up on beer.

Later we changed places and went to the conservative club in Danetree where Danny had the whole parish of old drunkards. The only way to get into the club was to go personally invited by a member, and they still made me sign a document at the entrance. The interior decoration was similar to that of a pub, but a little shabby, with a bar where drinks were served, some armchairs and a huge portrait of Queen Elizabeth presiding over the whole place. The people who frequented the pub were working class and not particularly cultured or posh, but very conservative and patriotic. At first, they looked at me with suspicion and hostility, but they were quickly pleased to have among them a young Frenchman to tell him about the countless virtues of the British Empire, the times they had beaten us in battle, as well as the decadent situation in which the country was due to left-wing politicians, the European Union and the disproportionate number of blacks and Indians now living in England.

For a while, I tried to make them understand that I was not French, but then I gave up and put all my effort into trying to drink the pint of beer and not throwing up the breakfast and beer I had had on the club's carpet in front of everyone. Finally, at two o'clock in the afternoon, it was time to go home, which I celebrated with relief. While we were waiting for Janet in the centre of town, Danny went into the local supermarket for a moment. "I'm just gonna get some cat's food" he said, which I thought was fine. After a while, he came out of the supermarket with a plastic bag in which there were indeed two cans of cat food and also a bottle of vodka. Apparently, someone hadn't drunk enough in the morning and was going to keep on rocking in the afternoon.

The first thing I did when we got home was going upstairs to take a shit. At first, I was going with the intention of vomiting, but then I decided that taking a dump would be more practical and less unpleasant. After this unavoidable moment that we all go through from time to time, I felt a little better and I lay down for a while to take a nap. "Holly crap with Sunday mornings" I thought just before I fell asleep "it's not even two o'clock and I'm already plastered again."

I woke up around six in the afternoon and took a good shower to clear my mind. Then I went down to the kitchen to get a glass of orange juice or similar so that I could swallow an aspirin that would counteract the persistent and annoying pain on the right side of my head. Danny was asleep on the couch with the TV still on, the half-empty vodka bottle on the table and a cat sitting on his lap. Janet was preparing something in the kitchen while watching TV also surrounded by cats. In that house there were cats everywhere, I think they had eleven in total, although a couple of them disappeared during my stay there, due to circumstances beyond my control.

I hadn't seen anyone that afternoon, but every day we met at the Friday's, and that Sunday with the World Cup final taking place, was no less. The bar was quite lively during the whole game, but with the Frogs triumph, the English were a little bit wilted and left gradually. As the working people have to get up early on Monday, the place got quite empty, so we decided together that instead of wasting time there we would go to the cemetery to make a small piss up of kalimocho. Luckily, the day had been quite hot and as it didn't get dark until ten o'clock, so we managed to convince Mario and the girls to come too. We all gave in a couple of pounds, which in exchange was five hundred pesetas, and I went to buy the wine, the Coca Cola and some beers, while the rest were looking for a good bench to settle down.

We only bought a bottle of wine and three litres of Coca Cola, apart from a few beers, because wine was, and is, terribly expensive in an eminently brewing country like England. The cheapest wine came from Romania, and it was fucking rubbish, although we wouldn't notice it much because we were going to mix it two parts of Coca Cola to one. I returned to the cemetery through totally deserted streets, because the British take the Sunday rest seriously, and I found a doubly pleasant surprise.

On the one hand, mixed in with our group of Spanish were several of the village girls we already knew. This was good because it meant that they had a good time with us and we would see them often, thus increasing our circle of female friendships. The other surprise was that three English boys were also there. One of them was the loner who had joined us the previous evening, but the best thing was that the other two were the aggressive energetic thugs who had led the attack on us the first week. These two kids were apparently the biggest troublemakers in town, always in the youth category, and they had come again looking for trouble. This time, however, two things had kept them from doing wrong. On the one hand, the disturbing sight of foreign girls appeased them somewhat, but above all, the imposing presence of our colleague Mario the battle ram convinced them not to go overboard.

I took their presence not as a threat or a nuisance, but as an opportunity to build some alliance with the natives that could be useful in the future. So I approached them and tried to speak to them in a language they could understand, as well as gain their respect. The first thing I did was to offer them a beer and start talking to them about how easy local girls were and ask them if they knew anyone who took it also in the ass. This mixture of alcohol and macho jargon was quite a success, and after a while, we were chatting amicably as if we were old friends. The two boys should be about seventeen and were among the strongest in the village in that age group. Their main occupation was a curious mix of school failure, unsuccessful job search and bullying. One of them was called Darren and defined himself as being able to drink a pint of beer (half a litre) in two seconds, which he showed me right there, as he always carried a pint glass for demonstrations. The other one we called him Skinhead and all I can say about him is that he enjoyed fighting other people.

As things were going well, to finish off the move I took them a little further away from the group and took out my block of hashish, cutting off a piece of it, making sure that they saw my knife, to make a joint and give them a few drags. This was the definitive blow because for them a guy who invites them to beer, reefers and carries a knife had to be a legitimate guy.

After becoming friends with the two knuckleheads, more out of interest than pleasure, I was able to concentrate on drinking and on the English girls, whom I chased around with great enthusiasm and relative success. By eleven o'clock at night we had run out of alcohol and both the English boys and girls had already left. As we had to go to school the next day and as there was nothing to do in that town at that time, we decided to buy fish and chips in the Turkish shop and go home.

The new week started with rainy weather and new challenges. Apparently, Bill had thought that all the kids would take an official final exam, something similar to the First Certificate, but with less pedigree. This was great, because it meant getting a certification of the level of English we had achieved, but also that we had to study and make a bit of an effort, which I didn't like very much.

Because of this, the second week's classes received a little grammar reinforcement and were no longer as funny as the first week's ones. Besides, we began to prepare the listening test, which consisted of hearing absurd conversations recorded on a cassette tape and then transcribing them onto forms prepared for this purpose. This was the case in the second week, during which we did not do anything particularly important in the afternoon either, apart from playing football in the sports centre and harassing a small group of teenagers who were passing by.

In the evenings we followed the routine of meeting at Friday's pub at eight o'clock and then having a drink at the cemetery. Depending on how lively the pub was, Mario and the girls would come with us, and even Bill would drop by sometime to see what we were up to. Fortunately, we were also able to count on the presence of our group of English friends who, although they were quite young and rather average looking, at least gave some life and colour to our evening meetings.

Monday and Tuesday were good days, and we had a good time drinking kalimocho and fooling around with the girls. I, personally, started to consider the possibility of hitting on two of them, the ones that gave me more attention, although I had not yet decided which one. There was a brunette named Abbey who I liked quite a lot and who also showed an unmistakable interest in me. The other, a tall blonde who went by the name of Kelly, was a bit hotter and I liked her better than Abbey, but I wasn't so sure I had a chance of hitting on her.

On Wednesday I had planned to make an even greater approach to both of them to sound out the terrain, but unfortunately that day the English girls didn't show up and we had to make the little session ourselves. Soon after we arrived, a group of about six local kids appeared, whom we had never seen before and who were quite drunk. We tried to ignore them and get on with our business, but there was no way. As soon as they heard voices in a foreign language, they had to come and see what we were doing and, of course, look for trouble. At first, Mario and I made a pathetic attempt of fraternisation, talking to them and offering them beer while the rest of the Spaniards took refuge behind us. This effort was in vain because from the beginning their attitude and body language showed that they did not want to drink or make friends, but to fight. We began to slowly retreat while they were already advancing on us and just as the leader was throwing the first punch at Mario I came up with an idea that would save us from further trouble. I quickly grabbed Henry and said:

"I saw Darren and the skinhead sitting on a bench at the entrance of the cemetery. Go and tell them to come and help us with the fight.

Luckily, I had noticed that our two friends were there, and I had even talked briefly to them before getting on with our business. Henry left and when it seemed that the break-up of hostilities was imminent, our two mates appeared like a whirlwind and started to harass the leader of the attackers, with whom it seemed that they already had a score to settle. The other five villains stopped in their tracks and no longer seemed so daring without the leadership of the punk. Mario and I stood up to them then, he with his impressive physical strength and I with my knife, as for occasions like this I had brought it, and they decided not to go on. Then Darren started talking to them and said:

-Whatcha doin lads, these guys are our mates, don't fuking mess with them, awright! -which was for them an order to get the hell out.

After the fight and a cigarette to calm our nerves, we tried to continue with what we were doing, i.e. drinking kalimocho. In addition, we invited Darren and the other one to join us, partly out of gratitude, partly out of fear of being attacked again. I suggested to the Pili and the others to be extra friendly to them, as they had saved us from a good one. Later, when we finished the wine-cola we took them to Friday's and invited them to a pint each to reaffirm our gratitude to them.

As expected, the next day nobody felt like going back to the cemetery and meeting the same assholes as the day before. As it was Thursday, we decided to stay at Friday's, hoping that it would cheer up us a bit that day. The night was not bad, Matty and Mark spent some time there and thanks to that we could agree to meet them on Friday. We also talked a bit with some girls and played a couple of games of pool, but in general, the night didn't take off completely.

At eleven o'clock the pub was closed and we went to the Turkish place to eat something. As that day had been somewhat dull, I decided to reward myself by getting something tasty to eat instead of the salt and vinegar chips I asked for every day. I looked at the price list and thought about buying something expensive. Apparently, the star dish of the Turks was a kind of roast beef sandwich with salad and sauce, which they called Kebab. Of these, there were several types: Donner Kebab,

Sish Kebab, Tavuk Kebab, Adana Kebab and some more. In the end, I asked for the Donner, which seemed to be the most representative, and I watched with curiosity how the Turkish man made it as he went along. First, he cut some slices from a huge piece of meat strung on a skewer and put them on a bun. Then he finished filling the roll with lettuce, onion and tomato, and finally, he sprinkled it with a red and white sauce before serving it to me. I took the kebab carefully and started eating it, first with caution, then with real gluttony. "This is so tasty, it's as good as a hamburger, but more exotic - while I was spilling all the sauce due to inexperience, will these kebabs ever get to Spain? - I asked myself. I don't think so, this kind of weird food will never succeed there".

The weekend finally arrived and with it Friday, a magical day on which I had placed most of my hopes for a good time and above all for a fling. As always, everything started at Friday's pub where we would meet at eight o'clock. Continuing with the tone of the previous day, we decided to stay at the pub instead of tempting fate by hanging around the cemetery. Luckily, Bill sent the little ones home at around nine o'clock, just when the place was starting to fill up, so we weren't bothered by the staff and could relax a bit. Later on, our friends Matty and Mark arrived with a large group of their friends, among whom there were some girls as well. Mario and I soon joined this group and made an attempt to approach the girls, with little success. This made me think and rethink the myth that when you are a foreigner it's easier to pull, because of the exoticism and being different. This may be true in enlightened and cosmopolitan environments or holiday resorts, but in small towns, chicks tend to look at you more like a weirdo than any other thing, in my opinion.

We continued drinking in the pub for a while longer and then the next step was to go with Matty and some of his friends to a nightclub. This was called The Cat's Whiskers and was quite far away, so it was necessary to go by taxi. Luckily, we found one quickly and shared it with Matty himself and one of his girlfriends who was really fit and drove us all crazy on the way to the joint.

We arrived at the club in less than ten minutes, got in the queue and waited for a while until it was our turn. When it was our time to go in, I saw Mario go by first and then he was stopped in the hall by some huge guys. I asked Matty for a second before I realized what was going on. "They're searching him, and I've got a pocket knife on me." I Panicked, jumped out of line under the furious gaze of the bouncers, and said to my mate Matty, "Sorry, I've forgotten my wallet in the taxi," loud enough for the doormen to hear me. Then I moved away a little and hid the knife under the hedge in a nearby garden, trying to memorize the exact spot where I left it to pick it up on the way out. When I returned, they were all inside, but luckily I didn't have any problems and I was able to pick them up, after paying the ten pounds that the entrance fee was.

Once inside, same old story. A lot of drunk guys who want to pull, and a few half-drunk girls who want to have a good time and defend themselves as best they can against the tide of testosterone that assails them. As most of the blokes don't get what they want, they drown their frustrations in alcohol, which increases their euphoria and false self-confidence, and makes them come back with renewed strength. At the end of this macabre dance, the guys always end up frustrated and drunk as a skunk; and the girls, disgusted with the male sex. The only one who benefits is the businessperson who runs the show and makes a great profit on behalf of the sexual desire of idiotic young men.

Despite being fully aware of the process I was part of, the desire to philosophise was taken away from me when I drank the first pint of beer. Even if it was stupid, I decided to have fun and play my role in that comedy as the canons say, that is getting drunk like a beast and being touchy-feely with the chicks at the slightest opportunity. However, there were very few opportunities, rather none. A lot of uncoordinated dancing and a lot of alcohol, but neither Mario nor I managed to pull, although we didn't try that hard anyway. It is curious how alcohol, which is always seen at the beginning of the night as a means of disinhibiting oneself and increasing one's sociability, as the party goes on becomes more of an end in itself and one ends up drinking for the sake of drinking. At three o'clock in the morning, when they were about to close the club, we began to suspect that our names were not on the winner's list that day, so we decided to go straight home.

Unfortunately, we couldn't find a free taxi, so we had to walk a couple of kilometres to get to Danetree. Halfway through the walk, we were shocked when we saw that it was getting light and as I was not wearing a watch I figured it might be very late. This worried me a lot because the next day we had to be at school at nine o'clock for our weekly excursion and Bill would not forgive us if we were late or didn't make it. The trip was sacred and you could go after a sleepless night, with a hangover, a boner or a stick up your ass, but you had to go no matter what.

Mario laughed for a while at my whining and paranoia. Then he reminded me that England is two thousand kilometres further north than

Madrid, and because of that summer nights have very few hours of darkness.

"Don't worry, it's only half-past four."

"Really? How is it possible if it's almost daylight?"

"Fuck, how ignorant you are. The further north the days are longer and the nights are shorter. That's in summer; in winter, the opposite."

"Ah, awrigh."

"Well, imagine yourself in the North Pole, always in the daytime or always at night."

"What does it matter if no one lives there but the penguins?"

"It was just an example for you to understand better."

"Man, I think I'm going to throw up..."

"Come on, don't fuck with me and walk, I want to sleep at least for a couple of hours!"

When I finally got home, I looked at the clock with concern and saw that it was five o'clock. I took off my Adidas and threw myself straight into bed, dressed, to sleep the three hours I had of rest until eight.

I woke up with a splitting headache and feeling a bit sick. It was twenty past eight, so I had to hurry if I didn't want to be late for the excursion. As I was already dressed and didn't have any desire to eat, everything was very easy; I just went to the bathroom where I peed, brushed my teeth, washed my face and put on deodorant like that without showering or anything. That was more than enough for the stupid excursion on duty. Then I picked up the lunch that Janet had prepared for me and put it in my rucksack, so I was ready to leave the house. This time the walk to school took longer because I was a wreck and when I finally arrived, I was really glad that the bus was already there because I got into it to sleep without even saying good morning to anyone. I spent the rest of the day doing only one thing: fighting hangover.

Luckily, the week's excursion was to a huge shopping centre in Milton Keynes, where the other kids would spend their time and dosh buying gifts for the family back in Spain while I vegetated on a bench. The good point about our trip to Milton Keynes was that I didn't have to walk anywhere if I didn't want to, and there would always be a toilet available for me to take a hungover dump if necessary.

During the bus ride, I tried to sleep, although holding a plastic bag with my hand in case I felt sick and had to relieve my stomach. Once we arrived and made clear the meeting point for the afternoon I sat on a bench and begged the other kids to pick me up in a couple of hours. During that time I bought myself a fruit juice to hydrate myself and to accompany the aspirin I needed, and I also took the aforementioned dump in the bathroom. When I finally got back together with the others, I felt much better and was able to continue with the excursion almost normally.

Thank heavens, at six o'clock in the afternoon we were in Danetree again and I was able to take a little nap before going out that night. In fact, I asked Janet not to cook me any food, making up the excuse that I was going to attend a dinner party in the evening, when in fact all I wanted was to sleep peacefully for at least a couple of hours. I got up around eight o'clock and took a shower to clear my head. Then I got dressed, put twenty quid in my pocket and marched once more to meet my mates at Friday's, passing by the Turks' shop to buy myself some food. On the way, I had come across several groups of drunk and rowdy teenagers, whom I had avoided by taking some detours or changing paths, and this made me think that going to the cemetery with the kids maybe wasn't the best idea. I didn't know what was going that year, but the local yobbos, fifteen and sixteen-year-old idiots were giving us a lot more trouble than I had expected.

After finishing the fish&chips I had bought for myself, sitting on a bench near Friday's, I went inside and joined my friends in a night out that would be quite similar to the previous one. A lot of beers in the pub and then off to the disco with Mario, Matty, the girls and more people. There, lots of hot chicks; techno versions of well-known songs, including the world-famous song by then-mass idol Ricky Martin, and above all more beer. This meant that we ended the night quite damaged but happy not to have to get up early the next day.

On Sunday I slept until one o'clock in the afternoon and only woke up when Janet told me that the food was ready. Again she had prepared the traditional British breakfast, but this time it felt much better because the hangover was much lighter and, besides, I didn't have to wash it down with several litres of beer. Danny next to me was telling me several unconnected stories about when he served in the merchant navy and while I listened to him, we both watched TV out of the corner of our eyes. When I finished my breakfast I went up to my room to lounge around a bit, tidy up my clothes and also to watch some of the porn videos I had brought back from Spain. Unfortunately, for now, that would be the closest I had come to sex since I had arrived at Danetree. This situation had to change no matter what it took because the moment the Spaniards left, my social life would be dramatically reduced and with it the possibilities of meeting new birds.

Thinking about what had gone wrong in the previous days, I decided that I had to work more in the park area and less in the discotheque. Now it was clear to me that in the club all the girls were older or at most the same age as me. In a way, I was too young for most of them. A girl of twenty-five is not going to be attracted in the least to an eighteen-year-old boy like me, who also had nothing special to offer. Dark-haired but pale-skinned, short in a country of tall-ish people, thin in a town full of beefy lads and, moreover, without a penny in my pocket. The best I could do was to be realistic and put all my hopes and efforts into the age group that naturally suited me, i.e. the girls from fifteen to seventeen.

This was a resolution I could not have made on a better day. All week Bill had been convincing us to go to an underage alcohol-free party at the local Leisure Centre that Sunday. This party was like a proper club but alcohol was not going to be served, adults were not allowed in and it closed at ten o'clock. I could understand Bill's reasons for sending the little ones there. In his innocence, he thought that at a non-alcoholic party the group would be safer and he could retire home early to get some rest without fearing that any of his pupils would be beaten up by violent drunks.

Mario was not coming because he had been invited by Mark and the others to attend a football match in Coventry. The girls were all sleeping over at one of their houses, so they were not going to show up either. This left me with all the underage kids at the under 18 party. I didn't want to go either at first, but after some thought, I realised that it might be worth having a look.

As the party started at seven and lasted until ten or so, at six we all met in the centre and I bought them some beers to drink some alcohol before going in. There were seven of us in total. Apart from me, there was Henry, Xavi, Dieguito, Fran, his cousin Albert and a fairly small-town kid from Leon whom we called Alfreditu. They were all sixteen or seventeen years old, so I told them not to be afraid of trying to hook up with as many chicks as they could, no matter how old they were. For me, it was different being eighteen, not because the girls would report me to the police or anything, but because making out with a fourteen-year-old girl would be totally disgusting, sick, pathetic and humiliating.

When we finished the beer cans we went into the Leisure Centre, where Bill was already waiting for us. The party was inside a kind of large conference room, set up for the occasion with disco lights and a bar to serve soft drinks. Two huge bouncers stood guard at the doors of the site and Bill approached them and introduced himself as the head of a group of well-behaved foreign students that should be protected with special care. The bouncers must have thought Bill was a fat cat because they had also seen him talking to the director of the Leisure Centre, so they assured him that he had nothing to worry about. These words sounded like heavenly music to Bill, because he was looking forward to going home and relaxing a bit for the first time since we got there.

"Chencho," he said, "I'm leaving you in charge of the group. Here inside the Leisure Centre, you are safe, so don't go out there. There are girls at the party and I'm sure you'll have a great time. When it's over, tell them to go home."

"No problem Bill," I said and he left as happy as Larry.

Unfortunately, before that Bill had also told the bouncers that I was the instructor of the group, that any problem should be consulted to me and also that I was of legal age. So when we were about to enter, the bouncer stopped me at the door and told me politely but firmly:

"Sir, you can't go in if you are over seventeen. Sorry, it's the rules."

Luckily, at the Leisure Centre, there was also a bar where parents who came to pick up their children from swimming class, or anyone really, could have a beer in peace. There I was left alone with a pint and smoking a cigarette while the other kids went into the club to have fun. After a while, Xavi appeared and sat down with me to tell me how everything was going, how many girls were inside and how things were going in general. This gave me an idea. As Bill had made me the boss, I decided that I would be like Al Capone when he was imprisoned, that is, I would pull all the strings at the party from my exile in the bar.

"Take note," I said to Xavi. "It would be great if from time to time one of you came to inform me of everything that is going on inside and the progress you are making. You can take turns doing this, although the next one to come should be the Henry, with an exhaustive report on all the chicks at the party," I said jokingly, acting like if I was Marlon Brando in The Godfather.

Xavi laughed and went back. A while after he left Henry came and told me how everything was going. The good news was that many of the birds we knew from the cemetery were there; and the bad news was that many of the little chavs we had had problems with, too.

This regular reporting system worked well for the next hour and as a non-alcohol party is not really fun, most of the time I had some of the kids telling me how it was going, and drinking of my beer discretely. After that time I decided that I had to start phase two of my plan, so I told Henry when it was his turn to come:

"Henry, you know who Kelly is, don't you?"

"Yes. The hot blonde, isn't she?"

"Do you think you could bring her here or tell her to come up?"

"I don't know, it'll be a bit of a hassle, but I'll try."

Said and done. He left and minutes later he came back with Kelly and another friend of hers to my headquarters. The three of them sat down with me and we started talking about nothing in particular. Surprisingly, the girls were very friendly and I'd even say a little merry. "How is it possible if it was a dry party?" Anyway, that suited me better. For the next fifteen minutes, all my efforts were directed at getting Henry to take Kelly's friend out so that I could be alone with her. For this Henry was more than willing, but not so the girls who didn't want to separate. We carried on fighting like this for a few minutes until the situation became untenable, and then they left us both there.

But I didn't despair and repeated the same move, this time with another girl named Abbey. She came alone and much happier than the other two. In the end, after talking a little with her and buying her something to drink, I asked her if they had been drinking alcohol at the party. She told me that some guys had come in quite drunk and had even managed to get some booze in.

This worried me quite a lot because it meant that the kids might have problems, but I decided not to deviate from the issue I was dealing with. "Okay, first I'll snog Abbey and then I'll come down and see," I thought as I smiled at her and got closer. For a couple more minutes the situation evolved favourably. To begin with, she hadn't left, which is always a good sign, and she seemed to enjoy being there with me. She laughed with my jokes, touched her hair sometimes, looked at me and smiled. I think I had read somewhere that women's pupils dilate a little if they like what they see, so I went event closer to appreciate any change. Well, at first glance there was no difference, but everything else was going well. Marilyn Monroe once said that a man would pay more than a dollar to know what a woman was thinking, or something weird like that. I would have paid a lot more to know what Abbey was thinking in those critical moments. "Snog now? Not yet? Do I wait a bit? What should I dooo?""

At that moment the Henry arrived again, but this time with a very bad face. "No, please, not now, don't fuck with me, I'm about to..." He looked at me and before opening his mouth he knew more or less what he was going to say:

"Chencho, you got to come with me man, they're attacking us!"

We left the bar in a hurry and entered the party at full speed. There we saw that a group of kids were threatening and holding back the Spaniards while so many others were kicking one of our own on the floor. I quickly charged at the one who seemed to be taking the lead and threw him to the floor with a push where I put all my weight. The other little shits turned on me, and I was already punching another one when suddenly the bouncers appeared and pushed us apart as well. Apparently, two of the yobs had staged a little scuffle outside to distract the bouncers while the rest of the kids were raging at poor Fran, who was now lying on the ground with a black eye.

It didn't end there because the boy I had thrown to the ground, a ruddy, lanky individual barely fifteen years old, started fighting with the bouncers right there. I don't know what the kid would have taken, but he was totally out of it, like a berserker from the Nordic sagas. The door guys, huge, big men, had serious problems controlling him and the bad thing is that in the meantime his buddies kept trying to attack us. I threw a few punches the best way I could, but they were too many. There was a moment when we had to run out of the room while pushing and hitting the attackers to breakthrough. "Come on, Fight back. Defend yourselves!" I shouted at the others as we descended into a massive brawl in the hall of the Leisure Centre, between sports instructors and parents who came to pick up their children. Luckily, someone called the police or we would have been lynched right there. Then the Leisure Centre employees told us to go into the bar and they closed the doors with us inside. Outside, two police patrols were trying to control a pack of twenty-something mad teenagers who were screaming:

"Kill the foreign scum!"

We were locked up for half an hour while the situation calmed down. The police took away what appeared to be the leaders of the attack to the police station; the lanky chav, whose name was Josuah, and a mulatto boy called Jerome, whom we nicknamed the Muppet because he was so ugly. What worried me most about all this was that I had now made enemies in town, who would still be around when the Spaniards left. We knew both kids by sight, and I'd even given Josuah a cigarette once. Even worse, I knew Jerome from the previous years. Before, there was only mistrust, but after I threw one to the ground and smacked the other in the gob that night, it was clear that now they would be coming after me.

"You have to be kidding, why are they so aggressive with us?" I thought to myself in dismay as I tried to bring some order and calm among the kids. Apparently, the people of Danetree still had quite a lot of Viking blood running through their veins, as we had had occasion to see that night. Not surprisingly, even the name of the village, Danetree (the Danish tree or the Danish tree), was of Scandinavian origin. To make matters worse, the town's coat of arms depicted a Viking holding a battle-axe on a sign:

"Dane tree sigillum".

"Who would think of coming to study in a village with such coat of arms," I wondered as I imagined that Viking, the great-great-grandfather of our attackers, creeping forward with the axe in his hand, ready to pull a trick on the first unwary peasant who got in his way. Later I learned that sigillum in Latin did not mean stealthy, but 'seal'; but that night I could not help but dream of stealthy Vikings attacking us without quarter.

After the fight at the Leisure Centre, the journey home was an odyssey. At eleven o'clock at night, the employees of the Leisure Centre, who had been very kind until then, began to insinuate that they had to close the joint and therefore we had to leave. Outside, in theory, the police had dispersed our aggressors or at least were holding them back from us.

One possibility would have been to call Bill to come with the car and take us all home in a couple of trips. That is if I had been farsighted enough to write down the phone number of the lady he was staying with. As this was not the case, our only option was to venture out into the dark and deserted streets of Danetree, hoping not to meet the angry mob who wanted to lynch us.

At half-past eleven we decided to go out and try our luck and left the safety of the Leisure through the back door. We also decided that we would not separate, but that we would all stay together until we left the centre and then accompany the youngsters to their homes. A few meters in front of the main group I went, as if I were an explorer, to detect the presence of possible enemies in time. At the rear of the group was Xavi, also with the task of keeping watch so that we would not be surprised from behind. If they found us, there was little we could do against twenty scumbags, but even so, we would not be caught off guard.

Luckily, we didn't meet anyone, friend or foe, on the way home. First, we went to the neighbourhood where some lived, then to another neighbourhood where we left others, and finally, Alberto and I went back to Southbrook, which was the area where we both lived. Once home I smoked two cigs in a row to calm my nerves and went to sleep as best I could.

On Monday morning we couldn't stop Bill from noticing Fran's black eye, so we had no choice but to tell him the whole truth. The man was quite angry and we could all understand his reasons. During the course, his main concern every year was to avoid returning to Spain with a wounded or bruised student and having to explain himself to his parents, and that was just what was going to happen if the bruise took too long to heal.

Fortunately, and also fairly, he did not blame us but took Fran directly to the police station to file a complaint. His surprise was great when he was told that the person who had caused the bruise had reported Fran himself and also the bouncers who had reduced him. Apparently, in England, it was a very serious offence to hit a minor even if he deserved it and that's why the bouncers were in trouble. Fran didn't have to worry, because she was also a minor, and I was glad that Joshua forgot to report me too. With my coming of age and my background in Spain, it would have been a big problem to be accused of aggression. Luckily, and thanks to alcohol and drugs, a time gap in our young friend's memory saved me from that fate.

Now I could understand why we had had so many problems with the local shits. No wonder in a country where children do whatever they want with total impunity. The lack of discipline and respect for authority at home, in school and on the streets had created a generation of little monsters with no respect for anything, who were beginning to be known as "Yobs", "Yobbos", "Hoodies" and many other names.

How can I describe the Yobs that were giving me so much trouble during my stays in England? More than an urban tribe, they are a youthful subculture that emerged from the British culture of alcohol and violence during the late nineties. In practice, the Yobs are groups of white teenagers, from lower classes and dysfunctional families, who drink alcohol and take drugs like crazy and then have fun destroying things, assaulting people and bringing chaos to the city centre during their nights out. Someone might say this is already happening in Spain and in many other places, but that is wrong for several reasons:

To begin with, we can say that violence and drunkenness also tend to occur in Madrid, but to a much lesser extent and in a different way. In the England of the Yobs, violence is an end in itself and always appears as an indispensable part of a night out. Another difference is that in Madrid violence was always directed at something or someone in particular. This or that gang, the police... The Yobs, however, acted erratically, indiscriminately and totally out of control. It doesn't matter whether they attack other Yobs or their own friends, a passer-by, an old lady or burn a car. Violence changes its purpose and is no longer a way to hurt or harm the being or the thing that is hated, but a way to amuse the one who practices it.

I don't intend to make a sociological study, but after much thought, I have come to the conclusion that the culture of the British Yobs is, apart from the existence of abundant Viking genes, is a consequence of the teenage single mother culture conveniently mixed with a new pedagogical fashion consisting of not punishing those who deserve it.

The culture of the teenage single mother occurs in UK when thousands or hundreds of thousands of very young girls decide voluntarily to bring children into the world despite not having a partner. I don't mean that a poor girl is abandoned by an irresponsible bastard, divorced or even widowed, but that she decides when she is barely a woman, when she is seventeen or eighteen, to get pregnant by anyone and take care of the child on her own. Why do they do this? The reason lies in the juicy state benefits that the government of this country gives to single mothers, from a free house to a monthly salary. Many young women see these benefits as an alternative way of life to working, pursuing a career and paying off a mortgage. The consequence is that girls in their early thirties suddenly see themselves as mothers of teenagers who have never done well at education and who are now becoming uncontrollable. If managing a teenager is already difficult when there are two of them, a grown-up father and mother, for a girl alone the trance is even more difficult. I don't want to sound chauvinistic or traditionalist, but I know from personal experience that a mother and father together can be a very effective force in controlling the irrational and troublesome animal that many teenagers become. Just look at me as an example. To top it all off, kids who have no father figure at home and almost no mother figure at all find themselves in an educational system where punishment is forbidden and in a society where minors are untouchable and can break any rule without any consequences.

All this has to be seen in an aggregate way. There will be individual cases of children from dysfunctional families (for that is a single mother who has children just to get a financial benefit) who end up being lawyers, doctors or members of the Parliament, and children from very stable families who end up like the guys I knew when I was in detention. Seen from a statistical point of view, however, it is not unreasonable to suggest that those from broken homes are more likely a priori to be on the wrong track.

After all this reasoning I came to the conclusion that the Yobs are not to blame for being the way they are, as they are a product of society. What I find most frightening is that I, Chencho, am also a Yobbo. A Yobbo, though, with a father who was strict, who didn't hesitate to scold me when I did something wrong, with teachers who would tell me off at times and in a society where there was still some respect for others. A Yobbo, yes, but closely watched and guided on the right path, surrounded by a healthy environment and without money problems. You should have seen me if I hadn't been born into a white-collar, middle-class family. I am a yobbo, the only difference with them is that I'm not poor.

Continuing with the description of the Yobs, we can say that they are usually found in the council states, cheap housing districts that the local government rents out to poor families, generally single mothers, so that they can raise their white or sometimes mulatto trash there until they become Yobs and go on to fail at school, become unemployed, live off the state and start a life of crime, in that order. The Yobs have no respect for anything and imitate American hip hop culture with little success, dressing up in baseball caps, hoods, gold chains and sportswear in general.

Well, with the little sympathy I had for these fucking Yobs I would have to put up with them for a couple more months if I decided to stay in England. For the first time, I started to think that maybe it would be better to go back to Spain with the rest of the troupe and forget about this country of insufferable teenagers. What was the reason for staying if you couldn't even go out for a drink at night without the fear of being beaten up for no reason?

I decided that I would think about it for the next week and make a decision according to how the situation evolved. In the meantime, it was my turn to focus on the English exam that would come at the end of the course.

Another challenge came in the afternoon when after classes and sports we had to decide what to do that night. Many didn't feel like going out after what had happened the day before, and in fact, we agreed that for a day or two we would return to our old tactic of avoiding the town centre and the cemetery until the situation had calmed down. In fact, that Monday we all went to the Peppermill, our haven of peace, and spent the afternoon drinking beers and looking apprehensively at any local kid who came within three metres of us.

This tone continued throughout the week, although it gradually faded, especially when we learned that most of our attackers came from Stefen Hill and The Grange, two distant neighbourhoods and that they only dropped by the centre from time to time. From Wednesday onwards, we returned again to Friday's and the cemetery and found that everything was more or less quiet. The negative point is that our English acquaintances, both the girls and Darren and the skinhead, had scattered and we were unable to find them. On Thursday the same thing happened again, so we ended up buying a bunch of beers and making a little party for ourselves at the cemetery. Once again we didn't see anyone we knew, although we weren't bothered by any troublemakers either.

I found all this quite depressing, because I had been trying to work out how to meet people so as not to be alone, and now, almost a week after the Spaniards would leave, everyone I knew had vanished as if by magic. Mario and I also went to the Friday's for a while to see if Matty and Mark were there, but nothing, they didn't show any signs of life either since we last saw them last weekend. Again I started to wonder if it would be worth staying in this town for a couple more months by myself. Everything indicated that it was not, that it would be wiser to go back with the rest of the Spaniards, but during the weekend something happened that made me change my mind.

FARAH

That Friday, July 24th, I woke up thinking that it was probably going to be my last weekend in England. I had been considering about it all night and had decided that on Monday at the latest I would inform Bill of my intention to go back to Spain with them so that he could book me a seat on the same plane. Realistically, there was no point in staying in a town where I had few friends, many enemies and where I didn't know how I was going to spend my time either. I had thought about working when I was in Madrid, but now I couldn't imagine how to get a job. As if that wasn't enough, I was running out of money and what I had left was not even enough to pay two months' rent.

With this idea in mind, I spent the morning classes and midday sports. Now the plan was to have fun that last weekend, do well on the exam for the English diploma and get on the plane the following Thursday to Madrid. For some strange reason, I didn't communicate my decision to my hosts and even during dinner, I told them that I hadn't decided anything yet. After I ate the delicious roast beef they served me, I took a shower. When I was getting dressed I received a phone call that would change things.

"Chencho, there's a phone call for you!"

"What, a phone call for me? Who the fuck is it?" I picked up the phone and it was my mate Dieguito."

"Chencho listen, there's a girl here asking for you!"

"A girl, who, Pili, Vanessa, maybe Abbey, or that blonde bimbo that I like so much…?"

"No Man, it's an unknown girl asking for you. She says that she knows you from town… She's asking if you are gonna come."

"Hold on a minute. First of all, where the hell are you?"

"We're in Town, in front of Friday's. I am in a booth and there is a girl who wants to meet you. Do you remember the Hindu?"

"The Hindu? Let's go back one day in the past," I said to myself. I could remember that I had been sitting on the benches in front of Friday's with all the Spaniards. Suddenly a dark girl passed in front of us. She was like Indian, but an Indian from India, not from the Apache. We all stared at her, because she was fit, even though she was a bit skinny. She must have been about twenty years old. I remember I said something to her and she ignored me, just like all girls used to do. She was just one of those thousands of hot girls who come for two seconds in a man's life, looks him down and then fades into oblivion. I didn't give it any more attention and focused on my business, which was to gather the money and buy the beer at the supermarket.

Fifteen minutes later, when Alfreditu and I returned from the shop carrying our bags full of lager cans, we found the same girl walking down the street again. Again I said something to her: "Do you wanna come and drink with us?", or something equally pathetic. Again I was ignored and that was the whole story.

"Ok, let's see. Diego, you telling me that the Indian girl is there and she is asking for me?"

"Yes."

"Okay. D'you think I'm a sucker and I believe one bit of it? Look, I'm sorry that I'm late, but I had things to do. Go and play your tricks on someone else!"

"No man, honest… she's fucking here."

"Put her on the phone." I heard a girl's voice mumbling something in English and laughing.

"Diego, I'm on my way. Tell her not to leave. Oh, and I'll kill you guys if all this is some sort of prank, d'you hear me?"

I hung up the phone and quickly began to dress with a mixture of excitement and apprehension. "A girl wants to meet me, why?" I wondered. "Most likely this is all a joke, I'm sure it's one of these bastards idea", I repeated to myself over and over again. Well, that was quite likely, but not the only possibility. On the one hand, it could be that a girl simply liked me and wanted to meet me. With this in mind, I took special care in choosing my clothes, combing my hair with gel and brushing my teeth to have a fresh breath. Another possibility was that just the opposite, my compliments and insinuations would have offended her. In this case, maybe she had intended to come back to tell me off and humiliate me in front of my friends. Who knows, maybe she was one of those gun-toting feminists who enjoy castrating men.

Well, that didn't make much sense either, because if it had, I would have got verbally beaten yesterday without the need for waiting for today. Worse still, she had felt insulted by my drooling and had brought her boyfriend, brother or husband, who conveniently hid behind a hedge waiting for my arrival to beat the shit out of me. That made more sense, considering the ethnic character of the girl who could well be Indian, Iranian or even Arab. The father, the brothers, the Moors, who knows what bearded and swarthy mamelukes I would have to face just for the simple fact of having said hello to a lass who was passing in the street.

Well, I wouldn't tolerate that, or at least I wouldn't be caught off guard. I put my knife in my right pocket and on the other hand, I decided to carry an empty beer bottle that could also be used as a weapon. As soon as I saw a suspicious bloke I would brandish one in each hand with a threatening gesture and depending on how strong they were I would choose to fight, run away, negotiate or beg for mercy.

Thus, without knowing very well if I was going to an appointment or to the crusades, I threw myself into the street and walked for ten minutes towards the centre while I became more and more nervous. Another idea that came to my mind was that the girl was simply not interested in me, but in my companion, Alfreditu, the Leonese yokel. If that was the case and when I arrived I found them making out in front of all, I would take advantage of the knife to commit suicide and leave this fucking world rather than suffer the humiliation of being defeated by a goat herder. Well, whatever had to happen I would see it in a minute, as I was already turning the corner and entering the main street, where Friday's Pub was.

When I approached I saw that the Indian girl was indeed waiting for my arrival in the middle of the street. As soon as she saw me, she also started walking in my direction, so we were finally face to face, at a safe distance from the Spaniards, who were looking at us with great curiosity. As I didn't know what to say, I just said hello while checking that she was alone. My suspicions were unfounded, as there was no threatening presence around. Then I realised that I was holding an empty bottle in my left hand and that this would not make a very good first impression. As it was too late to throw it away, I disguised it as best I could and prepared to engage in conversation.

"Hello, how are you?"

"I'm fine thanks. My name's Farah. Yours is… Chencho? Right?"

"Chencho is a nickname. My real name's Inocencio."

"What a weird name. D'you mind if I call you Chuckie. It's easier for me to pronounce and sounds cute."

"Yeah, no problem. I actually hate my real name too. You can call me as you want."

"What's that bottle for?"

"What? -This bottle! No, nothing... I found it and I'm gonna put it in the recycling bin."

"Ok, for a minute I thought you were gonna hit someone with it."

"Of course not, just recycling."

Once we were face to face I examined her from top to bottom, albeit discreetly. She was about my height and very thin. Her skin was tanned and her hair was super dark and very straight. Her eyes were brown and slightly slanted. I thought she was very pretty, although her features were strong, so I had the impression that she must have come from northern India or Iran. However, she was wearing western clothes, jeans and a lilac-coloured jumper, but showed no skin except for her head and hands. I was curious about her origin, so I decided to ask.

"Where are you from?"

"Well, I was born here in England but my family is from Israel, I guess you mean that. And you're Spanish, yeah?"

"Yes, I come From Madrid."

"You look French; I thought all Spanish had a tan."

"And you look Indian; I thought that Jews were white."

She didn't find my last comment very funny, so I decided to leave the issue of nationalities for later and focus on the important bit, which was to get her to come with me that night or at least a date for another day.

"Are you doing anything tonight? Why don't you come with us?"

"Sorry I can't, I have to go home in a minute."

"What about tomorrow night?"

"No, I don't go out at night here in Danetree. It's boring."

"So, is there any time that I can see you again?"

Fuck, she was the one who had called me and now she didn't want to meet me anymore. "What a strange thing. I think women enjoy driving us crazy," I thought. Then, looking at her oriental face, it occurred to me again that maybe a traditional and strict family would have something to do with it. As a child, one of my best friends at school had been a Moroccan girl, so I had already had the opportunity to learn that there are many cultural differences in this world and that what seems to us Westerners to be the most normal for others may be unacceptable. With this in mind, I decided to be patient and after a little more chitchat we agreed that we would meet on Monday morning during my break from school, as she felt this was the most appropriate time. "Stranger things have been seen", I thought with resignation and kept talking to her to find out more.

I was not very happy to discover that she had four older brothers, who also lived in Danetree. I asked her if she had a boyfriend too, mostly to make things clear from the beginning. It had happened to me in the past going out a couple of nights with a girl to later discover that there was a boyfriend, ex-boyfriend or special friend competing with me. She told me that she had broken up with her previous boyfriend and that she didn't want to see him anymore, and I took this as a no.

My new friend asked me how long I was going to stay at Danetree, I guess to see if I was a good investment. I didn't think it was a good idea to tell her that I would be leaving the following week, although I didn't really know what she expected from me either. So I told her that I would be staying all summer until the start of college in October, an answer that seemed not to like much. We continued talking for a while more until she told me that she had to leave. I offered to accompany her a little towards her house like a good gentleman, but she looked at me in horror and said that it would be better if I did not. I didn't have anything else to ask, so I said goodbye to my new and mysterious friend by giving her two kisses, one on each cheek, and reminding her that on Monday morning we would meet at school.

When the girl left, all the Spanish kids asked me what the story was about, but I confessed that I didn't know very well. The only thing that was clear to me at that time was that I liked her and that our first meeting had had a special chemistry. Something that didn't make me very happy was having to wait until Monday to see her again, especially since I didn't have much time to get to know her a little before going back to Spain on Thursday. On the one hand, this Farah would be a good reason to stay here for a couple more months, but it could also be risky to plan the rest of the summer around a girl I had just met and knew absolutely nothing about.

That night at Friday's I asked Bill how much advance notice I had to give him to confirm whether I would return to Spain on Thursday with the others or stay. Between beers, I had matured a plan that consisted of using those last days I had left for two purposes. The first was to get to know Farah better so that I could decide whether it was worth staying for her or not. The second would be to try to sleep with her and going back home with the indelible memory of having made love with a Jewish princess. Bill listened to me carefully but told me that I had to give him an answer by Monday at the latest so that he could call the airline. That meant that my plan was not worth a damn, as I only had the weekend to decide and I wouldn't even be able to see Farah then.

Seeing the indecision on my young face, Bill advised me to do the following. "If I were you," he said, "I would put myself in the worst position and book the flight with the rest of us on Thursday. Until then you have time to get to know the girl better and see what suits you best. If things go well with her and you see that you fuck a lot and well, you can always miss the flight and buy another one for later. But I advise you to talk about it with your host family to see if they agree."

I thanked him very much for his advice and decided to do so. If everything went wrong, I would be happy to have that seat in my name. If everything went well, losing the 200 quid from the flight, on the other hand, would be extremely painful. I decided not to worry about the flight until Monday and to have fun at the weekend. As Friday's was very lively, we stayed there until they closed at eleven. Matty and some of our other acquaintances dropped by as well, so we had a great time. I even had some success with a Scottish girl, fat and ruddy, who threw all her attentions at me. In the end, nothing happened because I didn't like her and I couldn't stop thinking all night about my next date with Farah.

The next day we had our typical Saturday excursion. This time it was nothing more and nothing less than London, so on Friday, we left early so as not to have a hangover and take advantage of the only trip that was really worth the effort. Luckily, Saturday was a sunny day and we enjoyed hours of walking around the centre of the British capital, seeing Victorian buildings, charismatic monuments and hotties everywhere. I had been to London before, but I always found the city spectacular. "I wish Farah could have come, I'm sure she would have had a great time with us," I said to myself while wondering if I wasn't getting too obsessed with a girl I'd barely known for a day.

On Saturday night we also went out in Danetree, but I wasn't really looking forward to the party. I was mostly tired after kicking around London all day, but I was also feeling a bit weird. On the one hand, I was a bit angry about having to wait until Monday to see Farah again, but I was also a bit nervous about the prospect of our second date. What I wanted most in the world was for everything to go well on Monday and for us to start going out together, mainly because having a girlfriend in Danetree would make my stay there much more interesting and enjoyable. Saturday night and all of Sunday passed slowly and without anything happening worth noting apart from my growing nervousness about Monday's important date.

Finally, the big day arrived when I would see Farah for the second time. I got up very early that morning and dressed up a lot more than I used to on a normal Monday. Then I went to school and swallowed two hours of classes that went on forever until the clock told me that it was already eleven o'clock, the agreed time for our second meeting. Feeling a bit nervous, I went to the school hall and waited there. Farah arrived a little later and after saying hello to each other, we stood there a little shy, looking at each other like fools and not knowing what to say.

As there were more people in the hall and we were not comfortable, I proposed her to go out for a walk so that we could talk more calmly. Two seconds after leaving the door of the College, without having said anything, we started to kiss passionately. After five minutes of making out, we decided to continue with the walk we hadn't even started. We didn't get very far, because after ten meters we stopped again to kiss and we didn't move anymore.

During all the time we were snogging we managed, however, to exchange some phrases that helped me to know her a little more. The first thing I made sure of was to arrange a third date, that very afternoon. This was vital because I didn't know her phone number or where she lived, or even her last name.

She tried to play the sex card to impress me, and the truth is that she more than succeeded. While we were kissing, she stroked my fly and asked me if I had had sex before. I answered yes and to this, she added that she would like to have sex with me. Excitedly I asked her if she lived alone, but she said no, that we could not go to her house because there were other people, but if I had a place we could go there.

"What a nympho", I thought; "these foreign chicks don't mess around. If they like a guy they sleep with him without caring what people say." In a way, I even got a little dizzy thinking that a guy could also be used, fucked and thrown away like a tissue by a modern, independent man-eater. Suddenly I felt a bit insecure in front of a woman like her, who seemed to have a lot of experience and little shame in sexual matters. I was scared that if I didn't meet her expectations quickly, her initial interest in me might disappear.

After half an hour she left, leaving me happy though somewhat paranoid about the sexual issue. All weekend I had made up my mind that she would be a rather shy girl, but now it was clear that I wanted to get serious as soon as possible. This should make me happy because theoretically macho guys like me always want to fuck immediately, but in a way, everything was going too fast.

During the following classes, I asked the kids I trusted if any of them had the house free to take a girl there. Most of the answers were negative until Henry told me that the members of the family he lived with never came home before six in the evening. So I asked him to let Farah and me go for a couple of hours at midday, and he said it was OK as long as we left before six.

Well, I already had a date for that afternoon and a place. Now all I needed were condoms, so I thought I'd go home quickly to pick them up, but Henry told me he had some in his room, which I could use if I wanted. He then handed me the keys, giving me instructions where to leave them when we left and wished me good luck.

At two o'clock in the afternoon, I met Farah again in the school hall. After we kissed a little I told her that I had a place where we could go and have some privacy. She seemed surprised at how quickly I had managed to find a room for us, but she agreed to come. As the house was quite far away, and I was quite anxious to get there, we took a taxi which dropped us off in five minutes and charged me ten pounds.

Once inside the house, we agreed to go up to one of the rooms and lie down together on the bed. I had imagined that a veritable hurricane of lust was about to break out, but after a few kisses, I began to realise that we weren't going to get very far, mainly because of her refusal to take off any of her clothes, but also because I didn't feel any desire to pressure her into it either. Lying there on the bed we kissed, talked a lot and even she fell asleep in my arms for a while. All the explicitly sexual insinuations she had made to me in the morning came to nothing in the evening. Now the tiger no longer looked so fierce in her sleep resting her head against my shoulder. Later, when we got to know each other a little better, she confessed to me that she had used the subject of sex that morning to impress me and that she was actually very afraid of sleeping with a boy. She had never been to Spain nor did she know anything about Spanish customs. All she knew were the stories about sex and drunkenness that the English told about holidays on the Costas, from which she deduced that the Spanish must be a bunch of perverts obsessed with frottage. So, she couldn't think of a better way to act than to brazenly insinuate herself, offering something that she wasn't really willing to give.

Around five in the afternoon, still lying in bed, we started to hear some noises downstairs and assumed that the owners of the house had arrived. We went quiet and got scared as hell. How were we going to explain to the geezer or the lady who owned the house what two perfect strangers were doing taking a nap upstairs in their shack? A few distressing minutes passed and we heard nothing again, so I opened the door of the room slowly and checked with relief that no one was there. It must have been some neighbours in some house nearby. Still, we took this as a warning and decided not to stay there any longer. After leaving the house, we walked back to the centre and then I accompanied her a bit to her neighbourhood.

On the way back I started to get used to some of her peculiarities that would become the tonic of our meetings. At one point along the way when we were arriving at busier areas, Farah told me to walk behind her, at a safe distance, and to act as if I didn't know her.

"My parents and especially my brothers," she said, "wouldn't like to see me hanging around with a bloke."

Then, when we got near what seemed to be her neighbourhood, she decided that it would be better to say goodbye there as a precaution. I asked her when I would see her again and she replied next day, same place and at the same time.

After leaving Farah I went straight home, which was not far from there while thinking about everything that had happened to me that Monday. At first, I was satisfied to have been with her, although somewhat disappointed that we hadn't slept together, in its metaphorical sense. I figured it was better that way anyway, to take it easy and not force the situation when I had almost two months ahead of me.

When I got home Janet had already prepared dinner, which I devoured with canine anxiety. With all the excitement of seeing Farah and the expectations of bonking her, I had forgotten to eat something at lunch. After having two full plates and ice cream for dessert, I went to my room for a while to rest. In the evening I didn't feel like going out, just staying home and thinking about Farah, but I decided to go to town and show some signs of life because the others hadn't seen me since one o'clock and might be worried. I turned up at Friday's around eight and gave the relevant explanations when some people asked me how my afternoon went, although without much detail. I told Bill that I had been on the verge of sleeping with a girl and that I hoped that it would happen tomorrow or the next day. The purpose of this was to have an excuse to get away from the afternoon sports and go with Farah. I knew that if there was a good reason for it, Bill wouldn't object to me leaving the daily routine and my partners behind. Luckily, the next day we had the English test, so we left quickly and I was able to retire home to rest.

The English test didn't go badly at all, although I admit that if I had been more mentally focused on the subject I would have done better. While I was answering the questions, completing the listening part or writing my composition, all I could think about was that at two o'clock in the afternoon I was going to see Farah again. I didn't think I was in love, but I saw this longing to be with her as a desire to take advantage of something I hadn't had for a long time. Regarding the girls that I had known all these years, I had noticed the existence of two subsets. One was the girls I liked and the other was the girls who liked me or at least I had some chances with. For many years the intersection between these two sets had been zero, a fucking empty set, but now and after a long time attracting only crazy unattractive girls, it finally seemed that luck was starting to smile on me.

This time I was more cautious and decided not to forget to eat, so when I finished the exam I went with two other kids to the canteen. As soon as I finished my sandwiches I went into the College hall and sat down to wait impatiently for Farah's arrival while I leafed through a magazine I found over there. She finally turned up at half-past two and as soon as I saw her I forgot about telling her off for being half an hour late. For thirty long minutes, I was in a state of panic at the thought of her not showing up, until I saw her come running through the entrance.

After greeting and kissing each other shyly we decided to go for a walk around the College, which was a very beautiful area, full of trees and green meadows. As we walked we held hands and started talking about various irrelevant topics. Before, while I was waiting, it had occurred to me that she was a complete stranger, so I had been thinking about a battery of strategic questions to get more information of the type "what are your parent's names or what job do you want to do later in life", but now that I was with her these things didn't matter. I simply gave up on that nonsense and put all my energy into kissing and holding her all the time. What seemed to me the most normal thing to do was not, however, the same for her. From her body language and her reactions, I deduced that she didn't like too much the touchy-feely. Because of this and because she told me: "We don't have to be kissing all the time, you know." It seemed that she wanted a bit of personal space too. For her, a kiss when we met, another one when we said goodbye and the occasional holding hands seemed to be enough, always after checking that mine were clean.

Even so, the two hours we spent together flew by. When she told me that she had no choice but to leave, it was like a smack of my face. "Do you have to go now?" I said, "It's not even four o'clock." She told me that she was having dinner early at her house and that she should be there at that time so nobody would suspect anything. In the face of these disconcerting words full of mystery and vague threats, I could hardly object, except to accompany her a little in the direction of her home, always careful not to be seen by anyone. Again, we said goodbye when we reached the point where she felt we were too close. I had already started calling that particular point "The Limit" and I didn't put much enthusiasm into finding out what dangers might lie behind it either. Knowing that she had four older brothers at home was enough of a deterrent to keep me out of the forbidden zone.

I didn't like the fact that Farah had to leave so soon, either of her own free will or through no fault of her own, so I went home too because I didn't feel like seeing the rest of the Spaniards playing ping pong or basketball. Once there I lay in bed with a small attack of anguish when I realized that we had not arranged for Wednesday. With the disappointment that she had to leave I had forgotten to ask her if we would meet the next day in the same place and at the same time. Now not only did I have to wait twenty-two endless hours to be with Farah again, but I also didn't know for sure whether she would show up or not.

I spent the rest of the afternoon lying in bed doing nothing, thinking about how much I wish I could spend more time with her. In a way, this feeling of uneasiness and anxiety reminded me of the time I had spent locked up in the Moratalaz police station. Now, as then, I was stuck in a room cursing so that time would pass more quickly, although for very different reasons. Luckily, Janet called me for dinner and this distracted me a little. I liked the food quite a lot, mash & bangers, and also the chat with Danny was productive. As I had already told them that I was going to stay in England for another month or two, we were working out all the details. From how much I would pay them weekly in rent to where and how I would be able to find work and earn a little money to support myself.

Dinner cheered me up and I decided that, at least for now, it wasn't just Farah in this world, as I still had the Spaniards to go out for a while at night. By eight o'clock I was back together with them all having a pint and determined to make the effort to be cheerful and rowdy. The others were going back to Spain in two days-time, so I wanted to be remembered for my more vital half and not as an anguished, obsessive bundle of nerves. To make this last effort I had the invaluable help of my friend alcohol, although it wasn't the same without combining it with my other friend "sex drive". Even so, the night was very interesting. During the last few days, my recent obsession with Farah had prevented me from seeing some curious approaches among the group. As always in this type of courses, passions run high and Spaniards end up getting mixed up with each other when they see time running out. Specifically, Pili got involved with Albert; Vane, with his cousin Fran (Alberto's cousin, not hers); and Maria, with Dieguito, although everyone knew that these ephemeral summer romances would last until the plane landed in Madrid. Of course, I didn't care about that at all, as I didn't care about the suspicions that my friend and former ally, Mario the Battle Ram, would have had some romance as well. The guy in question had been very quiet and somewhat distant this past week. At the beginning of the course he had told me that his adoptive family was a divorced woman, or maybe a single mother, and her two kids. When I saw the woman later, one day when I accompanied him to his place, I could see that she was beautiful and not older than thirty-something. From that moment on, Mario and I started to joke about whether he would end up shagging the woman or not. Whenever we drank a few too many beers, the joke would spontaneously come up until one day it didn't come up anymore and a wall of silence was erected around the subject.

I, of course, didn't think about it again, since it didn't affect me at all, but that day it occurred to me that something might have happened. Who can imagine how hard and lonely the life of a single, working mother is. One day that mother decides to make ends meet by renting that extra room to a foreign student, but instead of a girl or a geek with acne, the student turns out to be a big, manly twenty-something like our friend Mario. Who knows how many days, how many months, if not years, this single mother has gone without it because of her selfless dedication to her children. However, there is now a male nearby. She no longer has to find a babysitter or leave the girls with Mummy to go hunting, the male sleeps in the next room and is surely as horny as she is. After many doubts and detours, everything rushes in one night when she can't take it anymore and slips into Mario's room. At first, she just wants to talk, to be listened to, but she starts crying. As soon as she starts to let go of her sorrows Mario hugs her to comfort and Bob's your uncle. When they realise that they are both naked, kissing in bed, they can only stop for a second, just enough to get a johnnie out of the cupboard drawer. The next day is all remorse and talk. If it was a mistake, I'm so sorry, it's my fault, it won't happen again, and all that other nonsense, but the one who has already sinned once has it complicated so as not to fall back into the pleasures of the flesh. I will never know if this happened or not, but sometimes what people keep quiet is what tells us most about them, and the truth is that Battle Ram was very quiet the last two weeks. Thinking that my friend was going back to Spain happy and having preformed like a stallion made me happy for him and also took my mind off Farah, my new obsession, for a few minutes.

Wednesday morning was a moment of hangover and goodbyes. A hangover because we had been drinking the day before and a farewell because it was our last day at Danetree Tertiary College. As we had already taken the exam and didn't really feel like doing anything, both teachers and students decided that the best thing to do would be to watch a film. After the film and lunch, I went hopefully to the place where I had met Farah the other days. There I waited and waited for almost an hour until I finally gave up and accepted that she was not coming. That was a shame because I didn't know where she lived or her phone number, and she didn't know that I wouldn't come to the College anymore because the classes were over. "Well, I'll have to keep coming at two o'clock or look for her in the streets," I said to myself trying to console myself. I hope she doesn't think I've given up on her".

The rest of the afternoon was spent playing football with the other kids and worrying about the possibility of never seeing Farah again. Luckily, she must have read my mind, or at least thought the same thing, so she unexpectedly turned up at Friday's at eight o'clock just like the day we met. This time she didn't come alone, but with another girl of the same ethnicity with whom she must have been related. As she arrived she motioned to me not to kiss or touch her, so I concluded that the other one must not be a trustworthy person.

Under the attentive supervision of the new girl, Farah and I had a friendly chat, but without much affection, in which we nevertheless managed to set a new appointment for Friday at noon at the College. In an oversight by her friend I managed to give her a sneaky kiss, touch one of her tits and hand her a small sheet of paper on which I had previously written my name, address in Danetree, telephone number and blood group just in case. I came up with the idea that afternoon during my fruitless wait and the purpose was that she could always contact me, even if we had not agreed on an appointment. I also suggested to Farah that she and her friend should stay with us for a while, but there was no way. Again, she brought up the subject of very strict parents waiting for her for dinner. It seems incredible that at first, I took her for a modern, liberal and somewhat slutty girl. Now she was revealing herself as almost the opposite.

Well, in a way it was better that he left because that way I could focus on saying goodbye to my fellow Spanish exclusively. Again we had a few beers at Friday's and again the couples got sentimental and hid in a corner of the pub for kissy-kissy. Mario looked sad but relieved to finally be going to Spain, where his University exams and many hours of revision were waiting for him. "Well, at least you got laid this summer, mate," I thought to myself as I told him:

"Well, Mario, you didn't get it this year" just to see his reaction. For a moment, his eyes shone and I think he was very tempted to confess to me that he had been shagging the woman every night several times, but he managed to restrain himself and told me instead:

"Yes, it's a shame, but that's life."

"Yeah right, let's just hope you didn't make the poor woman another baby, she's got enough on her plate with two little ones."

Thursday finally arrived, the day of farewell for the Spaniards. That day we didn't do anything in the morning, because in theory, it was time to say goodbye to the host family. In the afternoon they had all arranged to meet at five o'clock at the Tertiary College to be picked up by a bus and go to the airport. Although I was going to stay in England, a decision I had taken in the last few days and only because of Farah, I thought it would be decent to bid farewell to my fellow adventurers for a month. There, in the school car park, just before getting on the bus, host families would crowd in to say goodbye to the students, with varying degrees of enthusiasm. Some were literally smothered with kisses, while others were dismissed with British coldness and a veiled "see you never". I, too, said goodbye to everyone trying to put some emotion into it and gave kisses, hugs and pats on the back left and right. The last conversation I had was with Bill, who gave me some advice and wished me luck in my new solo adventure. Then the bus left and I realised that I had been left alone.

For the first time since I had arrived in Danetree I stayed at home for the night. It was quite strange not to get ready after dinner to go to Friday's for a drink, but I didn't feel up to it on my own, so I spent the time watching TV in my room and went to bed early. The next day I had a date with Farah and this was enough excitement for me for the time being. Unfortunately, this date would make me discover that Farah was not always the sweet kind girl that I had imagined.

This time we met in the town centre at midday. As there was no need to go to the College any more, we had agreed to meet there and avoid us a long walk in the sun/rain. She arrived almost an hour late and in a very bad mood. No matter how much I asked her what the reason was for her bad mood, I was unable to get anything straight. I didn't think it was appropriate to ask her if she was having her period, but I had heard that women were getting super-altered in those days because of hormones. I tried to calm her down as much as possible but was not very successful. As we sat on a bench all I could do was listen to her as she called her family all kinds of different names, though not for any particular reason. I seemed to understand that they had argued with them and was fed up of them. After a while, she exchanged her family for a woman who had just passed in front of us as the object of her anger. In a second he called her a whore, a slut and several other names with such a load of hate that I asked him if he knew her at all. "No, I don't," she answered, "She's just one of the slappers that we have over here." For a while longer she continued being vicious to other people, known and unknown until she exchanged bad mood for crying and self-pity. "I have very bad luck in life and everything goes wrong for me," she said. "I'm jinxed". During this new phase of her tantrum, she also started to whip our new-born relationship, which he said was not worth it and that it was better to be just friends. All my attempts to calm her down or to reason with her simply did not work, so making a supreme effort not to tell her to fuck off I took her for a walk in some nearby meadows to see if she would calm down.

The rest of the time our date lasted we just walked side by side without talking and without going to any particular place. When the time finally came for her to return home, I was almost relieved. "What a cow," I thought, "I've stayed for her and look how she pays me."

I went home quite disappointed with her and in a very bad mood. I just wanted to have a good time and she had ruined it completely. As if that wasn't enough, she had also broken up with me, because if not, what the fuck she meant when she said she only wanted to be friends. Now I was really alone, without friends, without a girl, without a job or an occupation and with little money. I had almost made up my mind that I had a girlfriend and now I had to go back to being single again, and with very bad prospects because my social life at that time was zero.

I don't exaggerate if I say that I spent the rest of the weekend at home. Apart from going out for a while on Sunday to have a pint with Danny, I didn't do anything at all. I just didn't feel comfortable going out on my own like some pathetic, lonely loser. Maybe if my personality had been a bit more outgoing, and I was in a more welcoming place than cold and unfriendly Danetree, I could still have gone out and meet people. As I wasn't far-sighted either, I forgot that one of my objectives should have been to strengthen my friendship with some of the acquaintances I had, to get their phones and to know where they hanged out to hook up with them. When Farah came into my life I gave up on all this, thinking that I no longer needed friends and now I was all on my own.

Both Friday and Saturday nights I regretted that I had not paid more attention to Matty and his mates. They would have been happy to welcome me as another drunk in their group, but now I had no way of locating them and I wasn't going to go round all the pubs in Danetree looking for them on my own. Going to the cemetery to see the other acquaintances, the girls and other riffraff would not have been a good idea either. Now I was alone, I no longer had any familiar people around me to support me. I was just vulnerable, insecure and a social outcast. Honestly, I think if I had shown up they would have treated me with contempt, like I was a bum, and maybe even beaten me up.

These two days of confinement in the safety of my room were spent thinking about my new situation and the ways I could improve it a little. The first thing I did was to convince myself that I really wasn't that bad compared to how I would be in Madrid in August or on holidays with my parents. In both situations I wouldn't have any friends to go out with either, so the truth was that I wasn't missing much. At least in Danetree I was in a foreign country, with all the challenge and adventure that this entails, and the time I was there would be also good for learning English. All I needed was something to fill my time and at the same time give me the possibility, at least in theory, to meet people. For this, there was only one viable option: to get a job.

Another equally desirable idea would have been to take a course in something, but there was little of that in a small, working-class town. Realistically, the only course I would have had a chance to take would have been an eight-hour shift in one of the factories or warehouses on the outskirts. To get this desired job, some enlightened minds had told me to go factory by factory and warehouse by warehouse asking the managers. This seemed too stressful and ineffective to me, so on Monday morning, I left my house with the intention of signing up for all the ETTs in town so they would find me a job. Danny was particularly adamant that these agencies were very bad because they took commission and I couldn't convince him that I didn't care if they paid me a few pennies less as long as they found me something fast.

The first agency I visited was called Premier and it was like a kind of office on the street. Once I went inside and all the people, employed and unemployed, were staring at me, the nerves and insecurity suddenly appeared. I had never been to a temporary employment agency, nor had I ever worked, so I did not know what the procedure was in these cases. Especially in a strange country where I didn't speak the language either.

The employees didn't seem to help me much, because they just kept looking at me as if I was a zombie or a ghost. After an uncomfortable time standing there not knowing what to do, I gathered my courage and approached an apathetic fat woman who was acting as a secretary and told her:

"I'm looking for a job."

The lady stared at me as if she was crazy and after a while, she told me to sit on a chair and wait like everybody else. Apparently, not knowing the protocol of acting in this kind of places had made look like a fool. In these companies, you arrive first, sit down and wait until you are called. When they call you, you just tell them you'd like to join in and not "I want a job, bitch!" as I had just done.

When they finally deigned to listen to me, things didn't get much better. With my broken English, I tried to make the woman who interviewed me to understand that I wanted to sign up with the agency to get a job, but the woman didn't seem to cooperate. She put all sorts of obstacles in my way and asked me for a series of documents that I didn't have and didn't know I needed. I thought that with this European Union thing it was a piece of cake and that they were going to give me a job just like that, but apparently, it wasn't that simple.

Thinking that maybe that particular agency was too strict, I tried a couple of other agencies, this time without making a fool of myself, but with the same results. In the end, the morning had turned out to be a disaster in all but one respect. On one of my trips from one agency to another I had met or rather recognised, a fellow countryman.

The boy in question was called David and was Catalan. During the last week of our course, he had come to our class a couple of times, although without much enthusiasm. Thanks to this I knew him by sight and I knew he was Spanish, although I hadn't said a word to him either.

It's funny what human beings are like. A week ago, surrounded by my classmates and friends, I hadn't paid any attention to him, but now that I was alone and desperate I approached him with enthusiasm.

"Hello, David. How are you? You look great! How are you doing? What do you do for a living?" And a lot of other questions, trying to be as nice and affectionate as my sullen character allowed me.

Luckily, David was a decent chap and received me with cordiality and open arms.

"*Molt bé*, I'm glad there's a Spaniard here" he said half in Catalan, half in Spanish and then offered to help me with anything I needed. I didn't miss the chance and quickly told him about the sorrows and pains of my first day looking for work.

"Don't worry," he replied, "we'll go to my agency right now and I'll talk to them to see if they can get you a place where I work."

Thanks to this chance meeting, and also to David's kindness, I found out that to sign up at the temp agency and apply for a job I only needed two requirements, a bank account and a British social security number. The first was easier, just go to the bank, open an account and pay in a minimum amount of £20. The second was more complicated, I had to go to the local Job Centre with all the relevant documents and fill in an application. After that, I had to wait for a notification that would come in the mail, giving me an appointment at the Social Security office nearest to my address. There, an interview would take place and if everything went well, I would be given that bloody number in a few days.

Luckily, David did not have to work that day, so he agreed to accompany me to the Job Centre to take the first step in the long process of finding a job. There his help was invaluable because as he had recently gone through this, he even knew the number of the form we had to ask for from the official. Once this was done, we just had to wait for the notification and as I was very grateful I invited him to a beer at Friday's, although as he didn't drink he had a Diet Coke instead.

The next day I managed to get Janet to accompany me to the bank to open the account. David had told me that sometimes foreigners were asked to provide a guarantee, so I thought that no one was better than Janet. Once there, all I had to do was fill in a form with my details and give them a £20 note so that they could open an account in my name, although the debit card would still take a few days.

So, with all these preparations and the occasional visit to the public library to kill time, the days went by. I hadn't seen Farah since I broke up with her on Friday and I didn't think much of her either. Forget and move on had been my philosophy all week and so I was shocked when she showed up at my house on Thursday, after our supposed break-up.

"What the fuck are you doing here? What the hell do you want?" Or, "Didn't we just break up?" were some of the questions that came to mind when I saw her arrive after a whole week without seeing her. However, I tried to be calm and when I addressed her I did so more diplomatically for several reasons:

1 She was a girl.

2 She was hot.

3 There was still a possibility of sleeping with her.

4 I was all on my own and having a friend would be great.

"Hello Farah, how are you?"

"I'm okay thanks, and you?"

"I haven't seen you for a long time."

"Sorry I've been so busy. Can you come out?"

"Yeah sure, just give me a minute."

As Farah didn't like the animals or the strong smell in my house, she stayed outside waiting while I got dressed. When I left the house I thought she wanted to talk to me seriously to clarify if we were going to have a relationship or not. Nothing could be further from the truth. Farah had to do the shopping because her mother had ordered her to do so and as she did not want to go alone, she decided that I could accompany her and help her bring the packages. For the second time I was tempted to tell her to sod off, but once again I decided to be careful and see what she said to me on the way. In the precarious situation I found myself in, I couldn't afford to lose a female friend just like that, as I have never been what you call a ladies man.

As we walked to the supermarket I told her a little about the conversation we had last week about us and my impressions. To my surprise, she didn't remember much about it or give it much thought. She was simply upset that day, though not for any particular reason. I was beginning to realise that Farah was a girl with a high propensity for drama and ephemeral tantrums, and I decided not to take what she said to me so personally in the future. Apparently, everything remained the same. We were two kids who had just started dating, who were still getting to know each other and she seemed excited about it.

So we talked all the way through, and even she told me not to pay too much attention to her when her dark side came out. Of course, she still wanted to see me and be my girlfriend if it was okay with me.

And what could I say? She was hot, I had the hormones of an eighteen-year-old, and I knew hardly anyone in the village. I wasn't going to say no to the only source of sexual and emotional satisfaction I had at hand.

As had happened before, our meeting was shorter than I would have wished. After passing by the supermarket to buy the supplies demanded by her mother, we went straight back to her house and I left her just as we reached the limit. As the next day was Friday, I asked her if she wanted to do something and as she looked at me with some interest, I quickly told her that we could take a bus and spend the whole day in the nearby town of Northampton on a sightseeing tour. She didn't think it was a bad idea and said she would try, so we agreed to meet at eleven o'clock in town.

The next morning I was already at ten to eleven waiting at the bus station, dressed in my best clothes and eager to see her again. Farah arrived a little later and together we decided that we would take the 11:30 bus to Northampton because it was the most direct.

When the minibus arrived we got on it, paying the three pounds that the return ticket cost, and trying to sit as far away as possible from a small group of rowdy teenagers who were making a fuss. I had made up my mind that on the way there we were going to be cuddly with each other and do some holding hands stuff, but she cut me off when I tried to make an approach.

"You smell like dogs," she said. "Don't take it the wrong way, but it really stinks and I don't like it." I explained to her that there were several dogs and cats in my house and that it wasn't my fault for smelling like that. She replied that she understood, but that I still shouldn't get too close.

As physical contact had been forbidden, I talked to her instead of kissing and touching her. Little by little I learned more about Farah and her somewhat peculiar personality. The first thing that became clear was that she was fanatically obsessed with cleanliness. Nobody likes dirt and bad smells, but she took this to an almost impossible extreme. Not only did she dislike the smell of animals on my clothes, but she wouldn't let me touch her if I hadn't washed my hands beforehand, especially if I had touched food or some kind of street furniture such as a bench or a cash dispenser. For Farah, the whole world was a dirty, germ-ridden place that had to be disinfected before touching it. To do this she always carried a small bar of soap in her bag, as well as scented antiseptic wipes. Naturally, this affected her life quite a bit and it started to affect mine as well. Someone like that has difficulty performing some actions that for other people are normal. She couldn't sit on a bench because it was dirty, she couldn't eat in a restaurant because she didn't trust the cutlery, she wouldn't dare to touch a railing because it is unclean, and she would never sit on a toilet other than the one at her house. Lying on the grass or going to the swimming pool would be totally unthinkable things. As we arrived at our destination, I was amused to see that she was not even leaning against the back of the seat. -It's dirty," she said, unable to suppress a grimace.

Another thing I discovered about her that day was her great love for fashion. From the time we arrived in Northampton until we left, we spent ninety per cent of our time in shops like Zara or similar. Inside these clothing stores, hitherto unknown to me, she seemed to get into a kind of trance that forced her to run from place to place picking up rags, looking at sizes and trying things on. I would just go behind her, sometimes acting as a coat rack and saying yes to everything. After two hours of shopping marathon, I was so sick of seeing clothes and cute girls that I suggested to go for a walk in a park. She looked at me in disbelief and said:

"Are you crazy? I haven't had time to see anything."

At midday, I tried to make her understand that we needed to go and eat something, but as she didn't listen to me I had to drag her out of the shop. "Only five more minutes," she said, but the same trick wouldn't work for her for the fourth time.

Despite Farah's eccentricities, it can be said that we had a good time that day in the big city. After satiating her fashionable overalls, and eating at a fish&chip restaurant, she was more affectionate with me and even allowed me to hold her hand and touch her ass from time to time. To get back we took the five o'clock bus because she had to be at home by six. Luckily, she had already gotten used to the smell of my clothes, so this time the trip back was more pleasant. When we arrived at Danetree I accompanied her to the limit and before saying goodbye to her I begged her to see each other the next day. She didn't seem very convinced at first and told me

"Look, it's not that I don't wanna see you, but if I spend too much time with you my parents will know I'm with a boy. They're so strict and definitely, they wouldn't like me going out with anyone."

"Why, haven't they been boyfriend and girlfriend when they were young?"

"Well, actually no. They had an arranged marriage when they were eighteen. One week before they tied the knot they didn't even know each other."

"That's terrible!" I said in horror.

"It's their culture and their traditions. Their identity in this foreign land we live in."

"And you agree with that? I asked her with a small panic attack."

"No silly, if I did I wouldn't be with you, don't you think? I believe you should marry the person that you fall in love with, but I don't wanna confront my parents. After all, I live with them, don't I?"

"And I guess that if they found out they would get really annoyed."

"Yes, not only a boyfriend but also an English one."

"What the hell are you talking about? I'm not English."

"Yes you are. For us all Europeans are English. *Gorah* or *Farangyi* is how we call you."

"So, having an 'English boyfriend' is the worst thing that you can do?"

"Well, there are worser things than that, like losing your virginity or getting pregnant before marriage."

After this last indirect wake-up call, I was silent. Until now I had always believed that I was a foreigner dating an English girl, and now it turned out that I was the English and the girl was the foreigner. What a crazy world we live in.

Deep down, I imagined many of the things Farah had said to me, but even so, her confirmation had fallen on me like a jar of cold water. All this conversation, like all the others, was completely in English. As my English is far from perfect, it's possible that I misunderstood something, but in general, the idea was that our relationship was forbidden, had no future and was dangerous. For fear of the answer, I didn't ask her if his four older brothers thought the same as his parents, although I assumed that the family and his little sister's honour would be important to them too.

Despite all this, I managed to get Farah to be with me on Saturday. As I had no way of contacting her I stayed at home all day waiting for her to come and pick me up. I had promised her that I wouldn't show up at her house or call her on the phone, but she had absolutely refused to give me any personal information about her. After two weeks I still did not know her phone number, where she lived or her surname. All I knew was that she claimed to be Jewish, that her parents were very strict and that she had four older brothers.

Farah appeared around midday and we went for a walk in town. Like almost every time we were together, all we did was walk to no particular place and talk about our things. I sometimes tried to break this dynamic and kiss her, but she refused outright, claiming that there were people in front of her. "Fuck, it's just a kiss, not a romp," I would complain, and then she would agree to give me a quick one after many precautions. During these walks, my secret intention was that we would lie down on some lonely lawn and get some intimacy, but I rarely succeeded. According to her, even the slightest blade of grass on her clothes could give away our relationship to her parents, and in the face of such reasoning, I could do little to convince her.

That day, after much walking, I left her on the limit at three o'clock in the afternoon and went home to eat something. When I was about to sink my teeth into a sausage and bacon sandwich that I had prepared, I was surprised when the bell rang. As the door of the house opened to one of the kitchen windows, I looked out to see who it was. It was a big surprise to find Farah there again, so much so that I had to hide the sausage sandwich under a sofa. When I opened the door she told me that I could not enter her house because I had no keys and there was no one there. "What a shame," I said trying to conceal my enthusiasm. "If you want, you can stay with me all day. Jan and Danny are out" I added with a silly smile.

She looked at me very seriously and said at the same time that she was pulling me out:

"You have to help me to get inside. Otherwise, my parents will know I have been messing around."

"Awright, let's go and see what I can do."

For the first time, I crossed the border and we went up a small hill road with villas and gardens on either side. Then we turned a street to the left and came to a row of terraced houses, although they look posher than mine. There we stopped in front of the last house and Farah pointed out to me that it was that one.

After checking that the front door was indeed locked, Farah said that there was a back door, which might not be locked. That was the first obstacle, as the gate led to a back garden, which was surrounded by a wooden fence as high as I was and pointed at its upper edge. I managed to climb to the top of the fence without pricking my balls and jump to the other side. Once inside I was disappointed to find the back door closed, although I opened the garden gate to Farah from the inside. -At least you are now inside your property. When they come you can make up some story, that you went out for something and forgot the keys.

My girl seemed unconvinced by this and pointed to a half-opened window on the top floor.

"If you could climb up there and sneak in, then you could open the door for me and I would be so grateful," she said, emphasising the word "grateful."

I didn't think twice and started climbing while thinking about the risks I was taking. The first one was to fall and break my neck, but there were others. What would happen if once inside the door the siblings or parents arrived and surprised me there? Would Farah come out in my defence assuming her guilt or would she play dumb saying she didn't know me at all? I thought I could trust her, but I didn't know how afraid she was of her family. "The last thing I needed was to be arrested in England for breaking and entering," I thought just before reaching the bathroom window, sneaking in and giving myself a considerable blow to the floor.

"Farah, am in!" I shouted enthusiastically, to which she replied that I should not dare to step on the carpets with my street shoes. After taking them off, I came out of the bathroom and went down the stairs, all excited and cursing myself for not having brought a condom.

I opened the door to Farah and she came in and took her shoes off, leaving them on a mat in the hall. Then she invited me into the living room to sit on one of the sofas.

"Hang on a sec, now I'll show you how grateful I am," and disappeared into one of the rooms.

"I'm sure she'll come in naked," I thought. "Maybe fuck not yet, but make out for sure". After a while, she appeared with a small tray on which she brought a cup of tea and some pastries, which she offered me saying

"You can take your time to finish it, my parents will take at least one hour to come back." Then he started vacuuming and ignored me completely.

As it was obvious that there would be no sex at all, I was amused the time I was there gossiping and trying to find out things about my dear Farah. I could see that the house was very clean and tastefully decorated, with lots of carpets and cushions, which created a cosy atmosphere. There was a strange smell of spices in the air, which together with the above gave the whole place a vaguely oriental feel. On the wall, there was a painting of a kind of temple in an exotic style and in the kitchen I had seen another of those temples on a calendar also written in a very strange alphabet. I tried to look for some photographs where the members of his family were so that I could recognise them in the future and see if the brothers were very buff. I found few and she went ahead and hid them in a drawer while telling me: "You can't look at that." I also looked for some symbols or signs of the religious affiliation of the family that lived there, because the story Farah had told me that she was Jewish was beginning to sound like a porkie. Of course, I was not an expert in Judaism, but it seemed to me that Jews were forbidden to do any kind of work on the Sabbath and even to leave the house. If this was the case and her parents were so religious, how could they have driven so many miles to Birmingham to do the week's shopping? Wasn't this in contradiction to the Torah?

In the absence of sex, I decided that researching this mystery would be a good way to spend my remaining weekend. When a prudent hour arrived, Farah thanked me and politely kicked me out of her house. "My hero," she said as she threw a kiss in the air and then closed the door. I knew that I wouldn't see her again until Monday, but luckily I already had something to do, so when I got home I went up to my room and started making a list of all the words I could remember from the language Farah spoke from time to time instead of English and the meanings I knew or could deduce:

Gorah: White (a European person, usually referring to the English or to me)

Kala/ kali: Black/black (derogatory comments towards some black women we saw in Northampton).

Pili: Yellow (Farah used to call me pili teeth in allusion to my slightly yellowed teeth due to nicotine)

Aloo: Potato (an affectionate nickname with which Farah sometimes called me: Aloo face, whose literal meaning is potato face).

Korah: Horse (another affectionate nickname).

Koota: Dog (her favourite insult).

Chalo: Come on (used to hurry up in any situation).

These seven words were going to help me to shed some light on the mystery that for the time being enveloped my dearest Farah. With them, I wanted to at least discover the ethnic origin and confession of the girl's family and this would help me to know what I was dealing with and what to do in case I was discovered or presented.

On Sunday morning I put the list in my pocket and took a little walk to the public library. Luckily, it was open on Sundays until three o'clock in the afternoon and was also quite well stocked with what I had come to get, i.e. language dictionaries. First I sat down at a table far enough away from the small groups of children who came to the library to disturb and took out my list. Then I calmly took all the oriental language dictionaries that I could find and that I thought were representative. The first ones I found were of Arabic, Hebrew and Hindi. Farsi, Turkish and Punjabi cost me a little more, and almost when I was about to leave, I found one for Pashtu and another for Bengali.

Some of these were fat academic dictionaries and others were little more than simple conversation guides. Some I had to discard because the words did not come in the Latin alphabet and others were simply incomprehensible, but in the end, I got a good representation of all the languages of the Middle East and the Indian subcontinent.

From then on the procedure was simple, I compared the list with each of the languages to see if the words matched more or less. To begin with, I tried the Semitic languages, Hebrew and Arabic, without success. Turkish was also nothing like the words on the list, but things changed when I compared it to Indo-European languages, especially Hindi and Punjabi. After checking the results a thousand times and deliberating deeply, I came to the conclusion that the language spoken by Farah was probably Hindi, Punjabi, Bengali or similar, and that her religion could not be Jewish.

The next step was to take the encyclopaedia and look for Punjab, the land of the five rivers, divided between India and Pakistan, populated by Indo-Aryans, whose most important religions are Hinduism, Islam and Sikhism, which also led me to look for information on these three religions to see which one Farah could belong to, and so I was looking at bookshelves almost until the library closed. I did the same with India and Bangladesh but I almost fell asleep and I had to give up.

With all this nonsense I spent a relatively entertaining weekend. As I had no friends, I couldn't go to the pub on a bender and I didn't really feel like doing this in a town full of Yobbos either. Now instead of drinking or going out, I filled my time by being with Farah or failing that by thinking about Farah, because after going out with her for two weeks I had no choice but to admit that I was completely and madly in love with her. Accepting this was a good step to begin to better understand my situation in that town and those circumstances.

The next day, Monday, I saw Farah for a while, although we did nothing but walk and talk for half an hour. I didn't tell her anything about my discovery so as not to upset her, although it wasn't necessary either, as she never talked about her ethnic background unless specifically asked about it, and then she just did it reluctantly and changed the conversation as soon as possible. More important than this was the call I received from the Social Security, where I was given a day and a time to be interviewed about my application for a UK Social Security number. The appointment was on Thursday morning at 12 noon at the Northampton office, where I would be interviewed and my situation analysed to decide if I would be given my Social Security card with which I could start working.

I really needed this, because my money was running out and I barely had enough to pay the rent for a couple of weeks. In addition to this anxiety about being evicted, I was frustrated that I could not save or give myself a little treat. Not a beer, not a meal out, not a gift for Farah, nothing because I was on a budget. During these last days, I only ate what Janet had in the fridge and the cigarettes I brought from Spain were getting dangerously low. I didn't even know if I had enough money to catch the bus on Thursday.

At my next appointment with Farah, I told her that I had the interview with the Social Security on Thursday and I asked her to come with me for moral support and to help me with the language if I had any problems. She did not seem very convinced, but I promised her that afterwards, we could see all the clothing joints she wanted. She could not say no to this, so on Thursday we met again at 11 am at the bus station, ready to spend a pleasant and productive day in the city.

This time I didn't try to get my hands on her during the trip, because I was quite nervous about the interview I had to face, and on which my future in England depended. If I didn't get my Social Security number or took too long to get it, I wouldn't be able to work, I would run out of money and I would have to go back to Spain leaving Farah alone to be taken away by another son of a bitch. This could not happen, so I had been rehearsing the interview in my head the day before. I simply had to appear to be a working person willing to stay in England indefinitely, and my European passport would do the rest. At least in theory that was what I had been told at the Job Centre.

Once in Northampton we went to the Social Security offices, which were not far from the station, took a number and sat down in the waiting room. After a while, I was called and entered a small room where there was a table, a couple of chairs and a young officer who would be interviewing me. After the introductions, I asked him if he wouldn't mind that my girlfriend was present to help me with the language. "Is your girlfriend in the waiting room alone?" he asked me in surprise. "You better tell her to come in with us. There are some really dodgy people coming here," he said, trying hard to restrain himself and not telling me all his troubles.

The first thing I had to do was fill in some rather long forms with my personal details, my address in England and some other questions. This took me ten minutes, then we made some photocopies of my passport and finally came the dreaded interview, which was as follows:

"So you want to work in the UK, right?"

"Yes."

"Very well, we will send you a card with your social security number to your address. You will receive it in a few days."

"Thank you."

"Good luck with everything"

"Goodbye."

Everything had been much easier than I had imagined, so to celebrate we went shopping, Farah and I, although not to buy, but to fantasize about what we would buy when I finally had money and a well-paid job.

Until the day I got my social security card home, there was little I could do except wait and spend the days in comfortable boredom. There is nothing more pleasant than being forced to do nothing since in this way laziness is justified and there are no regrets. As the only thing I did these days, apart from eating and sleeping, was to see Farah sporadically, it occurred to me that as she was my girlfriend I was neglecting a little my obligation to try and sleep with her. For now, we were not making any serious attempts to maintain relations, limiting ourselves to walking around the village holding hands and talking about nonsense. We had been going out for several weeks now, so this might well be the time to put a little more emotion and carnal touch into our relationship.

At this point and to my regret, I think it's time to address a topic that I've been avoiding throughout the story, sex, as I don't want this story to resemble something like Tintin's adventures in his younger years. I'll speak plainly and unambiguously, as difficult as it may seem to me due to my early education in the values of a sanctimonious and vaguely repressive Catholicism. The first thing I have to say is that being straight and eighteen years old, my libido was constantly sky-high. Ninety-five per cent of my thoughts were related in one way or another to girls and sex, and the ultimate goal of any action I took in leisure time was to pull. My lack of success as a Casanova was compensated by the consumption of pornography and the noble art of playing the oboe on a daily basis. I wasn't bad enough to go whoring yet, but I had even thought about it. To sum it up, I was what you would call a normal guy.

But sexual desire was not the only emotion related to sex. When you are a teenager, sex also makes the difference between being a boy or a man, and that influences your identity and the image you have of yourself as a person. If you haven't had sex, you're a kid and a sucker, and no one will have the slightest respect for you. This subject among friends was quite delicate, and although in general, we tried to avoid it, deep down we all knew more or less which winners had already succeeded and who had not. I personally made sure that everyone believed that I had already fucked by telling some lies, but the truth, the harsh truth was that at eighteen I had not yet premiered.

The worst thing was that I didn't know if I was a virgin or not since from another point of view I had done some things, but this was such a complicated and personal issue that I couldn't ask anyone their opinion about whether I could still consider myself a virgin or not. I'll tell the story briefly so readers can draw their own conclusion.

I kissed a girl when I was fourteen. From then until I was seventeen I did nothing more than snog some chick I met one night and at most touch her ass. I didn't have any girlfriends either because all the ones I liked didn't pay any attention to me or those who liked me were mingers. The day I turned eighteen I realised that I was already an adult and still a virgin, and I decided that I had to do something to change the situation. In my class, there was no clear objective plus I didn't like having a girlfriend in the same school and being the target of chatter, I thought I should look outside my immediate environment. Luckily, I still had the phone numbers of the girls I had recently hooked up with, three in my last year, so I decided to try this way and see what happened.

I called them three with the excuse of seeing how they were and proposing to meet for a drink. One of them ignored me, another one told me to fuck off, but the last one was receptive, so after a bit of pantomime, we started seeing each other from time to time. At first, it was all about going out for a few meetings, drinking and generally meeting up with her friends. Little by little, we started to gain confidence, although I didn't even like her very much, and I don't think she felt anything special about me either, except for the need to look cool in front of her group of friends. There came a time when I started to stop by her house when her parents were away, usually on weekends, and everything continued to progress naturally. First, just visiting; then, a little more action, until we started to think about making love.

We tried twice, but we didn't succeed. Nervousness, inexperience, anxiety and poor condom quality made the task so difficult that we had to give up and comfort ourselves with mutual masturbation. Our third attempt was already on the right track. I had managed to put the condom on the first time, I had a powerful erection and a strong desire to impale her, but when I went to put it in there was no way, it was like hitting a wall. I don't know why this happened, as I'm not a doctor, but the truth is that the muscles or whatever were not dilating and it was impossible to achieve full penetration. In fact, I tried to put a finger in first, but it barely went in and she was already screaming in pain.

Disappointed but very excited we decided to try several different positions to see if there was any luck. First, she got on top of me, but we saw that this way we were not going anywhere. Then she got down on all fours and I tried to go doggy style, but we didn't succeed either. Finally, she lay face down on the bed and I lay on top of her with the idea of putting my thing between her thighs and so, with the lubricant of the condom and the friction with the buttocks, at least give me the illusion that I was shagging. Then the miracle happened and I realized that without knowing very well how I had put it in her.

"Wait, it's going in," I said, and she gave a little shriek of pain and surprise.

"I don't think it's in the right…," she said, "Damn it, you put it in the wrong place."

I asked if she was all right, pretending to be concerned. I interpreted her "yeah" as a green light and started to move my hips rhythmically while repeating the question from time to time to make sure everything was OK. She seemed to enjoy it, at least at first, although in the end when I was close to the climax she told me that it was starting to hurt and to take it out. I told her no way, that I would finish first and then take it out, and she saw me so determined that she endured the pain a little longer, just long enough for me to reach the goal. As soon as I finished and took it out, she ran to the bathroom and I didn't want to know what for. When she came back to the room she was already half-dressed and told me that I should leave, as her mother would be arriving soon.

After this day we met a few more times and also tried again to make love without success, contenting ourselves with other love practices. Little by little, we became more distant and lost contact until one day we stopped seeing each other, which was not particularly traumatic for her or for me.

Until now this was all my experience in sex and that is why I didn't know whether to consider myself a virgin or not. Technically I hadn't fucked, but I had been with a girl in a very intimate way. Sometimes I considered myself a virgin, sometimes not; sometimes I was disgusted with myself, but in general, I burned with the desire to make love as God commands with a woman and if it could be with someone special like Farah, all the better.

But to make this dream come true, I had to move on, because I wasn't going to stay in England forever and what was worse, there was little chance that our relationship would survive two thousand kilometres of distance and many months of absence. That's why I wanted to lose my virginity with Farah and at the same time be the first one for her. This, even if life forced us to separate soon, would be an indelible memory that we would both keep for the rest of our lives.

On my next date with Farah, I decided to talk about sex, but when I saw her unconvinced I immediately aborted the mission and went off the deep end telling her an irrelevant and absurd story. However, it was not difficult to understand her reluctance to love. A fuck meant nothing negative to me, but the possibility of getting pregnant, as well as her family discovering that she had been eating chorizo, filled her with terror. At that time I could have tried to convince her of how difficult it is to get pregnant if you take the right precautions and how unlikely it is that anyone will find out if you act naturally, but instead, I opted for the strategy of trying to fool her.

"You know... we could get a film and watch it in my room. They don't mind if I bring people home, as long as I ask them first."

"Your house is filthy, and it stinks like dog's poo."

"Nay," I insisted again, "My room's clean. I don't let any pets to come in."

So we continued to argue for a while until she promised to come in for a try during the weekend. This made me very happy, but when I got home I was struck by the harsh reality. I was so used to living there that I hardly noticed it anymore, but the house was a real mess and smelled of animals. When I entered my room I discovered that one of the dogs had sneaked in and shat on the carpet, leaving an unbearable smell. "Here Farah comes once and not only she doesn't come back but breaks up with me for being a dirty git."

That was the day to day life of living in a house with carpet floors, three dogs and eleven cats, in which even in the hypothetical case that someone cleaned from time to time, there were fourteen small pooping machines leaving hair, piss and poop everywhere and making every effort useless.

I didn't despair and resolved that even though the house was lost, I could still try to make my room into a clean and tidy bunker in which to try and seduce Farah, so I took my last ten pounds and went to the supermarket to stock up on cleaning supplies. In total, I bought a spray air freshener, a top-up air freshener, a special carpet soap and a liquid that eliminated the smell of animals. With all this, I went home and started the hard work of purifying my room. The first thing I did was to remove the dog shit, which was not an easy task because it had already dried out and was stuck to the carpet. Then I tidied up the whole room so that there were no things to bother me, putting clothes, books, shoes and in general everything in the wardrobe.

With the room clear I set out to mop the carpet with the special liquid. This sounds a bit drastic, but given the sorry state of the carpet, it was absolutely essential. Once it was clean I let it dry a bit and then I vacuumed the whole room, and I mean the whole room and not just the floor, to remove hairs and traces of dirt. Then with a cloth soaked in disinfectant, I went through the places where the filth had become strong. Finally, I sprayed the air freshener in such a way that I could hardly breathe, closed the door swearing that no four-legged creature would ever get through it again and opened the window wide, determined not to close it again, day or night, until my departure in September.

The cleaning operation was a success and when Farah finally came into my room, she changed the grimace of disgust and displeasure she had made when she entered the house into one of relief and satisfaction at seeing that everything was clean and smelled of lavender air freshener. The plan for the evening was to watch a previously rented film from the local video store and drink a bottle of white wine bought at the supermarket for the occasion. As I didn't have two chairs, we both lay down on the bed, turned on the video and huddled together to watch the film. After a while, we were already kissing, completely ignoring the plot and also taking off some of our clothes. At that moment I could have put in more pressure, taken her panties and my undies off and see what would happen, but I decided not to do it. If she had a good time and felt comfortable, she would probably want to come back often; whereas if I pushed it, I risked that she would never want to come again.

For this reason, I let her take the initiative, and I was even surprised to go further than I expected, even if we did not consummate the act itself.

Later, when I accompanied her home and left her at the limit, I congratulated myself on how well things had worked out. For now, we had a safe place to enjoy a little privacy, and I was sure that it wouldn't take long to repeat the performance. Little by little my great goal of making love for the first time, the one for which it was worth sacrificing everything, was becoming more feasible. Very soon I would stop being a virgin and feeling uncomfortable every time the bloody subject came up on stage. I had almost succeeded and I still had many weeks left in the UK to make other attempts that would surely be fruitful. Best of all, I really liked Farah and was very much in love with her. Losing my virginity to her and taking hers as a gift would be a beautiful way of both taking such an important step in life and putting an end to our relationship before the inevitable separation in September. It definitely had to be Farah the one.

ORANGE

With all this nonsense of being in love, the days passed quickly, until one Monday morning I discovered that among the mail there was a letter for me. The sender was the British Social Security and inside was a small red, white and blue card with my name on it and eight digits that I identified as the desired number that would open the doors of the job market for me. I hurriedly dressed and gathered all my documents, passport and other things, in a large white envelope and went to the temp agency to register as an applicant.

While I was walking I was mentally reviewing everything I had to say to make myself understood. In this kind of procedure, I felt a bit insecure with the language, because my command of English was rather limited to the business of drinking in a pub or walking around with Farah, so I used to get lost in the technical-legal jargon. When I arrived I realised that luck was smiling on me, as there was my friend David the Catalan arranging a matter about a day's holiday. As soon as he saw me, the lad greeted me effusively, and when he found out that I had all the permits and requirements in order, he insisted that I let him talk to the agency employees. I don't know how he did it or what he told them, but after ten minutes I had a job in the same place where he was working.

The employee who assisted me afterwards was very nice and helped me quite a lot with all the formalities. Her name was Amanda and although she was well over thirty, you could tell she enjoyed provoking the male workers at the agency. The tight white dress she wore that day was quite see-through and when she got up to get a document or something, all the men in the office could see that she was wearing nothing underneath it except a tiny thong. She would then smile, aware of all the attention she was receiving and sit back down, crossing her legs in the manner of Sharon Stone in Basic Instinct. Despite her little games, Amanda was very kind to me, informing me of everything and providing me with a pair of steel-toed boots necessary for the performance of my work.

"This isn't a present," she told me "the cost will be deducted from your first wages. Sorry, but you got to wear them for safety reasons."

"What a surprise, I thought steel-toed boots were just for kicking Nazis and beating up at punk concerts, and it turns out they are for work. Well, you learn something every day."

Luckily, or unfortunately, I had to start working the same day, in the afternoon shift at a warehouse owned by Orange, the mobile phone company, in nearby Chipping Wardington. The best thing was that I would be working in the same shift as my mate David, so I wouldn't be going alone. Also, the salary was not bad, almost six pounds an hour, which would be about two hundred a week by my calculations. To get there, a minibus would pick us all up at half-past one in front of the agency and bring us back at ten.

As it was still twelve noon it gave me just enough time to go home, change my clothes and prepare something to eat there. Once I'd done all this and got myself together to face the first day of work of my life, I showed up at the right place at half-past one, got on the minibus and sat down next to David. Around us were about eight other people. Most of them were young students who were taking advantage of the summer to make some money, although there were also some old losers and some immigrants who had no choice but to work for an agency. Once we were all inside, the driver started up and took us along a series of secondary roads through the English countryside, showing us a green and well-kept landscape. The truth is that the countryside in the UK was really beautiful compared to some of the cities which were quite sad. On both sides of the road, there were meadows, wheat fields, groves and a bit of sheep grazing. Occasionally we also passed through some picturesque villages, barely touched by the black hand of industrialisation, but this bucolic landscape changed when we reached our destination, a huge industrial warehouse where we would spend the next eight hours working.

The first thing we did when we arrived was to go to a kind of locker room where people got changed and left their belongings. Then we entered the warehouse itself. This consisted of two different parts, some very high shelves where there were lots of boxes with orders in the back and the area where the employees worked just in front.

The dynamics of the work were simple. Tractors called forklift trucks took pallets full of boxes from the shelves and carried them to rails located parallel to tables. At these tables, the employees, i.e. us, opened the orders and took out the small boxes with their mobile phones. Inside these boxes, where the terminal was already, we put the Sim card and sometimes instruction and advertising leaflets. Then we would make huge packages out of these boxes and put them into trucks that would take them to their destination.

The work itself was not complicated or physically hard, but tiring and quite boring. Every two hours we had a five-minute break to pee, drink or smoke, and in the middle of the day twenty minutes to eat something. At first, I stood at the same table as David, there were about twenty of us employees, but it didn't take long for us to separate. For eight hours I tried to be helpful, learn as much as possible and appear friendly to my colleagues. At the end of the day, we went through a security check and a metal detector, to make sure nothing was stolen, and we went back to Danetree in the minibus.

When I got home I found Danny and Janet a bit worried. As I had to leave immediately for work I didn't realise that I hadn't warned them and they didn't know what could have happened to me. As I told them the whole story, I became aware that this day had been a historic day, the first day of work in my life.

The next day I got up late, got dressed and prepared to see Farah, as Janet had told me that she had come to pick me up the day before and had left worried that I was not showing any signs of life. She arrived around half past eleven and we went out for a walk and bought some things. I had been looking forward to telling her that I had a job, but when I did, I was surprised that she did not seem very enthusiastic.

"When are we gonna see each other if you spend the whole day working?" she said.

"Well at least we can see each other at the weekend. If I didn't work, I would have no money to stay here."

This last reasoning seemed to convince her, although not completely, so we didn't talk about it anymore and went to do our errands.

When I came back at one o'clock I had a quick bite for lunch and again worked for eight hours in the Orange warehouse. This second day was much heavier than the first day when everything had been new. After the second one came a third one and so I gradually got used to the routine of working until I completed my first week. Every day hundreds of mobile phones passed through my hands that I manipulated them and left them ready to be distributed in the shops. Strangely enough, that was the first time in my life that I had some of those jalopies in my hands and looking at them closely I was still not very convinced that those gadgets were really useful. At the tables where we worked, we were forced to stand up for some strange reason. In my, and many others, opinion, the effectiveness of our work would not be affected if we could have a stool in front of the table to sit on from time to time while operating on the mobile phones. No, some human resources shitbag had figured out that the riffraff like us worked harder if they were forced to stand, and even the managers would give you a bollocking if they saw you sitting on a box or table.

Between four and six of us worked at each table. At first, I tried to be always with David, whom I became very close to, but this was not always possible. Most of the time, I don't know if it was unintentionally or unwittingly, we ended up being put in a different corner of the warehouse because of the demands of the job. This was a bit frightening for me because, in addition to the insecurity on the first days, I was surrounded by unfriendly-looking foreigners. However, just as it happened to me in the cells of Plaza de Castilla Court, the boredom made me start talking to the person in front of me after a while to make the work less boring. When I finally let go a bit and my colleagues saw that my English was relatively good, I started to make acquaintances among the rest of the Orange staff. This suited me very well for practising the language, as until then I really only spoke to Farah, Janet and Danny. New people with different accents and a desire to chat enriched my lexicon and accustomed my ear to registers that I had not had the chance to hear before.

Inside the warehouse, there were three types of workers. The permanent workers were usually middle-aged or older English people who had been with the company for many years and knew the score. There were two types of temporary workers, students and immigrants. The students were British university students who took advantage of the holidays to earn a little extra money to pay for the very expensive university fees in that country. Immigrants were people who had just arrived in England, from Eastern Europe or Africa, who were willing to work at anything and do anything to stay in the UK.

I personally got on well with people from all three groups, because it was really like a mixture of immigrant and student. The immigrants considered me an equal to them because I was a foreigner, and I identified with the students since I was going to start Business Management at University in October. The old English workers also gave me a lot of conversation when they found out that I was Spanish because for them Spain had a reputation for being a paradise for holidays, sun and cheap alcohol. During the sandwich and cig breaks, we formed the immigrant gang, which was David and me, a Ghanaian boy and two Romanian boys and a girl posing as Italians. It was with these people that I felt most comfortable, both at work and during the breaks. The English were generally kind and patient, but sometimes I could sense a certain distance in them as if they didn't want to be seen mixing too much with the foreigners.

As we finished every day at ten o'clock at night, on Friday we decided to go for a beer at Friday's after work with our new friends. I was looking forward to this, it felt like I had mates again, although none of us felt like hanging around after closing time. Now that I had a girl I had no interest in the nightlife that Danetree could offer me, as the risk of being beaten up by lager louts was not compensated by the possibility of pulling some birds.

With great joy, I set out to enjoy my first weekend as a working man. There's nothing like working long hours every day to appreciate how wonderful Saturday and Sunday are, even if, as was my case, you don't have a penny in your pocket. Unfortunately for me, the employment agency always paid us a week late. I never managed to understand why this practice, but it seems that it was common to all agencies and universally accepted, so I had no choice but to put up with it. At least, even if I didn't have any income I still knew I would have one the following week, so I was able to get my hands on the rent money. With this little cash, I decided to take Farah back to Northampton to look at shops and even considered giving her a little present.

Time flies when you have a girlfriend and money, so by the time I realised it was six o'clock and we were catching the bus back. Farah was very happy and had a great time, although she complained a little about always having to take that old bus. -I wish you had a car, I hate this smelly bus," she said as we paid for our ticket.

“Well, I said, this is your country, so you should be the one with a car so we wouldn't have to depend on this wreck full of children and ball-busting teenagers.”

“Driving is more like a boy's thing, innit,” she replied, ending the conversation since I had nothing to say in the face of such an unusual argument. Apparently, Farah's family had brought her up to live in a world where men did everything outside the home, women only had to worry about looking good, maintaining decency and one day finding a good husband to support them. Farah had accepted all this quite naturally, even though it was not very practical at the end of the twentieth century, and she seemed to be only interested in fashion, make-up, jewellery and boys. All girls' things, in her own words. For some reason, I had always imagined that when I had a girlfriend this would be a modern, independent and dynamic girl, but for some time now I had begun to sense that Farah was nothing of the sort, but a girl of Asian descent who had been instilled with very different values from those I had received as a child. I don't want to detract from the immense effort she had made by turning her back on her community to be my girlfriend. The huge step she had taken in a few days could be compared to what had taken many women years elsewhere. A foreigner, of different ethnicity and religion like me, could only bring her trouble and displeasure in the long run, and she had been very brave to start a relationship with me. However, although she acted as my girlfriend at times, this did not make her forget her roots and the values and customs in which she had been brought up.

That same Saturday night I found a piece of evidence that I thought was definitive to prove that my Farah's family came from the Indian subcontinent. That day, after leaving her at the limit, I had gone home and had had a quiet dinner. I had no plans, but fortunately, Janet had rented a film that I wanted to watch and had not yet returned it to the video store. Just before I started to watch it, I thought that I would fall asleep sooner if I had a beer or two, so I went down to the kitchen to get one. Janet had recently bought some beer, but Danny had gulped it down in a day, so I had no choice but to go out to the corner shop for a couple of cans.

As I approached the shop I saw three Indian women coming in the opposite direction from me in the distance: "How funny, maybe they're related to Farah", I thought with perverse irony just before I went into the small establishment that was serving as a late-night shop. I took two beers out of the fridge and waited in line for the kids to pay their jelly beans and piss off. Meanwhile, the three Indian women passed right in front of the shop and I could see them clearly. At first, I noticed their colourful clothes, like big robes they were wearing over their breeches and a veil on their heads. Two were young and an older one seemed to be the mother of the others. One of the faces looked familiar, so familiar that it turned out to be Farah, stuffed into a bright blue salwar-kamis.

I was amazed, I couldn't believe my eyes. That Indian woman had been my girlfriend for a month and I could hardly recognize her dressed in such an exotic way. The three of them passed by and luckily didn't see me, because I made such an astonishing face that even the clerk at the shop, also an Indian, asked me if I knew those women. "Not at all!" I answered, paid for the beers and got the hell out of there.

The next day I invited Farah to come to my room with the excuse of watching a film. While we were kissing in bed I didn't want to say anything, but once the situation calmed down a bit I asked her if she had done anything on Saturday night. She answered that she had gone out with her mother and cousin to see some relatives who did not live far away. I then innocently confessed to her that I thought I had seen her pass by my house when I went to buy some things. In a second Farah transformed herself from a sweet girl into a beast and accused me of having been spying on her, even threatening to leave me if I continued to harass her. In fact, all this anger came because she knew that I was very close to discovering the whole truth. As she couldn't stop me from knowing, at least by making a fuss she would make sure that I didn't dare, out of fear, to bring up the conversation again. Her tactic, however, worked well and I seriously considered not asking her any more questions about the origin of her family so as not to piss her off and spoil how well everything was going. I had no idea why she was trying to hide her background from me, but as this did not affect our relationship in the short term either, I decided not to stick my nose into her family affairs again.

After a full weekend in which I had unwittingly upset Farah, on Monday I started the working man's week again, eight hours a day preparing telephones that Orange made available to a customer eager for new technologies. The warehouse was full of orders, so they had brought in new workers and a big-headed manager to get us started. As far as the work is concerned, the week was similar to the previous one, with the same type of procedures and tasks to be carried out. In the mornings I still saw Farah, although we didn't enjoy much time together, and at night I went to sleep quite tired. The only significant event occurred on Friday afternoon, just before I got into the minibus when I went by the office to pick up what would be the first payslip of my life.

I was paid about £220, of which about £20 in tax was deducted and £10 from my metal-toed boots. If I received a similar income every week, I would have no money problems while in England and could even save a bit. My expenses were only the seventy pounds a week which I used to pay Janet for food and lodging. Apart from that, the transport was free and I could spend thirty or forty pounds at most on the weekend with Farah, I still had almost a hundred pounds a week to save. I didn't need to pay for my return ticket to Spain, as it was already booked, but I was sure that I would probably need money for other things. Mentally I had been working out a plan to come and visit Farah over the Christmas break and although that was still a long way off, I thought it would be best to have some savings just in case.

This dynamic of working for Orange in the afternoon and seeing Farah in the mornings continued until the end of August. Although this was not a life of luxury and fun, I was happy with it because it allowed me to be with Farah on a daily basis and even enjoy intimate moments during the weekends, although, for one reason or another, we never physically consummated our love. I wasn't too bothered about this, convinced that the day would soon come, and sometimes I even wondered what would happen if I forgot about University and stayed in the UK with my girlfriend as a mere factory worker. Maybe if she had proposed to move in together, I would have left everything and stayed in England, but we were still very young and both of us were very afraid to challenge our families.

Paradoxically, our quiet life was disrupted when Farah came up with the idea that she wanted to work in Orange and earn money too. Several times I had seen a glint in her eyes when we were going to get money out from my account and I would buy her something, but now I realised that it was not only admiration but also dirty envy that she felt for my buoyant economy.

Said and done, one day in the morning I accompanied her to the agency and she filled in the registration form right there. Everything was going well until Amanda told us that only the first shift, from six in the morning to two in the afternoon, was available.

Farah didn't want to make this shift because it would mean that we wouldn't see each other during the week and I begged her to wait a bit to see if there were some positions in the afternoon, but no. In the end, greed and lust for money won and Farah started working in the mornings the next day.

I tried to conceal my anger as best I could and pretended to support her, but deep down it had made me feel very disappointed. Everything was going well until Farah came up with the idea of messing up and altering our peaceful life. For me, the only reason to work in Orange was to be able to be in Danetree and the only reason to be in Danetree was to see Farah every day. If the latter was taken away from me, there wasn't much point in everything else.

That week was very hard for me, as I didn't see Farah until I arrived at the warehouse and then only fleetingly as I went in and she came out. Most days we didn't even have time to talk for a minute, as the minibus had to leave and she had to go with it. I was tempted to stop working in Orange and sort my ticket back to Spain because to be like that there was no point in staying. I had been thinking about other alternatives, but it was too late to start a new job and the morning shift at Orange had no places. It was almost September 1st and on the 21st I had to be in Madrid to register for university.

That weekend I met Farah at Mc Donald's in Danetree to have lunch and tell her my impressions, although, in the end, I ended up blaming her for choosing work over me in our last days together. I understood that she wanted a job, but what was the rush? Why not wait two weeks until I had left to start working? The conversation grew in tone, and we started to argue until she finally revealed her reasons to me.

"If I've started working," she said, "it's because I want to save enough money to go to Madrid with you." This was the last thing I expected to hear that Saturday afternoon.

"With me to Madrid?" I asked, "For good?"

"No moron, just on holidays. This way we can be together for a bit longer."

"What are you gonna tell your parents?"

"I'll make up some crap, don't worry."

Great, the idea of Farah coming with me to Madrid on holidays was so exciting that I couldn't help but wonder why I hadn't thought of it. It probably seemed so unattainable that I hadn't even dared to propose it to her. Once the euphoria subsided and I calmed down a bit, I began to consider the difficulties that our plan might have. On her side, we had to convince her parents, whom I didn't know, but who seemed to be the strictest chums in the world. For my part, I also didn't know how mine would act if I brought a foreigner home, although in principle I didn't expect any negative reaction. They had always been progressive and liberal, although with these recent times of increasing immigration to Spain I didn't know quite what to think either. My main concern would be to find out whether they would allow Farah to stay at home for a few days, as we had an empty room, or we would have to spend the dosh on a hotel.

For the time being, we decided that I would continue working in Orange until my departure and that Farah would come a day or two later when I would have the situation under control. I also thought it would be a good idea for her to start telling her parents about a supposed Spanish girl friend who would be the excuse, when the time came, for Farah to travel to Spain.

That Sunday we didn't do our film session in my room but met up to talk about how to organise ourselves. I knew that I was going to book my flight on the 18th or 19th and I thought that Farah could come on the 22nd, staying with me until I started classes the second week of October. The public library had an internet connection, so we went there to see how much the flights cost, but before deciding anything we agreed that the first step before getting our hopes up would be to talk to our families.

I called home that afternoon and told my mother that I had a friend, a female friend, who was coming to Madrid on holiday. "Would it be possible for this girl to stay at home with us for a few days?" I added without letting her speak and taking the bull by the horns.

My mother was cautious about this and told me she would talk to my father about it. I knew that if there was a problem, it would come from Dad's side, as Mom was the most condescending person in the world. "Well, I've already asked," I thought, "now let's wait and see what they say."

While I was waiting for an answer, the week passed slowly. Every morning I went to the agency to cry and beg them to switch me to the morning shift, but instead of telling them my real reasons, I made up a convincing excuse. "I've moved to a new place," I told Amanda, "and now I can't get there at night because there's no public transport that late. In the mornings I have someone to give me a lift, but not in the evenings," I added with a sad face.

She swallowed my lie and every day called the warehouse to see if they needed someone else in the morning. In the meantime, I went to work in the afternoon, resigned to the fact that I wouldn't see Farah for more than four minutes at the shift change either. Finally, on Thursday I was told that the following Monday I could report to the agency at half-past five and start the shift at six in the morning. One of the morning workers was on sick leave due to depression and needed to fill his position urgently.

Throughout the weekend I received more good news, as I was able to talk to my father and ask him very tactfully what he thought of my friend's affair. Surprisingly, everything was much easier than I had expected and my father did not object to "a girl" staying with us for a few days, as long as she went back when I started university and I focused on my studies. I think my parents were rather relieved that I was coming back to Spain and would start university, rather than staying and working there in the UK. They knew that immediate money and women can be very tempting for a young boy and were starting to imagine things.

Farah, on the other hand, was going to have a harder time convincing her family, as it seemed that in her culture it was not common for unmarried daughters to leave their parental home for any reason, let alone go on holidays to a foreign country to do God knows what. Unfortunately, Farah's folks would not agree to allow her to travel anywhere on her own. When I asked her what we were going to do,

Farah told me not to worry. "I've got something up my sleeve," she said enigmatically, "Everything will end up well, you watch."

On Monday my alarm clock rang at five in the morning, reminding me that I had to be at the agency at five-thirty to take the minibus to Orange. I quickly got dressed and left the house in a hurry, thinking how much I liked the afternoon schedule when there was no need to get up early. Besides being sleepy, I was very cold, because in England, in September and at dawn, the thermometer didn't even reach ten degrees. However, I was happy because I was going to see Farah and spend the whole day with her, well not in the most romantic place on earth, but at least we would be together.

After walking for a while I reached my destination and got into the minibus trying to hide as best I could. After a while, a black SUV arrived and stopped right next to us. In it was Farah and a man sporting a dark moustache whom I identified as her father. Out of the corner of my eye, I saw Farah saying goodbye to Moustachio, getting out of the 4x4 and getting into our minibus, sitting three seats in front of where I was without even greeting me. When we finally got going and lost sight of the black car, Farah came to sit next to me and kissed me good morning. "That was my dad," she said, "we better be careful in case he starts getting suspicious. He sometimes comes in the evenings to pick me up too, so don't come too near me then, right?"

Once in the warehouse, the day went on in a similar way as it did in the afternoon, although at a slightly calmer pace. Luckily, the fat cats didn't usually show up until twelve noon, so for most of the morning, we were under the supervision of a good-natured manager and worked at our own pace. What I was most afraid of was that Farah and me would be separated into different work teams, but this was rarely going to happen, as the working atmosphere was more relaxed and free than in the afternoon, when the bosses would start to get nervous about some crap not meeting expectations.

Working with Farah made my days more pleasant and time passed quickly. When we came back from work in the afternoon we would stay for a while in the centre or go for a walk before going home. It was on one of those days that we booked our flight to Madrid on September 19th. As we did it over the Internet we got a good price, although I still didn't trust this kind of virtual transactions very much. In the end, we decided to go together on the same flight to avoid complications. I wasn't sure how we would get from Danetree to Stansted airport, which was where the flight would leave from, so I asked Janet's advice to see if she knew of any direct buses. -Don't worry," she said, "My daughter doesn't live far from the airport. I'll tell her to come and give you a lift."

This seemed to be the perfect solution, as having someone local drop me off at the airport I wouldn't have to rack my brains trying to find my way there.

While we were making all these preparations we were rushing through the last days of working in England. On Friday 11th September we decided that we had enough money saved up so, after our shift at Orange was over, Farah and I dropped by the agency office to say goodbye to Amanda and thank her for all her help. In total I had spent six weeks working in that warehouse, having earned a total income of approximately £1,200, which was about 300,000 "potatoes" in exchange, and although I had spent almost half of it on accommodation and other stuff, I felt there was no point in working any more. I still had one week left in England, but I decided that this would be spent resting and preparing the last details of my holiday with Farah in Madrid.

BACK TO MADRID

Stopping work a week before I left was a pretty smart decision. The work itself, monotonous and repetitive, did not bring me anything positive and had only served to support me and pay the rent. Once I had the flight and everything was covered there was no point in spending my time in that warehouse manipulating phones. In fact, I was now beginning to think that perhaps I'd made it too long, as I'd even managed to save a lot of money. Happy not to have to step foot in that horrible industrial warehouse again, at least for a long time, I spent the rest of the day walking around the village with Farah while we did some shopping that she considered essential to enjoy a proper holiday. As she had never been out of the country on holiday before, something she reluctantly acknowledged, she wanted to take everything necessary to survive for two weeks in the Third World. At first, I went along with her, but later I had to dissuade her from buying many things because we already had them in Madrid, such as toothpaste or shampoo.

"No, Farah, you don't need that. We've already have one at home," I said over and over again as she answered "Are you sure?" making a rather comical face of incredulity.

The next day we went to do more shopping, but this time by bus, to the nearby city of Northampton. Apparently, Farah had decided that for her first holiday abroad it was absolutely essential to renew all her clothes. After a long pilgrimage through each and every one of the local fashion shops, the loot she got consisted of several bags full of different coloured rags which, according to her, were the basic things every woman should have for the summer-autumn season. I personally felt that there was no need to buy all that and spend a lot of money, but I kept my opinion to myself, as during the last few weeks I had understood that Farah and I sometimes worked very differently and that respecting and accepting these differences was the only way for our relationship to work.

On the way back to Danetree we continued to talk about our impending holiday in Spain and I tried to answer all her questions about the food, the shops, the customs and many other things. I also asked her some questions about her family and how they felt about her decision to go on holiday just like that, but I was left with some elusive answers. As I had done before, I felt that Farah was very uncomfortable talking about her family environment and wanted to end the conversation as soon as possible. "That's my business, not yours," she would almost always say, and then shift the conversation to something else without giving me the opportunity to dwell on it further. "Well, that's all right, that's what I need to know," I would repeat to myself trying to ignore the fact that I was burning with the desire to find out everything that my girlfriend seemed to want to hide from me. "Someday she will tell me the truth, in the meantime to enjoy and live in the moment."

Talking about all this we headed from the Danetree bus station to The Limit. When we arrived I returned the bags with everything she had bought, but she didn't want to take them.

"No, you keep'em. I got no room at home... and don't take anything out of the bags, just in case the dogs get it!"

"Very well," I said without understanding clearly what it was all about.

I didn't think about it anymore and went home to rest, but the next day when we met he surprised me again by bringing me a small suitcase, also to keep it in my room. When I asked her again why I had to keep it for her, she answered that because she did not have space in her room.

During the following days, Farah kept coming to my house with more things, make-up, underwear, a towel, and packing her suitcase very discreetly in my room. I found this suspicious because I had the impression that she was preparing to run away from home, packing in secret. In the end, I couldn't take it anymore and asked her directly if her parents knew she was coming to Spain with me.

"Of course not," she answered after some hesitation. "They don't know I'm going on holidays. They would never let me go abroad on my own. Not in a million years!"

"What are we gonna do then?" I answered, confirming my fears that she wanted to run away with me. Why else would she have taken the flight and packed her suitcase, if she knew that she would not be allowed to go? This worried me a lot, not because of the escape itself, which would be easy, but because of what would happen after the two weeks' holiday when I started college. There was no way I could afford to keep Farah in Spain no matter how much I loved her and I was very doubtful that her parents would ever admit her back to the house after she had run away.

"What are we gonna do then? I asked her straight out."

"Don't worry", she answered my question. "I've got a plan. Everything will be fine."

"Okay, but you better start explaining because I'm a bit lost right now."

"Do you know I've got a sister? Her name is Fozia and she is a nurse in London. She lives there since she ran away from my parent's home ages ago. Well, I just told my mum and my dad that I'm gonna spend two weeks at her house."

"Yeah, but what are you supposed to do there for two weeks?"

"Simple, I just joined a training programme at Marks & Spencer, and it is in London. I'll pretend that I'm there for two weeks."

"What happens if your parents go there to check on you?"

"They won't do that. They don't get on well with Fozia."

"What about your brothers?"

"Awright, I have something to confess. I hope you won't get annoyed..."

After a long conversation, I seemed to understand that she had an older sister, totally independent of her parents, who lived in London. This sister, called Fozia, was to be her alibi, as Farah had told them that she was going home for two weeks. Anticipating my question as to what she was supposed to do there, Farah told me that she had signed up for a selection process to work at Marks & Spencer and that the dates were deliberately set to coincide with our holiday in Madrid. "That's gonna be the perfect excuse," she said, "I even got the official forms at home." If the M&S people phoned her or wrote to her to ask for explanations, it wouldn't matter either, as she had given a false address. Best of all, her parents wouldn't stop by London to say hello either, as they hadn't spoken to Fozia since she ran away from home at eighteen and broke off all relations.

When I asked her what her siblings would think, she was silent for a while and then very embarrassed told me that she didn't have any male siblings, that she had made it all up when she still didn't know me well, to scare me and thus dissuade me from misbehaving with her. This, far from pissing me off, was a relief, for I was already seeing our plans to escape to Spain frustrated by four overprotective and meddlesome brothers. Actually, Farah hadn't lied to me at all, as she had four older sisters who she had simply changed sexes in her story to keep me in line. In fact, I had already met one of them during the first days I went out with Farah, although I took her for a friend or distant relative. I was surprised to learn that I had made a very favourable impression on this sister, as a boy who at first sight seemed honest and nice. This was fortunate because if the parents knew nothing about my existence and our trip to Spain together, the sisters were aware of everything. So many years living under the roof of strict and overprotective parents had created a strong feeling of complicity between them, so they often helped and covered up for each other in order to lead a relatively normal life without upsetting the old folks.

Still, as a precaution, the two older sisters before giving us their support demanded to know me a little better and also to have some facts about me. So Farah and I met them at the only coffee shop in town, something like a Yankee Starbucks, to have a coffee and talk. This meeting went quite well, because on the one hand I found them to be very nice and normal girls, and on the other hand I managed to give them a positive impression. Thanks to this they did not put any objection to our plans and wished us a lot of fun. "Don't worry, we'll cover up your little holiday. Our parents ain't that clever anyway," they told us, although they also asked me for some personal details of mine, like an address and telephone number to keep track of their sister. I assured them that I would take care of their little sister at all times and treat her with all the respect in the world. To convince them of my good intentions, I even left them a photocopy of my passport that I kept from my days as a worker, arguing that a person with bad intentions would never do something like that. Farah promised to phone them every day and behave herself during her stay in Spain, which was a euphemism that meant not getting pregnant.

Convinced that we had all the ends tied up, I had been making my preparations to return home when two days before we left Farah surprised me with a new problem. Now it turned out that her parents had made it their business to drive her to London so that she would not have to go by bus to mingle with the mob, with such bad luck that she could not refuse. Moreover, she had already said that her M&S internship started on Monday, so the old people did not want to take her on Saturday claiming that they would take her on Sunday. Our flight was on Saturday at five o'clock in the afternoon, so our whole plan was in jeopardy.

During a brief moment of crisis, we really thought that our trip was going to go to shit and that our elaborate pyramid built on lies was going to fall apart. Then, when we calmed down and stopped arguing, we started thinking about how to solve this last-minute problem.

"Awright, the only thing we can do," I explained to Farah "is that you miss your flight and I buy you another one from Spain later. It's gonna be expensive, but it's the only way."

"What am I gonna do all that time in London?"

"You can stay with your sister."

"No, that's just a cover for my parents. My sis doesn't know I'm using her as a cover. I can't go with her. I don't even know where she lives."

"What about a hotel?"

"Me in a hotel, alone in London? No way Jose!"

After much talking and looking at all the possible options, the only thing that occurred to us was that Farah could take a bus on Saturday to Northampton and from there another one to the airport without the annoying interference of her parents was that something should happen to the old man's car so that he could not take it that day.

So Saturday was not only going to be my last day in England, but also the most exciting because I was going to get up in the middle of the night to slash the tyres of my girlfriend's father's car without being seen so that it would be impossible to use it that day. As a complement to my plan, Farah invented that her London sister would not be home on Sunday, so she would have to go on Saturday. Needless to say, until she arrived on Friday, Farah tried hard to convince her parents not to take her to London, but as there was no way, at night I had no choice but to start the "tyre slashing" plan.

On Friday at eleven o'clock at night, I had all the luggage ready, so I told Janet that I was going to take a pint of beer to the pub to say goodbye to some English friends. She didn't suspect anything even though I was dressed in a black tracksuit, my black jacket, trainers and a black panty around my neck. In one pocket I carried my bumper, plus a huge, razor-sharp kitchen knife concealed under my trousers and the Lonsdale. In the other pocket, my ID card; just in case I was stopped by the police, at least to be identified, although that would certainly mean the ruin of my holiday with the loss of the flight.

I left home at almost midnight and headed for the area where Farah lived, trying to go across fields, across meadows and wooded areas instead of along the street. My aim was to reach the car park where Farah's father always left his car. It was quite cold outside, it was raining and there was nobody in the street, which is understandable as it was a suburban area. Decent people were at home and the partygoers were still getting drunk in the centre, so I didn't meet anyone until I reached a kind of grove that was situated next to the car park where Farah had indicated to me that her old man always left his car. When I arrived I hid among the trees to rest a bit and concentrate on the crucial moment of the night.

Before, in the afternoon, I had thought of waiting until five or six in the morning to commit my misdeed, when everyone was asleep. I then dismissed the idea, realising that it would be impossible for me to leave the house without the dogs making a fuss and waking up Janet and Danny, who would probably be surprised to see me sneaking out at dawn. So I decided that I would do it at midnight when the revellers hadn't returned yet. For this, there were mainly two problems. The first would be to meet a gang of rowdy teenagers who would frustrate my approach, the second would be for some resident with insomnia to see me through the window slashing the tyres and call the police. Until now, fortunately, I had not met anyone, but the fact that the neighbours were still awake and looking out the windows was something I had no control over.

Still, inside the grove no one could see me, for dressed in black I looked more like a shadow than a dodgy git. I walked to the edge of the trees and looked out towards the car park. Luckily, there was the black SUV that belonged to Farah's parents, not far from where I was hiding. I then curled up behind the last tree, put my panties on my face and grabbed the huge kitchen knife, although still hiding it under my Lonsdale. I remained silent waiting for the moment when nothing could be heard or seen that was suspicious, apart from the beating of my heart that was already beating at a 100mph rate. When I thought that the time was right, and I could no longer stand the pressure that fear and nervousness put on my chest, I decided to risk my holiday in an instant.

I walked quickly out of the trees towards the car and ducked behind it, hiding from any indiscreet windows. So far I had done nothing wrong, but in a second there would be no turning back. Then I took the knife out, leaned it against one of the wheels and pushed, although the blade didn't make it through the tyre, as it was harder than I had imagined. Very nervously I tried again, stabbing hard, and this time I did sink it into the wheel. When I pulled it out, the air started to come out making a great noise. I don't know why, but I had imagined that it would be quieter, so I had a little moment of panic and was tempted to run away. I controlled myself and said to myself, "it's still not enough", as I approached another wheel and stabbed it. Then I switched sides and stabbed another one before deciding that it was enough. I ran back to the tree line and hid there. In total, I had punctured three wheels and it had taken a little less than a minute.

Before I left for the countryside, I took one last look and saw that everything was quiet. Apparently, no one had seen me, but I couldn't delay in case a neighbour was now phoning the police. Through some meadows and parks, I quickly broke up the road as the nervousness and the fear gave way to a feeling of contained euphoria as I realized that everything had gone well.

When the park was over, the way to my house ran for a while along a long path with a very dense hedge on one side and a wooden fence on the other. As I was crossing that part of the path I came across the only challenge I would face on the way out. In front of me was approaching what looked like a young boy coming, the typical teenage Yobbo of the lower class, with his sports clothes and his baseball cap. I didn't want any trouble and my aim was to get home as soon as possible, put the kitchen knife back in the drawer where it belonged and go to sleep, but the boy kept looking at me as I approached him.

I decided to look at the ground and pass by as soon as possible. If there had been a choice, I would have changed pavements, but I was on a sort of pedestrian-only path. Closer to him, I saw out of the corner of my eye that the boy kept looking at me in a cheeky way and when we crossed each other he gave me a push while saying in a slumming accent: "What's your problem?" and he kept looking at me with a defiant attitude and a goofy smile on his stupid child's face. What the guy didn't know was that I was coming back from committing a crime and with adrenaline running through my veins like crazy. I stopped in my tracks even though I didn't confront him, but I watched him again out of the corner of my eye. The boy must have been about fifteen or sixteen years old and could well be one of those who had attacked us at the Leisure Centre over a month ago. Blond, thin and quite tall, he reminded me a bit of Joshua, and although I was sure it wasn't him, the guy met all the requirements to be one of those Yobbo bastards who make life a misery for so many decent people in England.

In a fit of rage, I put my scarf on my face, took out the huge kitchen knife with which I had slashed the tyres and I threw myself at him visibly waving them, shouting and exaggerating as much as possible my foreign accent: "I'm so sick and tired of you lot!..., you bastards!," while I kicked him in the chest, one of those moves that I trained in Taekwondo and that almost made him fall down. The guy was shocked at first and then, scared by my knife and my swearing in a foreign language, ran away like a rabbit and got lost in the distance. I ran away too, although in the opposite direction, and after a while I arrived home with my heart beating wildly, but with an incredible feeling of triumph going through all the fucking cells of my body.

What I had just done was a little bit stupid, because I don't even want to think what could have happened if the kid had decided to fight instead of shitting himself and run away. Still, I had taken infinite pleasure in attacking a Yobbo before I left the country and with that, I avenged in a symbolic way all the times I had been bothered by the unpleasant local louts.

The next morning I woke up at seven, had a shower, got dressed and went downstairs with all my luggage. There I said goodbye to Janet and Danny in a rather emotional way, as they had treated me very well and had got used to my presence. Then, carrying Farah's suitcase and mine, I walked to the bus station. Janet had insisted that she could give me a lift, but I told her not to bother. I didn't want her presence to hinder the second part of our "escape from England" plan.

Once I got there I sat quietly in a discreet place waiting for Farah to arrive escorted by her parents. It had been almost half an hour and several buses when I finally saw her arrive accompanied by Mum and Dad. I had seen the father from the Orange bus before, but now he looked sad rather than angry, as some heartless felon had slashed the tyres of his car. The mother, whom I had also seen once, was still wearing traditional Indian clothes and had been scolding the old man, probably because of the tyres incident. For a moment, I felt sorry for the man and wished I hadn't done it. Then I stopped looking, as they were getting too close, and hid behind a newspaper that I had brought with me for that purpose.

After about fifteen minutes the bus from Northampton arrived again and Farah, her parents and I got on it, sitting at a safe distance and hiding behind the newspaper again. At ten o'clock in the morning, we were already at the huge Northampton bus station, the ugliest building in England according to a survey, and we were still on schedule as we had to be at Stansted Airport at five to catch our flight. The problem there was that Farah's parents did not want to leave until they had left their daughter on the bus to London and as I could not ask Farah, nor could she tell me which bus that was, we were stuck there at the station.

For an hour we waited to see if the parents would bugger off, but nothing and time kept running against us. As there were half a dozen different routes to London, I couldn't just pick one at random hoping to meet Farah or find us there. Finally, Farah went to the ticket office and bought a ticket. Then she went to one of the boarding gates into which the station was divided and I followed her with my eyes. In a moment of inattention from her parents, she pointed out a sign to me: it was the Northampton-London route via Milton Keynes. Okay, I knew which bus to take, but not the time. Assuming that she had bought a ticket for the next one was too much to assume and I didn't want to risk going on another bus. At that time a mobile phone would have been the most useful thing in the world, but in 1998 few people had one. Luckily, at the ticket office, I was told that the ticket was good for any time, so I bought a one-way ticket for ten pounds.

After this little hurdle, I sneaked on the same bus as Farah again and waited for her to start and leave the station behind before I finally met her. For a moment I had thought that the old folks wanted to come to London too, but fortunately, this did not happen. After sitting next to her and kissing, we started to tell each other our respective odysseys to get to that moment. She told me that her father was very sad when he found his tyres flat and that he was very sorry for him "One tyre would have been enough, you twat!" she said to me with a certain reproachful tone, although deep down she was happy that everything had turned out well.

When the bus stopped at Milton Keynes station, we got off and bought tickets to go to Stansted airport, and a couple of hours later we were already there, looking forward to getting on the plane to Spain. The rest of the trip went on normally until ten o'clock at night on Saturday, September 19th we finally landed in Madrid.

In total, I had been in England for three months and the whole experience had been a success. I had returned all in one piece, with a much better level of English, quite a bit of money saved up, and a girl by my side. I couldn't ask for more. "What a great country UK is" I thought as a final epilogue to my stay abroad "Full of fun and opportunities. Even the weather isn't that bad. If it wasn't for the violent lager louts it would be paradise on earth. I'm so glad they're in the EU so I will always be allowed in there without worrying about visas and stuff".

Farah's first impression of Spain was the warm and dry atmosphere. "There's no air," she told me again and again, even though the hottest part of the summer had already passed. She also said that Central Madrid reminded her of London. "Well, what did you expect darling, a dusty, mud-hut, Hollywood-movie-style, Mexican-border *pueblo*? These *guiris*[8] are so dumb sometimes".

---

[8] Slang for foreign tourists.

At Barajas Airport, we took a taxi and half an hour later we were already at my house. There I introduced her to my parents and also, what else could I do, to *Piletus*, who started barking, pissing and pooping all around the place, making a considerable mess. Well, it would do the same whenever a strange came into our house anyway. My brothers were not yet in Madrid, as the schools were starting in October, so we had plenty of room at home. Farah moved into what had been my grandmother's room and once we had organised everything we went to sleep, as we were very tired.

On Sunday we took it easy. I showed her a little bit about the surroundings and the house and how most things worked. From Monday onwards we started to live according to a routine that we repeated every day and that seemed to me like being in heaven. The day started for us at half-past eight in the morning, which was when my parents left the house to go to work, leaving us alone. Five minutes later I got up and went to Farah's room, who was already waiting for me naked and with a condom on the bedside table. Then we would make love and sleep a little longer until we got up around eleven o'clock. During the day we would go for walks in the centre of Madrid, especially in the parks and other "beautiful places" that Farah liked so much, and also spent a lot of time shopping. Around six in the evening, we would start cooking dinner, as this way we didn't have to coincide at the table with my folks, and after dinner, we would go for another walk or a drink out.

Every day that Farah was in Madrid we had beautiful weather and, besides, my parents were very kind and nice to her, showing me that my fears had been unfounded. Farah did not like to go out at night too much nor did she drink alcohol, but we still went out one day with my mates. Not that I was particularly interested in seeing them, as I was going to be with them all winter, but I wanted to introduce them to Farah and show off my foreign girlfriend in front of them. Every day I spent with Farah was perfect and the next one even better. For me, it was like a dream to see her with me in Madrid, especially because we could be together all the time without worries and without the threat of her parents finding out about our relationship.

Far from them, Farah relaxed and became a happy and carefree girl, although she also confessed to me that she missed her family a little. Every night she phoned home to tell her sisters about the fun she was having and her parents about the training course she was supposed to be doing. As usual, the parents asked her a lot about her sister Fozia, so Farah also called her a couple of times to see how she was doing and to make the lie more believable. With so many phone calls abroad, the phone bill promised to come in loud the next month, but nothing took me out of the constant state of happiness I was in. There was only one thing that made me apprehensive and that was seeing the days passing by and the date when I would have to take Farah to the airport and say goodbye to her for a long time, or who knows if forever, getting closer and closer.

It was while we were rushing through our last days together in Madrid that we began to talk a little more seriously about what was going to happen to our relationship after she returned to her country. I personally had no experience in these matters, but I had read in dirty magazines that long-distance relationships only work in romantic literature, never in real life. Besides, my parents, seeing me so much in love, advised me not to have many expectations about the future, but to live the present and not worry too much. Bearing all this in mind, I decided to address the subject with a rational approach. Nothing prevented me from keeping in touch with Farah by letter or telephone and from visiting her on my next holiday if she was happy with it. If on the other hand the distance or absence broke our relationship, then no drama. We had our fun, *Je ne regrette rien*, we'll always have Paris, *hasta la vista* baby, and so on.

I also knew and accepted as an inevitable part of the game the possibility that she would find another boy there or I would find another girl here. This seemed fair and reasonable to me, as it would be our decision and ours alone. The only thing that worried me a little was Farah's family and their strange customs. I still didn't know exactly what ethnicity and religion they belonged to, but somewhere I had heard that these people from the Asian continent were very fond of marrying their daughters off to men close to the family. This idea of arranged marriages was hateful to me and just the thought of Farah in somebody else's arms made me sick. To prevent this from happening, I spoke to her very seriously and exposed to her in no uncertain terms that if her family tried to force her to do something she didn't want to do, she could always count on my help to escape, whether we were still together or not.

Farah laughed a lot at my remark, but then, seeing that I was worried, she was able to explain her situation to me a little better. When we first met, she had told me many lies and now it was time to know the truth, although there was no secret she could not have told me before.

Farah's parents were immigrants who had come to Britain in the late 1960s, I thought maybe from the Punjab, or some other border area between India and Pakistan, but Farah always refused to tell me which specific country of Asia it was. From Turkey to Burma anything was possible. Their grandparents had been in the British Army and this had made it much easier for them to get a residence permit first and British nationality later. Recently married and newly arrived in the country, the whole family settled in Bradford, a northern city famous for its large Asian community. There they did the same as everyone else around them, the father went to work in the textile industry and the mother got pregnant and brought up children.

The problem was that after having a daughter, just a year after they were married, another daughter followed the following year. After the third daughter came a fourth, and when they tried again to see if they could have a boy, two more daughters came. By the age of twenty-five, Farah's parents had six daughters and not a single son, but they did not give up and kept trying. A couple more pregnancies, in which the ultrasound scans showed that they were female, and in which the mother had two mysterious miscarriages, made the parents give up and take it as impossible. At the age of thirty, the mother was broken and the father was deeply grieved, for not having sons is a disgrace within the more traditional Asian culture.

Knowing their misfortune, family and neighbours began to pity them and also to talk about them behind their backs. When the level of gossip and patting on the shoulders became too heavy to bear on a daily basis, they packed their bags, took their girls and went to live in Danetree, an eminently English town where there were no ethnic communities. It was here that Farah grew up and went to school, and also where she learned to live in two worlds at once and to speak two languages, her own at home and English at school. Little by little as she grew up she realised how difficult this was, with different and often contradictory rules coming from one side of the family and the other side from the teachers and the other children.

Adolescence only accentuated the problems, as Farah was neither completely in one world nor the other. She found little support or understanding in foreign parents who were alien to modern British society, and within this modern British society, things were no better either. Respected, though not fully accepted, Farah and her sisters always encountered a kind type of racism in which they were treated by the English very correctly, but generally excluded from many relevant social interactions. Not surprisingly, Farah came to regard her sisters as her best friends, the only ones who understood her situation and those she could trust.

As she grew older and adolescent hormones began to take their toll, the issue of boys became a problem too. On the one hand, she wasn't very attracted to English boys, but she didn't trust Asian boys either because of experiences with older sisters where chauvinism and hidden agendas had been the norm. Besides, there were none in Danetree and she would have had to move to some big city to look for them.

Worst of all, the parents forbade any kind of relationship for their children, but they were not going to provide any solutions either. As I learned from Farah, in these traditional cultures parents start to introduce their children, when they are older, to the children of other families known to them. If they like each other and there is "chemistry", then they get married and love will arise. If there is no understanding, then they keep looking and fair play.

The big problem for Farah in the future, and above all for her older sisters, was that being so many girls, the father would have a hard time marrying them all, or even some of them, as it is very common for the parents of the groom to ask for money and gifts in the form of a dowry, even though this is not legal. In fact, three of his sisters were already well over the ideal age for marriage and no move had yet been made. With all this mess, having forbidden all approach to the English, and also the doors of the legal marriage quite closed in perspective, Farah saw everything very difficult. Until I showed up.

The first days we met at Danetree I was simply amazed. I didn't understand what interest that Indian girl could have in a foreigner like me. Then she explained some things to me and I could understand a little. Farah didn't want anything to do with the English, who she thought were promiscuous, rowdy and drunk too much. Neither did she like the Asians, who were (according to her) too chauvinistic, treated the girls badly and even tried to take advantage of them. I was neither one thing nor the other, but a sort of quite interesting Mediterranean middle ground and, above all, outside the above-mentioned categories. As the chances of their father being able to pay six dowries to families of good caste were almost nil, there was not much point in keeping virtue and virginity to please a traditional society that offered nothing and demanded everything from women. Moreover, marrying a fellow countryman in the traditional way was no bargain according to her point of view. To begin with, the candidate was chosen by the family, although the bride and groom could theoretically say yes or no. If there was a wedding, the couple almost never went to live on their own but moved to the husband's house, where the woman could end up being the in-laws' maid and subjected to all kinds of mistreatment, at least until she gave birth to a male child. If this did not happen soon, the level of abuse could increase and she could even be disowned.

So Farah decided to make out with *the foreign boy* she liked and take the opportunity to have some fun for once in her life. Whatever happened, the boy would soon be gone, without creating any problems or making her look bad. To make it last a little longer, Farah told some lies when she met me, that she was an Israeli and a few more that I believed very innocently. However, it later occurred to me that the purpose of those lies was not only to deceive me but also to create an image with which she would feel comfortable with herself.

At the end of the twentieth century, Farah was suffering from a disease that, although not new, had reappeared with particular virulence in Western Europe due to migration. This disease is called "uprooting" and affects millions of people, millions of Africans, Arabs, Indians and Latin Americans in Europe, but above all their children, who are from here but also from there, and who are looking for different ways to combat its symptoms. Farah's and her sisters' way had been to lie, and apparently, Farah's lies were nothing compared to the fantasy worlds, Arab princesses and daughters of Greek millionaires that her sisters had become involved with over the past few years to escape reality.

Of course, there was also some advantage to living in two worlds at once, such as being able to keep what she liked best in both. Farah was especially grateful for the freedom and equality she enjoyed in the West, as well as the fashion and hedonistic consumerism. From the Indian subcontinent, she kept the music, Bollywood films and traditional foods she loved, but apart from that, she felt more British than foreign. In fact, she had only visited the motherland once in her life, when her parents took them to see the poor village where they came from, and the truth is that she had not had a good experience. As she told me later, what she had liked best about the country was that it was so far away and so expensive to go that she would never have the chance to return again.

Quite happy to have finally found out almost everything about Farah, we kept talking about both the past and the future during the last few days, when we also tried to enjoy our time to the fullest in every way. Finally, at the beginning of October, the fateful day arrived when I took her to the airport and separated from her at the police checkpoint inside the terminal. The moment was quite emotional, although it was also hard, and we spared no kisses, hugs, promises and even a few tears. In total, we had been together a little over two months and had become quite attached to each other. It was now that we would begin to test day by day whether our relationship or at least our friendship, could survive many miles away and long months of absence. To avoid becoming too depressed, I consoled myself by thinking that at least I had made my debut as a man with a beautiful and very special girl and that we had had a great time together.

The first days without Farah weren't easy and I felt quite depressed, especially because once everything went well and I finally managed to be with a girl I really liked, it all had to end so soon. Little by little time went by and I started going to university. Luckily I already knew several people there, among them Gutierrez, who was in my first class of Business Studies. Other school friends like Diego, Nico, Manu et al were also studying on the same campus, so almost from the first day, I could count on a group of *compadres* who made the absence of the beloved woman and the melancholy of autumn much more bearable. The studies did not seem much more difficult than secondary school and little by little I got used to the routine of going to class in the morning, reviewing a bit in the afternoon and going out on the weekends. The university changed our partying habits a bit, favouring alcohol over joints, and the *cubalibre* became the star of our nights, replacing the circle of *kalimocho* and joints in a sordid alley.

That autumn I would try to have as much fun as possible, even though I remembered Farah very much. With her savings from Orange, she bought one of those mobile phones and thanks to that I was able to call her without arousing suspicion. Since her return to England, everything had gone well for her and she had not had any problems with her parents. She simply told them that she didn't get the job, and the matter was forgotten.

Far from losing touch, Farah and I started writing each other quite regularly, and even spoke on the phone sometimes, when she would call my parent's home or I would call her on her cell phone.

In mid-October, three weeks after Farah had departed I received one of these calls from her. She sounded quite upset so I asked her what the matter was. She started crying and mumbling inconsistencies "Can I trust you?" and stuff like that.

I told her that I quite did not understand what she wanted to say, and asked if she had had problems with her folks, or somebody else. Then she dropped the bomb: "Chuckie baby, my parents are gonna kill me when they find out... I think I might be pregnant!"

END